7:33am
"The Clock Is Ticking. Wake Up!"

A Love Story

by Monda Raquel Webb

Latebloomer2000 Publishers – Maryland

Copyright © 2007 by Monda Webb

This book is a work of fiction. Many of the characters, incidents and dialogue are drawn from the author's imagination and are not to be construed as real. Any resemblance to actual events or persons, living or dead, is entirely coincidental.

Some people and places are real, and are noted in the back of the book. These special people make up the pulse that produces the heartbeat of Washington, DC and her suburbs as entrepreneurs, exhibiting daily their vibrancy, spirit, vision and commitment to excellence.

All rights reserved. No part of this book may be reproduced or transmitted in any form or by any means, electronic or mechanical, including photocopying, recording, or by any information storage and retrieval system, without permission in writing from the publisher.

Published by Latebloomer2000
PO Box 1531
Olney, MD 20830

latebloomer2000@hotmail.com
www.latebloomer2000.com
www.myspace.com/monda_latebloomer2000

ISBN 978-0-9797827-0-1

Designs With Distinction
"Your Personalized Print Shoppe"
Sharon F. McCreary, CEO
Sharonflorita@gmail.com
Printed in China

Adult language is used throughout the book.

For information regarding special discounts for bulk purchases, please contact Monda Webb at **mondawebb@yahoo.com**

Layout and Design: DigiGraph Media
www.digigraphmedia.com

Cover illustration and seasonal glyphs: Rod Little

COVER ILLUSTRATION BY ROD LITTLE
INFORMATION·ILLUSTRATION
WWW.INFORMATIONILLUSTRATION.COM

"Guard your heart above all else, for it determines the course of your life"

—Proverbs 4: 23

This book is dedicated to my cousin Brie Anna Terry and my niece Brandye Washington, young ladies who are already comfortable in their own skin.

Acknowledgements:
- First and foremost, all praise and glory to Jehovah God for making the impossible possible.
- A big 'ol shout out to anyone who has found themselves in an uncompromising position and compromised.
- Special acknowledgement for genealogy. My paternal grandmother Hiawatha Webb loved to read, and my maternal grandfather W.W. Terry loves to write. The fusion of the bloodlines mixed in me, made nice, and a storyteller was born.
- Much love to my father Robert Webb and my mother Cynthia Webb for understanding my critical need to be true to the art and authenticate my characters. In other words, thanks Mommy and Daddy for accepting the "cussing." Albeit begrudgingly.
- Tremendous thanks to my good friend Hermond Palmer, who not only co-wrote and arranged the lyrics for the companion CD, but put some fire under my butt to complete this project.
- I am so extremely grateful for my friend and illustrator, Rod Little. You did a fantastic job.
- It will take me an eternity to pay back the staff at DigiGraph, Kevin, Mike and Vince, who exhibited the utmost in patience and flexibility for the layout and design of both of my books.
- A ton of thanks to my editor Thomas Mazza. Thank you for coming through on the humble. I will never forget it.
- I can't say "Thank You" enough to my girls, Stacey Brown, Aimee Dixon, Esther Ntim, Gail Pinckney and Nichelle Thomas, for enduring my endless questions and "what if" scenarios for the past 10 years!
- Special thanks to all my guy friends who broke the "man laws" and shared lots of "man secrets" telling me like it is… Darrion Anderson, Andre Colona, Winston Goslee, Derwin Hewitt, Jorge Santana.
- Many thanks goes out to my litmus testers, friends, family and Sorors, brave women who read bits and pieces of this story and provided raw, honest, feedback until I got it right… Bobette Banks, Ana Barraza, Amber Brown, Angie Clay, Sabreena Geddie, Tracy Jackson, Mia Joe, Barbara Floyd Jones, Norma McCowin, Penelope Morgan, Edith Covington Murad, Danielle Shanklin, Karen Tolson, Tyra Washington, Ciara Webb and Roblin Webb. Good looking out, ladies!
- I would be remiss if I didn't mention my mentors, Dr. Diedre Badejo, Ruth Jordan, Randi Payton, Doug and Debbie Mitchell and my cousin Floyd Robinson, Jr. and my real estate mentor Karen Rollings for giving me the strength, courage and chutzpah to pursue my dream with grace and determination.
- Special thanks to my attorney Derric E. Thomas for saving me from myself.
- Special thanks to my new friend and favorite printer lady in the whole wide world, Sharon McCreary. Thanks for making it happen.
- No words can be said about the music that infiltrated my soul and touched my core as I conceived, developed and wrote this story. Thanks to all the artists out there who have made music that inspires, motivates and transports me to the land of infinite possibilities and limitless imagination; especially Maxwell.
- I couldn't have written this book if it wasn't for all of the love and emotional uplift I received from friends, co-workers, relatives and just plain folk I ran into, shared my story, and boom—there was the love. So thank you, thank you, and thank you.

"Faith is the substance of things hoped for, the evidence of things not seen"
—Hebrews 11:1

The Faithful 2007
I'd like to personally thank each and every person who believed in me enough to offer their financial support before seeing a final product. Thank you for helping me reach my dream, and thank Jehovah Jireh, for HE does provide.

Colette Akande	Vince Earland
Melvin and Ayanna Alex Harris	Cathy Eastman
Samilia Anthony	Claude Etienne
Shanel Anthony	Lade Fatiregun
Jackie Ashton	Foluke
Ayinde	Diana Franklin
Carolyn Yvette Baldwin	Sophia Frimpomaah
Bobette and Medaris Banks	Tamara Garrett
Felicia Battle	Sabreena Geddie
Jon Bean	Lisa Goodnight
Ingrid Beckles	Georgia Goslee, Esq.
Sam and Murshell Bland	Melissa Green
Kenya Bradshaw	Minnedore Green
Syvella Brantley	Kevin Griffin
Amber Brown	Gary Guinn
Forest Brown	Stephanie Harris Jackman
Stacey Brown	Brenda Harrison
Nedria Brown-Wilson	Tonya Hartman
Edith and Stan Britt	Denny Hewitt
Donald Byrd	Derwin Hewitt
Phyllis Burke	Ophelia and Diana Hewitt
Laura and David Cambridge	Sandra Hines
Michael Carter	Lacey Hlavka
Donald Chandler	Tracy Jackson
Eric Croom	Asheley Jenkins
Donte Davis	Barbara and Rubin Jones
Raheem DeVaughn	Sashia Jones
Angelina and Magaye Diombokho	Bruce and Alia Johnson
Aimee Dixon	Diane Johnson
Kevin Dove	Donald and Terry Johnson

Maisie Dunbar
Marcus Johnson
Ruth Jordan
Juani
Billy Kearney
Dr. Ella Kelly
Alex Kinion
Michael Koch
Fred Leftrich
Alicia Lewis
John Linder
Rod Little
Sandra and Huey Long
Phillip Malone
Shirley Malone
Phyllis McCormick
Sharon McCreary
Mark F. Morgan
Darrell Miller
Doug and Debbie Mitchell
Myntoleah and Todd Monash
Temika Moore
Penelope Morgan
Matthew Myers
Renee Neverson
Portia Newman
Roxanne Newsome
Brenda Ntim
Esther Ntim
John Nullmeyer
Marilyn O'Neill
Hermond Palmer
Marc Palmer
Jill and Jon Patton
Karen and Randi Payton
Sharon Pratt

Todd Rexx
Terry Reynolds
Marinete Rinelli
Kenny Rittenhouse
Jackie Showers
Robinson, Dixon, Hodge and Grime Families
Arianna Royster
Angela Russell
Safori
Danielle and Darrell Shanklin
Heather Smith
Iris Imani Francis Smith
Lorri and Martin Strachan
Jeff and Lea Stiggle
Cliff Swindell
Keith Taylor
Rhonda Walton
BrieAnna, Melody and W.W. Terry
Sean Terry
Beverly and Dudley Thomas
Derric E. Thomas, Esq.
Nichelle Thomas
Ron and Geraldine Thomas
Victor Thompson
Estee Vaughn
Rhonda Walton
Tyra, Brandye, Chaz, Kennedye and Larry Washington
Rashaud Wayns
Ciara Webb
Cynthia Webb
Robert Webb II
Roblin Webb
Robert and Linda Webb
Sydney Williams
Langston Willis

Dedicated to all who shared their wallets, their time, their professional services, their advice, their essence, their gifts, to help me manifest my dream. This poem is for you.

Simply…Faith

Faith is peace
Faith is calm
Faith yields blessings
Without causing harm
Faith is clear
Faith is pure
Walking in faith
You can always be sure
Faith takes courage
Expressed by belief
Practicing true faith
Alleviates grief
Faith is something you renew every day
And isn't for the weak at heart
Faith can lead you, guide you show you the way
You just have to do your part
And Believe!
How can you possess something you cannot see with the human eye?
How can you embrace something you cannot be, trade, or buy?
It's quite simple, God doesn't lie…have Faith, be Faithful, live everyday Faith

Introduction

"This is my story. It is ripe for the telling. It took me a while, because I was in so much pain for so long, but in looking back, it may really be able to help other people who find themselves in a situation where they are sharing the same man or same woman. My story is so juicy, I think it could be a movie. It doesn't even seem real at times. The only way I was able to heal from the pain of deception and betrayal was to write in my journal; bits and pieces of which I will share with you. You can't get it all, now. Plus every page wasn't that interesting. But prepare to laugh out loud, holler, shake your head in disbelief, and embrace the lesson."

—Madison Robinson Terry, Author

THE PRESENT

**Early in the morning at Damion's crib
As told by Madison Paige Robinson— The Knock
June 2000**

I lay there, snuggled next to my honey reverse spoon-style, you know, arms wrapped around his person, my own personal, live teddy bear. I watched him as he slept. Umm, umm, umm, he was fine to me. He wasn't that fine when I first met him, but damn! The longer I stayed with him, the better looking he got. Isn't it funny how that happens? I know y'all know what I'm talking about. He looked so peaceful and happy after an unforgettable night of lovemaking. His smooth brown sugar coated skin had a slight glow, if I didn't say so myself. His chest, with just a splatter of soft black hairs, rose and fell easily with his steady, even, breathing.

I would have still been sleeping also, but the urge to smoke a cigarette overcame me and I bolted straight up. I stared at the Safori original above Damion's bed. The artist, a good friend of Damion's, used such vivid colors his paintings seemed to come alive by just looking at them. Color abounded. Rigorous reds, deep greens, tinted blues, a hint of purple here, a splash of gold, there. I even turned my head and squinted sideways. Yep, the piece still came alive. Damion's house was full of his pieces, giving it that lived in cozy feel almost as soon as he moved in. I'd met Safori once. Damion and I attended Queen Aishah's Thursday night comedy open mic a couple of months ago, and he was there. He stood up to greet us with a genuine smile and deep dimples. Safori was a beautiful man, slender, with clothes to rival any haberdashery, gentle, with iron resolve. He seemed…timeless.

Seemingly with no obvious things to tease him about, Aishah, a very funny comic, tore him to pieces. That was a good night. But back to the cigarettes, I must have been dreaming about it or something, 'cuz I could almost feel the nicotine coursing through my relaxed body.

I'd been trying to quit for two months, ever since Damion and I had one of our heart to hearts. In those sessions, we would be open and honest with each other about things we didn't like about one another. Well, as honest as we could be without crossing the line, that is. It's hard. I won't lie. It is *hard*. I mean, you know how it is, you say too much, crush your man's ego, and he's out. And, in case you're not from here, there are way too many women in DC who will take my place stroking and reassuring his ego. And, in case you didn't know, the women to men ratio in DC is just ridiculous. But, during these "honest" sessions, we would state our issue, and if it wasn't intruding too much in the personal, we'd try and affect change. In this particular session, Damion admitted he didn't like kissing me with cigarette breath. I weighed it, figured I could make myself like kissing more than smoking, and we shook on it. Actually, we kissed on it. I promised to quit. I looked at it this way. I could kiss on him the rest of my life, but smoking might take me out of here a tad early, and I wanted to prolong the END as long as possible. I mean, it's not like I'm trying to change for my man, or anything, we're just enhancing one another as human beings. I told him that I didn't like the way he spoke to everyone as if they were his best friend. He's all friendly with the world, especially with the ladies, "Because" he explained, "I want everyone to feel special." Sure you're right. That sounds great, but there comes a time when you need to differentiate with the special feelings and shower them on me, your princess, you know what I'm saying? Yeah, it was selfish, but he agreed to try. We then divulged the qualities we loved in one another and made fantastic love. It's important to have the balance, you know?

Tracing his body contours with my eyes and thinking about his wonderfulness made me tremble with a growing passion. The comforter was rumpled at the end of his new king-sized bed. I stress the new, because it made me feel good. I knew I was the only woman he'd slept on that bed with. The Ralph Lauren sheets I gave him as a housewarming present were hanging so sexily off his hips, it seemed as if he'd planned it that way. I contemplated pleasuring myself and then thought, "Self, why play when you've got this gorgeous man right here that will surpass your bony fingers any day?" Hence, therefore, ergo, I prepared to nudge him, but stopped short, index finger suspended right above his shoulder. Should I get up and brush my teeth, wash my face and scrub my figgy pudding? Ladies, what would you do? Hmmm, let's see. I looked at the clock. 7:30 am on the nose, a great time for wake-up sex. To me, anytime was a great time, but I'd say that to Damion and he'd get a kick out of it, my imagination, that is. So, as far as I was concerned, this round would be a wake-up round. "Wake-up sex, make-up sex, whatever the reason, it's time to flex!" I played with the word rhyme in my head, a possible editorial idea. Could I do this without brushing my teeth? Damn, I wanted a cigarette. My mind was all over the place, and I was going nowhere fast. I calculated the length of time we'd been dating. It would be…let's see, not including the first date…the week after Labor Day. I remember saying to my best friend; "Stacey, from this day on, I refuse to labor after any man. I have worked too hard in the past trying to make some fucked up relationship work, 'cause I'm so weary of being on the singles scene, and for what? Nothing. So from now on, I'm going to sit back, relax, and let the brother do the talking, as long as his words and actions match." Stacey looked at me, smiled and answered "True that, true that." She's been married twice. Although her last name, Norton-Shields only reflects one, it's actually her two married names, the maiden name was dropped. If you were to ask her why she kept both, she'd respond. "Darling, each of those men taught me an important lesson. One, money don't buy you love, and two, love don't buy you money. The next time, I'm 'gone get it right!" Interesting, I thought. Labor Day…we will have been together nine months on June 11. That's enough time to conceive, carry and deliver a healthy, bouncing, baby…whatever sex, it didn't matter. Damion loved kids. Whew! Maybe, just maybe, we should start talking about the next level.

"Oh forget it!" I hissed. I was too lazy to go through the proper hygienic motions. Besides, we'd been through the major embarrassing moments, such as the first time I had to tell him he had a big one hanging from his nose, to me ruining my bed sheets with a heavy period, to him gassing me out in the car. There's something to be said about being trapped inside a vehicle, while the stink permeates your whole being, in your skin, nostrils, clothes, etc. 7:32. Of course he thought it was funny. I didn't. What is up with men and farting? I don't know.

And WHY I was taking myself through such an agonizing thought process anyway, to wash or not to wash? Forget Shakespeare, *that* is the question. I decided not. I peeked at the clock, consummate clock-watcher that I am. 7:33. Just as I nudged him, there was a knock at the door. Who in the hell? The knock got louder, became more persistent. Damion had just moved in a couple of months ago, and hadn't met many of his neighbors yet. Who could that possibly be? I roused him, telling him to go get the door. He jumped up and flew down the stairs. He walked back in the room thirty seconds later looking sheepish. "I forgot my jeans."

"I know," I said, wrapping the sheets around me soap opera style, hoping it looked sexy. "They're over here by me." I reached down on my side of the bed and grabbed his jeans, still supporting the sheet with my left hand. That move was the Norton-Shields rule of thumb: "Give, but don't give too much, let them see, peek or whatever, but don't let them get too used to it. They'll take your precious body, your gift, for granted." Stacey's voice rang through my head as I thought briefly about my vivacious friend. She runs through men like I run pantyhose, sometimes as soon as I put them on. Now juxtapose the pantyhose for the men in Stacey's life. One run, one date. Sometimes you can wear a good pair two or three times. For Stacey, two or three dates. You get the picture. However, with all that experience, she could kick some serious man knowledge your way, and you better listen, because she KNEW what she was talking about. She'd been there.

Damion playfully snatched his jeans from me and I smiled widely as I noticed his growing sex. He caught me looking and grinned, 32 perfect teeth, just gleaming. I say 32 because some people have extra. I actually counted his. He then decided to moon me. Strictly man humor that I don't get or find funny.

"What you looking at?" He'd placed both hands on his butt cheeks to make it seem like they were talking to me. So immature.

"First of all, you never end a sentence with a preposition," I answered in my best naughty English teacher voice. "and second, I was thinking how much you need to lotion your ashy butt!"

I hoped my remark stung, but Damion just laughed, turned to face me and said, "You may lotion me upon my return," in a poor imitation of James Earl Jones. I shook my head and hissed a low "Whatever, negro. Just hurry back," and lay against the headboard, thinking how much I wanted to please him. I jumped out of bed and decided I'd take a nice, hot bath so I could smell good and be squeaky-clean. I reached in my overnight duffle and chose a light negligee, which was perfectly acceptable during the day, a bar of sandalwood soap, bath salts, moisturizer, and some deodorant.

Today, Sunday, was my day. Yesterday Damion went to the Capital Jazz Fest with his boys Todd and Rod. I know that sounds funny, but those are really their names, and they've all been best friends since they were like, eight. I wanted to go with Damion, but that would be breaking their tradition. It was man law, and no woman could ever break it. So, he promised that today would be my day and my day only. I compromised, although every Sunday at my parents was Soul Food Sunday and my mom had a hissy fit when I missed, but truth be told, I'd rather be with my man instead of my mom and dad, no man or woman law there, if there is such a thing.

I started my water, poured in the bath salts, and brushed my teeth, multitasking, true woman style. Watching the water fill the tub was so soothing and hypnotic, I forgot all about the cigarette, and remembered, instead, our first meeting at Home Depot. We'd come a long way since that day; the persistent knocking was, by now, a distant memory.

CHAPTER 2

**Madison—The Meeting
September 1999**

As Madison pulled up in the giant parking lot of Home Depot, she figured she'd do the bathroom today. Her monthly Sunday sojourn to the overwhelming store consisted of mental furnishing, one room at a time. Next year she planned to buy a townhouse. She wanted somewhat of a fixer upper, and aspired to renovate to reflect her specific taste and style. Madison figured she'd educate herself on the best manufacturers and products now, and comparison shop so she'd be prepared when the time came, for decoration and budget.

Madison maneuvered her way through the large aisles, each packed to the ceiling with all kinds of stuff imaginable. The glaring orange signs swinging above were reminiscent of the fabled Hansel and Gretel breadcrumbs. They seemed to be whispering "Just in case you get lost dummy, look up!" If she wasn't mesmerized by the gently swinging banners, she was blinded by an all too friendly associate in an orange bib asking if she needed help. Madison would respond glibly, "Oh, I'm fine, thank you, I'll just follow the orange signs." After which she'd look up, then pause, then look down at the puny associate, and he or she would bow away gracefully, thankful someone had enough sense to just look up. This store did have everything a customer wanted, though, for every part of the home. Madison took her time heading towards the bath section, reading the signs and glancing down the aisles. Anything anyone could imagine was here, including cement, nails, hammers, floor tile, rugs, paints, paintbrushes, electric saws, manual saws, windows, doors...random birds that played tag in the rafters, and on and on and on. Madison thought if all the supplies in the store were to come alive, humans would be defenseless. "I could see some clown coming up with a horror movie like that," she giggled to herself. "Supplies Alive" or some stupid title like that. And the sad thing is, people would go and see it. She finally made it to the far right backend of the store, which shone and sparkled like new money. Sinks, showers, bathtubs, toilets, you name it, they had it. Chrome was everywhere. She ventured toward the tubs and slowly studied them. She placed her hand on her chin and wondered if they carried the older, heavy tubs.

"You don't see what you want, do you?" said an unknown, yet familiar sounding voice. Madison spun around and thought briefly how she might *want* this guy. New movie. The scene opens and she and this tall, brown, honey are making out on one of the toilet seats. It might be titled, "Amazing Displays," and all the women would be lined up saying, "I want *that* toilet!"

This guy was very cute. She silently berated herself. It was time to stop being so shallow. She studied him and figured she would stop being shallow on New Years. "Resolution number one," she thought, making a mental note.

"No, I don't think so..." she began carefully, hoping he noticed that she exercised just the right amount of judgment in speaking to strangers.

"I'm looking for the kind of tub that when you drop a piece of soap, it goes thud... not clank!" Madison had a tendency to talk with her hands. He was standing so close to her she almost hit him. The stranger laughed loudly at her expressiveness and mentioned, "I know this brother who specializes in restoring old ceramic tubs, even the ones with the lion's paw. He'll hook you up too, with delivery and everything." Madison eyed him unscrupulously.

"I'm sorry," he apologized. "My name is Damion. I just like to see money made and saved in the black community, so whatever I can do to keep the flow going, I do." Madison wondered if he'd said 'I do' at any point and time. Instead she sassily replied,

"Damion? As in Omen? Yeah, I know a place where they need those heavy tubs to withstand the heat there, you may have heard of it, run by a guy named Satan? You know, got to keep that evil within the sinful community. Anything I can do to get him renters, I do."

"Ah, a mocking woman!" Damion laughed again. "I like that!" he said a little too loudly, admiring Madison from head to toe. Madison didn't mind in the least. It felt good to get the attention, from an attractive guy. Toothless, raggedy street urchins didn't count. Stacey would have said "Girl, a man who flirts shamelessly will say anything and act anyway to get your ass in the bed. He will wear a cape and become Superman if he has to, and remember, nine times out of ten, you ain't the only one he's 'flirtin with." Madison shook her head. Here she was, secretly sweating this gift that just happened to drop into her lap, and she was thinking about her best friend. Whew, she needed to get out more.

"I really like the ceramic tubs myself," explained Damion.

Madison absorbed his words. She really liked the way he spoke.

"I take baths often, and the old school tubs retain the water temperature longer than the plastic ones. It may seem silly to you, but in today's world, everything is moving so fast, with computers and technology, it's nice to take a moment and slow down and appreciate life's gifts to you. It doesn't have to be something big, just something that brings you pleasure." Damion took a moment to gaze at her. Madison was thinking, "Is it me, or is it that everything this guy says can be taken at talk level and at the gutter level?"

"You might think I'm soft for liking baths," Damion uttered, "but I assure you, I'm all man!" Madison started. She was so taken with the sound of his voice and his delivery, when he stopped, the warm air surrounding them suddenly turned cold. Truth be told, that 'all man' statement took her over the edge. She was visualizing him in one of those huge tubs with the lion claws, 'chillin, surrounded by candles and bubbles for effect, reading some fancy manly magazine and smoking a hand-rolled cigar while Denyse Graves seduced anyone who would listen in the background.

"Hello?" Damion gently nudged her with his voice.

"Unh, I don't think you're soft. I don't even know you, but after that soliloquy, I would think you were Shakespeare." Great comeback, she thought, after getting caught with her pants down, mentally.

"That's a good one!" Damion laughed wholeheartedly, exposing a set of picture perfect teeth. Madison was taken aback. It was as if the sun were rising behind him. This brother actually glowed.

"I knew you looked familiar. I've seen you during open mic night at Mr. Henry's doing a stand-up routine, right?"

Madison frowned furiously, creasing the point between her two eyebrows into several wrinkles.

"Got you!"

"That wasn't very nice you know."

Madison demonstrated her full-fledged perfected pout. With an older brother, she had to learn to do something when she didn't get what she wanted.

"Let me make it up to you and take you to dinner sometime."

'Good answer,' she thought.

Still pouting, Madison reached in her handbag and searched for her card case.

"My mother warned me about women with those endless handbags," Damion joked.

"She said anything can be found in there from address books to zinc."

Madison paused momentarily to give him a warning look that only a sister could give. If a picture is worth a thousand words, then non-verbal communication must be worth a million.

"You know you talk a lot for someone whose about to get the number."

That smile again. Good Lawd! He must be hard to resist. But mom references this early in the conversation was a good sign. They must be close. Madison's cousin Ingrid told her that the first sign a man will treat you well is how he feels about his mother.

"See, now how you 'gone play my mama?"

"Damion, you wouldn't lie on your mother would you? With an arrogance like yours you must be the only man-child," Madison reasoned while handing him a business card, hoping he would notice her newly manicured nails. She just couldn't believe it. Here she was in Home Depot of all places, looking right funky in her jeans, t-shirt, an old blazer, and some even older cowboy boots that had seen better days. She'd booked a honey without even thinking about it, or was he booking her?

"Yes, one boy, five girls," he ventured, while perusing her business card. He must know women extremely well, Madison thought. That could be a good thing, or work against her. She'd have to play it careful.

"Madison Paige Robinson," he read aloud. "Computer Specialist—Help desk. My bad, I didn't know you were a techie. I hope you didn't get offended when I was talking about technology and this fast-paced world, were you? If so, I'm sorry." Damion looked at the floor. He reminded Madison of a little boy who'd just told the little girl he liked she was a 'dumbo head', and then realized it was the wrong thing to say. It was so cute when kids were little and didn't know curse words, they would put any combination of words together in their limited vocabularies. Too bad adults weren't like that.

"No, not at all. I don't take people's opinions personally." Madison figured she'd take the soft approach, noticing his extra-long eyelashes, which probably made it very difficult to say "no" to, and mean it. Beginning to feel uncomfortable with the way this stranger was occupying her personal space and jumpstarting her fantasies, Madison felt the urge to jet.

"Well, Mr...Damion," she stuttered realizing she didn't know his last name, "It was nice meeting you. I'll get that referral from you at a later date, closer to when I'll possibly need it." Speaking of needing it, Madison felt like she could go behind the sink wall display right now and have this brother take her standing up. She hoped she didn't sound too clinical or too pressed. It was hard to read his facial expression.

"It was really nice meeting you, Madison," Damion said genuinely. "I'll give you a call at work tomorrow and we can make plans. I'd sure like to see those nails wrapped around a fork, watching you eat with that beautiful color would make my meal a lot more pleasurable." Madison was sure he was about to say '...watching those nails wrapped around my dick would sure make your meal a lot more pleasurable.' Her imagination had gone buck wild. It was time to go.

"Remember what I said about the little things in life." Damion winked, turned on his heels and he was gone. Madison stood there, rooted to the spot. Wasn't she the one that was supposed to be leaving? Well, whatever. She turned back to the tubs, but it just wasn't the same. Her concentration was shot. She abruptly turned to leave and knocked into a display table, hurting her thigh. She looked around to make sure no one saw and spotted Damion in the next aisle. He had his back to her, running his fingers over a chrome showerhead. Thank God. Madison pulled her cigarettes out of her handbag and rushed outside to the cool air. She couldn't wait to light up, and tell Stacey about this man. Had she looked a little closer, she would have seen his shoulders shaking from laughing.

CHAPTER 3

Madison—"Why Do Bitches Always Get the Man?"
September 1999

Rrring! Rrring! Madison could barely fit her keys in the lock. After fumbling for what seemed like hours, she flew into her apartment and sprinted towards the phone, her heart racing faster than her legs. Rrring. She had to get it before the fourth ring. She checked the Caller ID with alarming speed: Norton-Shields. 555-6453. Madison needed to talk to her anyway. "What do you want, tramp?"

"Look, trick. I've got a story to tell you,"

The name-calling was a sick, yet exciting game with them.

"Well, I've got a story for you too, wench."

"Pssst. Your stories are always boring, let me tell mine first," Stacey demanded.

Madison sighed. As usual, Stacey would take the lead and tell her story first, anyway.

"Hold on! Hold on! Let me get my packages from outside the door, I just got in."

As Madison walked towards the door she remembered she hadn't given Damion her home number. Normally, she would have. However, she made a promise to herself last week, Labor Day, to play the little cat and mouse game that seems to be necessary in the District of Columbia. Personally, Madison preferred not to play games. Stacey was a master, though. She told Madison she would have to learn the rules, unless she wanted to date white men. "Brothers are hunters, women are gatherers, she'd caution. They love to hunt, chase, capture and conquer. Let 'em, but the trick is letting them think they've won, when you've set it up from jump. Don't you know you have half the battle won if a man thinks you've submitted to him, wholly and completely? He'll fall head over heels in love, thinking he made you. But there needs to be some surrender time involved, two weeks won't do it."

Madison heard this loud droning noise coming from the receiver. Apparently, she was taking too long and Stacey was pressing #4 on the touch tone phone, which held the letters, G, H, and I. Stacey used it for the H. Which stood for 'Hurry the Hell up, Hussy!' They had been playing the H game for as long as Madison could remember. 14 years at least. Silly girl. Madison threw her packages in a clump on the floor and plopped down on her overstuffed sofa. She picked up the remote as she brought the phone to her ear.

"Alright Stacey, spill it!"

"Not before you put that remote down. I know you're about to turn the TV on."

Madison sighed again. Loudly. This reminded her of the scene in *Ferris Bueller* where Ferris is trying to get Cameron to come over and Cameron is sitting in the car beating his forehead against the steering wheel, debating on whether he should go or not. Ferris said something like 'I bet Cameron is sitting in his car, trying to decide if he should come over here or not.' It was the same way between she and Stacey. They knew one another too well.

"You know, Stacey, sometimes you're more trouble than you're worth."

"Das not wot de man on de corner say lass night, chickee, he say me was irie!" Stacey giggled, mimicking a West Indian accent.

"Whatever."

"Question. Why is it that bitches always get the man?" That was another game they played, the WHY IS IT? The objective was to bring up thought-provoking questions there were no known answers for and ponder them. The question was usually rhetorical. Madison gave the question the allotted for quiet time and looked around her living room. It was so funky, the idea right out of *Metropolitan Home*. The green chenille sofa with the multicolored throw offset the burgundy leather chair with matching ottoman and the antique coffee table. The chair opposite the leather was a soft plaid with greens and yellows. A large orange pillow dared the chair to come to life. The room was balanced with tall, ornate, candles and decorative lamps. Two wooden bookshelves, one painted yellow and one painted green, packed tightly with American classics and African American literature held up the walls. Madison loved her living room because it mixed warm, inviting colors with rustic traditional elements that created the feeling of the passing of time, but allowed you to peek into the future.

"As I was saaaying," stressed Stacey, drawing as many syllables as she could out of the word, "why do bitches always get the man?"

"Stacey, we are not in church and you don't need call and response. Get to the point." Madison picked up a magazine and began to leaf through it while waiting for Stacey to finish up.

"O.K. O.K. O.K. We were kinda slow at the store this evening and I was straightening the counter. I heard this bickering and let my ears do the listening. An attractive couple stepped off the escalator. The woman was a tiny thing, slim, light-skinned with freckles and long red hair. It looked real though, no weave action, unless it was like a Janet Jackson weave. Anyway, she was giving her man the what for. He would listen patiently, then he'd deny whatever it was she was saying or accusing him of. Well, let me tell you, Madi, I had no shame. I stared at them until they stopped in front of my counter. Then I was slightly embarrassed. So then I started cleaning the countertop with Windex. The brother cleared his throat and said "Excuse me, we would like to purchase a fragrance." The little dynamo just glared at me like, witch, you weren't that busy a minute ago when you were all in our conversation. Anyway, he asks her if she wants the Prescriptives, you know, the Calyx you like so much.

'Hell, no! I want Issey Miyake,' she practically screamed. Now, Madi, we're talking a $70 price difference, at least. This chick had on all the latest gear, matching handbag and shoes, the works. He probably bought her everything she was wearing. The brother didn't look too bad. He was tall, gentlemanly, conservatively dressed and you could tell he cared about her. He had that 'Baby, I'll drink your bathwater look.' So girl, he pulled the gold Amex out of his wallet while I pointed to the Issey. "The eau de toilette or the parfum extract?"

'The big one,' she said confidently.

"The extract?" Madi, that runs around $135 dollars. She rolled her eyes and said 'Did I stutter? Just ring up the perfume.'

Her man was like, 'Crystal, baby, you don't have to take out your anger on her.'

'Shut up, D, and you don't have to mind my business.' By this time, Madi, I was totally sick of her, them and my position as a sales associate, which is the only thing that kept me from punching that munchkin in the face. So I ask again, why is it that bitches get the man? Is it because men are dogs and they like women with a little bitch in them?"

Madison picked up an *O* magazine and wondered about the significance of this story, which seemed inconsequential.

"Aw, come on, Stacey. There are some really decent brothers out there, here, even in D.C., even with the overwhelming women to men ratio. It's all good. Now keep the faith. I have to prepare for tomorrow, I'll call you later ok?"

Stacey's silence indicated she wasn't too keen on Madison's response. She loved to be right, and when she was challenged, she withdrew a bit. Besides, Madison barely touched the perfume story. She wasn't in the mood.

"What's your news?" Stacey sounded like she was moving around in the background.

"It doesn't matter. My stories are always boring anyway."

"Madison, you're about the most sensitive trick I know. We're going to have to get you some hard lessons. Alright, holla at 'ya."

Madison hung up without saying goodbye. Stacey exhausted her, sometimes. She mustered enough energy to put away her items, pick out her clothes for tomorrow and brush her teeth. By the time she crawled between crisp, cool sheets and her head hit the pillow, she was already dreaming about bathtubs.

CHAPTER 4

Crystal Renee Leonard—Being a Judge Ain't Easy
September 1999

      Crystal rolled her eyes toward the ceiling in her hearing room, listening to yet another lie from a law breaker. A quick flip of the wrist and her Raymond Weil informed her that it was 11:30 am Why hadn't she heard from Damion yet? He was supposed to take her to lunch. She forced herself to pay attention to case #14587, a Ms. Johnson who was babbling aimlessly about buying Similac for her baby as opposed to paying her tickets. Crystal remembered her Dad telling her that anyone who repeated himself or herself was lying. And Ms. Johnson was threepeating herself. She sounded as if she were chanting...

"Similac, Similac, Similac—"

"Ms. Johnson," Crystal began tiredly. "You are in violation of the law, of which you have broken several times. In the past six months, you've received three moving violations, and that's just what you got caught with. You have twenty parking tickets, and..." Crystal paused on the 'and' as she flipped through some paperwork. "and one charge of indecent exposure to a traffic policeman. With all that, how can you be innocent?" said Crystal, glaring at the woman. Unphased, the woman continued her defense.

"You see yo honna, I got my doctor's note right here to explain."

As Ms. Johnson reached in what appeared to be a newly purchased street vendor imitation Gucci bag, a big black shiny cockroach crawled out and scuttled under the bench. Crystal tried not to recoil in horror. Ms. Johnson appeared not to notice, and triumphantly produced a slip of paper. "Here it is!" she exclaimed, gold teeth gleaming. Crystal motioned for her to bring the document to the dais. Despite being ghetto fabulous, the woman walked like a model. Ms. Johnson's brown cat suit blended perfectly with her tanned cocoa butter skin. Her leopard-belted waist was mannequin sized, and her matching leopard pumps added a good three inches to her slim 5'8 frame. As she handed the bailiff the note, her gold nails, which were curved like wilting ferns, sparkled like pirate's booty, a chest full of gold bouillons. When she turned around to walk back to the table, Ms. Johnson's earrings clicked and bounced off one another in rhythm with her jiggling behind. The men in the hearing room couldn't take their eyes off of her. Crystal noticed Ms. Johnson wasn't wearing any underwear and wondered if she did that on purpose? Probably. If she were a male judge the infractions would have been pardoned, and this heifer was probably hoping she got a male too. Ah well, not today.

Why did people always try to take advantage of her? She believed her height had something to do with it. She felt small on the dais, flanked by the DC flag and the US flag. She learned early on that many people took petite folks for granted. That realization, which kicked in at age 9, made her all the more tough. You had to be tough in this environment as a DC hearing examiner. During her tenure here, Crystal had heard some incredible lies.

People were always trying to get over. Occasionally, someone would just say, "I was wrong, I know I was wrong. I shouldn't have parked there, but can you come down on the ticket?" Because of their honesty, sometimes Crystal would. But this Johnson chick; con artist was written all over her.

Crystal put on her glasses to read the note that came from the roach coach. She reached for her gavel.

"Ms. Johnson, I am hereby charging you $500 for past due fines. Pay the court or your car will be impounded. Case dismissed!" she said, slamming the gavel with finality.

"But Judd," pleaded Ms. Johnson, "you see my letter."

"What I see is a note by a doctor who stated you had multiple sclerosis disorder as opposed to multiple personalities and besides, multiple is misspelled. This case is over, Ms. Johnson."

"Now you listen here, you uppity Judd, you know I 'caint afford no tickets, so I'm going to 'peal."

Crystal sighed heavy and long. Her patience was being tried, for sure. She wanted to say,

"I don't care if you have to borrow it, steal it or trick for it in your little see-through body suit. Get the money any way you can and pay the court. Now get out! Your APPEAL is denied!"

Instead she said,

"Impound lot, no impound lot; it's your choice."

The defeated Ms. Johnson slunk to the door.

"Take your roach with you," Crystal murmured. 11:45. Damion really should have called by now. She was frustrated as hell. She got that way when she hadn't spoken with him in the morning, or before she went to bed. She couldn't function right. But, she'd never let him know that.

"Hello, gorgeous!! You ready to go to lunch?" asked a friendly voice.

"Tony, hi! Sure, I'll go with you, but if Damion calls, I have to meet him."

"Damion Smamion," Tony smirked. "I'm sick of hearing about that brotha. Five years and he still hasn't asked your fine ass to marry him? What's up with that? What's wrong wit 'em, girlfriend?"

"Tony, please. Don't start in on him today. I do enough damage myself."

"See, that's your problem. That's where the brother has power over you. You keep pointing the finger at yourself, when the problem is him."

"Tony, I'm warning you!"

"Alright already. Come on, get off that dais before some disgruntled defendant comes and shoots at you with pistols in both hands, talking about 'You knew I didn't have the money, else I wouldn't have got no tickets in the first place!" Crystal laughed a short, piercing laugh. Tony joined her and their laughter echoed together in the empty chamber. She and Tony always said, one day, someone was going to go postal and blow the joint up, and their final words wouldn't make a damn bit of sense.

"Do I need money?" she inquired, reaching for her handbag.

"Do you ever need money when you're with me?"

Tony reached for Crystal's hand to help her off the dais. As they walked arm in arm out of the chamber, Tony glanced at the wall and broke into Florida Evans mode. "Damn! Damn! Damn! James, I'm so tired of living in the ghetto. The roaches could at least pay rent!"

Crystal picked up the cue and imitated James, "Well, you better call Bookman to come take care of it. Maybe he'll be able to do that right!" They continued with the "Good Times" imitations until they got to the food court.

CHAPTER 5

Madison—"Lunch?"
September 1999

"Help desk Madison speaking."

"Well, hello dear. How are you today?" asked a syrupy voice. Madison looked at the ID. x2296. Damn. It was Mrs. Portal. She was a nice lady, but she and computers did not make good bed partners. No matter how many times you'd tell her something, she'd forget. Mrs. Portal's phone calls alone generated enough volume for another full-time help desk position.

"What can I do for you today, Mrs. Portal?" said Madison, determined to be nice to this woman no matter what.

"Hee hee, you recognized my voice, eh?"

"No, Mrs. Portal," Madison patiently responded, "I'm looking at my Caller ID."

"Tsk. I can't use all that fancy stuff. Today is so different from 20 years ago." Madison groaned inwardly, thinking how much she'd like to get to Mrs. Portal's problem, today.

"Back in my day, we were happy to see typewriters."

Madison tensed, she knew a long, drawn out story was coming.

"You know, that's where shorthand came from, we secretaries had to write everything by hand, and with the way people talked, all fast and everything, you had better come up with a shortcut."

Madison motioned to her girlfriend in the next cube. She put an index finger on her lips and used her right hand to signal that Ayanna was to speak to her very loudly. Mrs. Portal's stories were always part truth, part fiction, and the sooner anyone figured that out, the better off they would be.

"And my old boss, he used to say, that—"

"Excuse me, Madison. I need to see you as soon as possible!"

Ayanna was right on cue. She should be, they practiced different scenarios often for times just like this.

"Oh, is that someone for you, dear?"

"Yes, maam, I don't have long."

"Let me try to explain my problem, then."

Madison gave Ayanna an O.K. sign and blew her a kiss.

"I can't seem to find the letter I was working on for Mr. Thomas," Madison heard Mrs. Portal punching keys.

"He's a VP, I can't mess this up."

Madison felt a little sorry for Mrs. Portal, this job was her life. She'd been there 25 years.

"I assume you are/were in MS WORD?"

"No, maam! I was working in WordPerfect, and I turned my back to answer the phone, and then everything just disappeared."

Madison could imagine the confused woman now; easily 280 pounds, loud perfume, red wig and stubby little painted nails clutching at her throat, helpless style, looking like the black Mimi from "The Drew Carey Show."

"Mrs. Portal, there is no WordPerfect in MS Office. But do you see any rectangular bars at the bottom of your screen shaped like a Kit Kat?" Madison figured she'd be able to relate to the candy bar thing, being food and all.

"Yes, I see. There it is. Madison, you're the greatest. The Kit Kat bar has the name of the letter on it! All I have to do is click it, right? Yes! There it is. Thanks, dear! Click.

Madison looked in the dead receiver and shook her head. As soon as she placed it on the hook it rang again. It was extremely busy for a Monday, it usually took folks a good two days to actually buckle down and do some real work.

"Help desk. Madison Robinson."

"Hi, Madi, what's up girl?" said a chipper voice.

"Nothing much, just the usual, you know, Mrs. Portal."

"Ah, the portly one. I'm sorry girlfriend."

"It's ok," chirped Madison. "How are Mitch and the kids?"

"The kids are psyched about school, Mitch and I brainwashed them all summer, and he just landed two major contracts."

"Excellent, Pilar. That's just wonderful. Girl, you know the Lord is smiling on you."

Pilar was Madison's favorite work buddy. They ate lunch together often and she'd visit her family on certain holidays for cookouts and such. Madison often used the couple as a litmus test for the new guys in her life. They were usually dead on in their assessment. Pilar and Mitch had met at least two of Madison's boyfriends. Kenny Langston took to Mitch like he was a long lost brother. Joe Willis felt like Mitch represented the father he'd never met. Mitch could do that to people. He had a way of making everyone feel at home and comfortable in his presence. Pilar was lucky. Besides two beautiful healthy kids, they had tangible goods, such as a McMansion in Upper Marlboro, a Lexus truck, a Benz, and a black Lab to boot. Pilar was a fox. 5'7, a buck thirty, and curves for days. You'd never imagine she'd had children. During one of their many lunches, Madison verbalized her respect for her friend.

"Pilar, I want to be like you when I grow up."

She admired the fact that Pilar was so good-natured and sensible.

"Madison," she'd say slowly, for effect, "It wasn't easy. I was 31 when I met Mitchell. 33 when we married, and you know the young ones came shortly after that. I never thought I'd get married, especially in DC. If I hadn't bumped into him in Fresh Fields, I'd probably be single, still. So keep your chin up."

After that conversation, Madison envisioned wearing a chinstrap. She needed one, as many times as she'd fallen on her face, relationship after tired relationship. She was 29 and had seen four serious boyfriends, one more serious than the next, or so she thought. She'd dogged at least two good men who wanted to give her the world, but she was younger then, and they weren't exciting enough. She thought she wanted that heart-stopping, mind-stimulating, body trembling stupid kind of lasting love—if it existed. Madison truly believed it did.

"So what's up Pilar? I know your problem will be quick and easy."

"I can't even begin to tell you my problem," she sighed wearily.

"Pilar? You ok?" The defeated tone of Pilar's voice was strange and new to Madison.

"Yeah, baby, you know me, always trying to do a million things at once. I'm fine. You know a black woman ain't allowed to get tired. Look here, I seem to be having trouble with the printer. I sent a document to the printer three times and nothing. The printer has plenty of paper and it's online."

Madison felt as if Pilar were talking about something else, but she held her tongue. If Pilar had something to say, she would tell her in her own time, in her own way.

"Hmmm, minimize your screen for me, Pilar. Now go into MS Office. You there? Good. Click on the control panel. Click on the printer icon. Double-click it. Now you should be able to see the printer's status. What does it say?"

"Printer not found."

"No problem, see that default right above your window? Good, what does it say?"

"All kinds of funny looking symbols, backslash, backslash, underbar and lpt2."

"Great, it's supposed to be printing to lpt1. Now use your down arrow and highlight funny looking symbols, double backslash, underbar Lpt1. Ok? Now what's happening? Ah, music to my ears. I hear it, now, baby."

"Madison, you're a genius," Pilar said gratefully.

"I'm broke like one too," laughed Madison. "Geniuses are only well-known after they die, they don't make shit when they're alive."

"Listen, Ms. Morbidity, do you wanna do lunch on payday Thursday?"

"Sure thing Ms. Moneybags. Thank you."

Madison hung up the receiver, smiling. This would be a good time to stop, grab a quick lunch, so she could work on her latest editorial. The phone rang. Madison glanced at the display which showed an outside call with a number she didn't recognize.

"Help desk, Madison Robinson."

"Hello, Madison. This is Mr. Cross calling. I need help with my appetite. Will you join me for lunch at Café Zados? Madison giggled.

"Dat sounds just especial," she said with a Spanglish accent. "I was going to go to wings, wings and mo wings and get some of that special mambo sauce. Zados is a step-up." Madison had only heard of Zados, although she'd been told it was very nice.

"Great. Where do you work?" Damion sounded very businesslike over the phone. Madison could tell he was on a cellular because of the traffic, but it seemed extra loud.

"14th and K streets, NW. I'll be outside by the circle, what time?"

Damion snorted. "So you working in that red light district, hunh?"

"Damion, please. You can tell you're from DC, that was over 15 years ago. The streets are clean now, dahlin! Now what time?"

"12:30, and I'm not from DC"

"Well, we'll discuss that when I see you. 12:30 is good."

"Alright. See you soon. I'm in a black convertible Saab 900 SE."

So that's why the noise was magnified. It was 12:15, he must have been close.

Madison grabbed her handbag and her pumps. It did not pay to ride the subway in heels. Sneakers and socks were the rule of comfort for the morning and afternoon. Forget looking cute. The phone rang. Forget about it. She ran towards the ladies room. She quickly brushed her teeth. Didn't want to approach homeboy with cigarette breath in case he was a non-smoker. She reapplied her make-up. Mac, don't leave home without it, she hummed, while dabbing her neck and wrists with a sample of Christian Dior's Dolce Vita. Before leaving, Madison checked herself out in the full-length mirror. No runs, check, no scuff marks on the pumps, check, hair and nails immaculate, check, mauve double breasted suit with gold buttons giving off the Chanel look, check! Just because she worked the help desk didn't mean she had to look like a junkyard dog. Madison stepped out of the ladies room head held high, and most importantly, chin-up!

CHAPTER 6

**Crystal—"No Lunch"
September 1999**

The food court at the Department of Adjudication was special. It was no ordinary food court. It featured a four-star seafood restaurant, sushi bars, fresh fruit and yogurt stands, authentic Greek cuisine, kosher delis, as well as the usual American foodstuffs. The only oddity was a Taco Bell, and Tony was drawn to that like white on rice. Crystal opted for a grilled chicken kabob from the Greek place. It came with basmati rice, salad and pita.

Tony looked around for a minute, and saw a table near a water fountain surrounded by real plants and filled with different kinds of goldfish.

"How about here?"

"Sure. I likes getting sprayed with the watah," Crystal chirped, *Gone With The Wind*, style, surveying the rapidly filling food court.

"We can sit somewhere else," said Tony obligingly.

"This is fine," said Crystal eyeing the pile of food on Tony's tray.

"I want you to enjoy your lunch before it gets cold, although it probably already is."

"Don't jone, now" Tony warned, "or it's on."

There was no reason for Crystal to take out her frustration on Tony. He just pushed a button when he talked about Damion not asking her to marry him, yet. She couldn't figure out what the holdup was. Tony had been a close friend since they graduated from Howard eight years ago. He'd been an ally at work for three. She could always count on him for support, advice and sympathy. He had a girlfriend, but they were doing the long distance thing. She was in a masters-PhD program at a school in Memphis. Tony treated her like a queen, when he saw her.

The insistent double-ring of her cellular brought Crystal out of her brief reverie. She quickly placed her tray on the table and answered. "Crystal Leonard, speaking."

Her face fell. "Yes, hi. I'd heard, but I wasn't quite sure, by credit card? Thanks. Yes I will. You too. Bye."

"Who was it and what was that all about?"

Crystal sat down and watched him unwrap his burrito and fix it with sour cream, salsa and hot sauce.

"That was Darrell. I won't have to hold court this afternoon. Case #32106 paid their tickets."

"Cool. You're getting these rogues straightened out, girlfriend, I'm proud of you," said Tony warmly. Crystal looked at him thoughtfully, munching away on his burrito. He was a good-looking guy. He made good money, had his own place, a good head on his shoulders. He was only 5'9, but he carried it well. After swimming in high school, he developed a strong, muscular upper torso, with a wide chest and nicely rounded shoulders. He dressed well, and had a good sense of humor. But there was something missing. They got along extremely well, which is more than she could say for Damion, whom she loved with a fierce love, although she knew, or felt, things weren't completely right. She couldn't quiet put her finger on it, but she dealt with whatever it was. She had this inescapable fear that one day, Damion was going to meet someone, someone really special to him, and that would be it. Crystal knew that by now she was just a habit. There were still some sparks in the bedroom, but she had to be honest with herself, that was about it. There hadn't even been much of that lately, either. She hoped her fears weren't going to become a self-fulfilling prophecy. She needed to get out of this funk.

"Tony, you'd be cute if you didn't have so many teeth."

She gave Tony a sly, coy look.

"Oh, Crys. Don't start! At least I don't have to use a stepladder to open my freezer."

"You got me. How was your morning? Any drama?"

Tony almost choked on his second burrito. He gulped down some of his Coke, and began to laugh silently. "Did I? It was All My Negroes in the office today, girlfriend. Starring the black Erica Cane, with a special appearance by Fire Marshall Bill from "In Living Color."

"Do tell," said Crystal. She looked forward to good juice.

"Whatever it is can't possibly top my morning."

"That's what you think, little Napoleon. Remember Raunchy Rita?"

Crystal's eyes widened with recognition.

"You mean half-black, half Puerto Rican, 'joo can't tell me nuthin,' broke down Lisa Lisa and the Cult Jam, always trying to get over with them four babies Rita?"

"Si, Senorita, that's the one!"

Crystal leaned forward while daintily munching on a piece of pita. She had a feeling this was going to be a good one. Tony managed a ceremonial "ahem", signaling the beginning of gossip that could top no other, at least for the moment.

"Since we grew up in the same neighborhood, I figured I'd try to help a sister out."

Tony sucked his teeth.

"She used to, or is, dating this fireman. Once in a while, dude freaks out, forgets she's a woman, and beats her like she stole something. Now, I'm sure Rita gives him a run for the money, but the last time he went too far and she ended up in Providence Hospital with bruised ribs and a fractured arm. Now, according to Rita he's stalking her and threatening to impregnate her. She's caught him peeking behind trees and ducking behind cars in parking lots.

"Yeah. Treeboxing."

"Right. Whatever, but she comes to me, her old buddy, trying to get me to have someone sign a restraining order. I buy her sob story. I figure Judge Goslee would be sympathetic to an abuse case, although I felt uneasy about asking the Judge for a favor like that. She is a very busy woman.

So Ms. Rita and I are in my office, and I'm explaining to her the implications of this restraining order since she claimed the police weren't very clear or friendly; trying to convince her not to go soft if and when dude shows up, when HE crashes into my office!" Tony is interrupted by Crystal's cellular.

"Excuse me, Tony," she said, holding out her hand to stop him from talking.

"Crystal Leonard, speaking. Oh, hi baby."

She fiddled with her rice.

"No, I didn't wait. I'm having lunch with Tony. He's telling me this juicy story, I'll tell you all about it when I see you. Which will be?"

She paused while taking in Damion's story, and rolled a black olive around on her plate.

"Really? A new one? Lots of money? I understand. Hmm mmm. Look, I've got the rest of the afternoon off. You want to go to the driving range, say around 4:30?

It's really nice out. Yes. I'll be home waiting, then. Love you, too. Bye." Crystal barely looked at Tony after flipping her phone shut.

"He's meeting a new client, right?"

"Yes, a new one whom he feels has a lot of potential."

"What's her name?"

Crystal didn't care for the accusation. She wanted to believe Damion. She needed to believe him.

"I'm sorry Crys, it's just that I care about you, and I want you to be happy, but that brother is suspect. I swear. He's one of those woulda coulda brothers. 'I was going to do this, and I could have done that, BUT, I had to meet a client.' What he needs to do is put a ring on them fine, but aging fingers of yours. You'll be 32 soon."

Crystal cut him off.

"Tony! Please finish your story. Please! You persist on badgering the witness here, please!"

"You know what they say in a court of equity, Crystal. Let us all come with equal hands."

"Tony, if you don't stop right now!"

Tony knew he had gone too far. He just wanted to push her buttons to make her think sometimes. She was a fool for Damion, and Tony knew what he was up to. He'd seen him out on more than a couple of occasions, escorting some long-legged honey to and from some chic bar or restaurant, talking about 'it's a client.' 'It's bullshit. That's what it is,' Tony thought bitterly.

"Alright," he said switching gears, "Where was I? Help me out, Crys."

"You were at the part when the boyfriend comes into your office."

Crystal reminded him, feeling as if she'd gotten the wind knocked out of her, mentally.

"No, *cumming* is apparently what he wants to do, with Raunchy Rita. I said he burst, meaning slamming doors open and everything, burst into the scene looking crazy. Rita saw him and don't you know that bitch, excuse me, that woman started smiling? He then turned to me, and Crys, this is a big dude. He's at least 6'4. You can tell he works out, because his uniform was a tad tight, and I'm being generous with the description. So he looks at me and squints his eyes, threateningly. All I could do was watch his jugular vein perform the Macarena. He pointed at my desk, which, as you know is overflowing with papers and shit, and said 'That piece of paper don't mean nothing to me. And if you mess 'wit me, I am going to burn your house up, and no one would be able to prove it, because I know what I'm doing!' Crystal, I was bugging."

"What'd you do?" Crystal clasped her hands like a little kid at Disney World who'd just met Mickey Mouse.

"I tore up the request while those two slobbed each other down. It was quite disturbing."

Crystal doubled over, holding her sides while her laughter resonated through the noisy food court.

"Now ain't that some shit?" Tony laughed slightly. The memory was a little too fresh and painful for him. Noticing his mood, Crystal finished her sparkling water and stood up, gathering his trash and hers on the plastic tray.

"People be tripping nowadays."

"Yeah, they be tripping alright," agreed Tony, "Now put that in your Ebonics pipe and smoke it."

They exited the food court much the same way they had entered. Arm in arm and laughing up a storm.

CHAPTER 7

**Damion Eric Cross—Life Is Good
September 1999**

A s Damion raced down North Capitol street he smiled broadly to himself. Life was all that. Aunt Linda told him that college would be the best time of his life. Aunty was tripping. 10 years later was even better. Damion's career was getting ready to blow up, he could feel it. As the voice of WJAZ's nightly mellow moods introduction, and sometimes DJ, his popularity was increasing, hell, the NEXT group had even labeled him one of Washington's most eligible bachelors.

The group consisted of young black urban professionals in the know. They were the next generation of doctors, lawyers, executives, politicians; in short, the group considered themselves tomorrow's movers and shakers in the Metropolitan area. They were advocates for career advancement, economic empowerment, and keeping the white folks on their toes and Damion was fast approaching membership.

Many of the members were married, power couples, and that posed a bit of a problem for Damion at the moment. He figured the most eligible bachelor thing was meant to jumpstart the dating game so he could choose a mate, knock her over the head, and drag her to his cave. That may have been exaggerated, but that's how Damion felt about it. Marriage just didn't appeal to him at the moment. There were too many honeys swarming around, too many willing honeys, too many willing, professional honeys. He had Crystal; they'd been together, more on than off, for five years. He loved her, but something was missing. That something led to steamy and heated affairs with Chaka, Kitty and Junie. For some reason, Chaka just stopped calling. Kitty was gearing up to become a psycho-bitch, so he cut her off, and Junie, Junie was just drama, but she was very creative behind closed doors. They were all very beautiful, intelligent sisters with long legs. Ah well, maybe that's why he hadn't asked Crystal to marry him, she was petite, with well-proportioned legs, but short. Plus she wasn't much trouble. She was into him, him and him. Crystal definitely had a brotha's back. Lately she'd been a little more difficult, but who knows why? Maybe her girls were making her feel stupid for not being married. Back in the day, he would have married any of them, but lately he'd been meeting class A sister after class A sister. He kept having this feeling that something was just beyond the horizon, and without a doubt within reach.

Take for example, the honey he'd met this past weekend. He'd seen her, of all places, at the Home Depot on Rhode Island Avenue. When he first spotted her, she had her back to him, but she passed the Levi's test. She passed with flying colors. They fit her snugly and comfortably. Her jacket split just right in the back to show the curves of her behind perfectly. Her blazer even had patches on the elbows. Her hair was jet black and healthy. Without even thinking he'd approached her with his best voiceover voice. "You don't see what you want, do you?" She'd turned around so quickly, it made him nervous, but when he saw that face, that face so alive with delight, wonder and curiosity, the nervousness dissolved. She was a perfect brown, with large, inviting eyes and the most delicate, full lips. Damion didn't remember much of the conversation, all he knew is that he wanted to see her again. She would look stunning in a short evening dress with those long legs. She had legs for days. He did remember getting her business card because her nails looked good. She didn't write down her home number, but he would get it. There was something about her. He felt the urge to explore her mentally and spiritually. The physical would come eventually. Of that he was confident.

Damion thought of Madison the rest of the evening. He felt guilty so he took Crystal shopping for some perfume she wanted, although her birthday wasn't until April. She was in her "asshole" mode, too. The sales clerk, her name was Stacey, looked at him like she felt sorry for him. He remembered her name because she had huge breasts, and Damion appreciated nice breasts, what man didn't? Sometimes he wondered why Crystal stuck with him. There were times when he just didn't want to be bothered and he'd disappear, not call, just distance himself. Crystal always thought it was another woman, which wasn't true. Occasionally, he needed space and time for Damion. This Damion time was a hard concept for Crystal to swallow. She'd caught him once with Junie. He was only planning to get with her one time, but Junie made a brother feel like a king, and he went back a few more times, until Crystal walked in on them after returning home early from a business trip. The door was unlocked because Damion was in the shower when Junie came over, and she'd forgotten to lock it, and he'd forgotten to check if she'd locked it. When the door opened, Damion and Junie were sitting on the sofa watching the Perky Pediatrician, a freaky nurse who played doctor with all her male and female patients. Damion was about to suggest that Junie role-play the perky, energetic ped when he heard the door slam. Crystal had knocked, but a patient was knocking on the doctor's door at the same time. Damion was so engrossed, he didn't see the door open, and what followed made for a great story with the boys when he went out drinking later that night. It was an ugly scene. No words. Just a flurry of hair, nails and cursing to rival any navy ship. Damion broke up the two women, holding his laughter, and kicked Junie out. He tried to get back with Crystal for six months. He'd crept with Junie just once more, but it wasn't the same. He kept visualizing her getting a beat down. Crystal may be small, but she was powerful. Thinking he might actually lose her made Damion straighten up, besides, dating two honeys was getting expensive.

On this particular Monday morning, he woke up feeling especially buoyed. When Crystal came out of the shower, he decided to surprise her.

"Baby, let me take you to lunch today," he volunteered.

She shot him a look as she lotioned her body.

"Damion, you haven't done that in so long, what'd you do?"

"Why a brother gotta be up to something? You look too deeply into shit, Crystal."

"OK. Lunch is good. People at work think Tony and I are an item we're together so much." Damion squeezed some of the scented cream in his hand, and began to lotion Crystal's back.

"Fuck people at work. Tony's probably gay anyway, always saying 'girlfriend this and girlfriend that. You funny Crystal, and so is your boy, and I don't mean the same kind of funny."

Crystal turned around and punched him in the shoulder.

"Well, since you don't have a 9 to 5, my friends don't think you have a real job."

"Fuck your friends, Crystal. That's why none of them have any men. They too critical. But, that's a conversation best saved for another day, I've gotta voiceover this morning, I'll call you when I'm finished, alright?" Damion sat on the bed while Crystal finished dressing.

"Sure. First the perfume, now the lunch. Studies have shown that guilty people overcompensate. I'll be anticipating your call.

Oh, and Tony's not gay, he's just in touch with his feminine side, and to me that's manly. And my girlfriends are not critical, just observant."

Damion, sensing things could get heated, decided to concede.

"C'mon baby." He jumped off the bed as she put on her earrings and grabbed her from behind. "The only thing I'm guilty of is being pressed for you, counselor," he confessed and kissed her lightly on the neck.

"Damion, please. I can't be late this morning, although my case probably will be."

They both laughed. Crystal studied their reflections in the mirror. He was so tall and scrumptious.

"Where's your gig?" she asked wrenching out of his inviting arms.

"Gary's Auto Insurance."

"No! Not Gary's!" Crystal exclaimed while pulling on her pantyhose. "Isn't he the one that uses that Go-Go music in the background of his tired commercials?"

"The one and only. Remember his last one? Talking about 'Wind me up, Gary, other insurance costs are scary. Wind me up, Gary.'"

"Yep. That one was over the top."

As Crystal finished putting on her clothes, Damion studied her intensely.

"You look good, baby. Smell good, too."

Crystal motioned Damion towards her. She stood on her tiptoes and kissed him lightly on the lips.

"Thank you, stinky breath. Don't forget to lock the top lock when you leave, and don't be going through my shit either." She smiled seductively and walked out of the bedroom, switching for effect, because she knew Damion was watching.

Damion laughed to himself as he watched Crystal leave the room. She was trying to act cute when she already was cute. Go figure. He waited until he heard her close the door and plopped back on the bed. He figured he'd chill for half an hour, run by his place, grab some clothes and scoot over to Gary's. He drifted into a deep sleep wondering how long it would take him to hit the national scene. What a story; from Gary's Auto Insurance to NFL Monday Night color commentator, kicking it with John Madden. That would be sweet!

Damion woke up later than he expected. He jumped up, took a quick shower, shaved, wrapped a towel around his waist and searched through his part of Crystal's closet for something to wear while brushing his teeth. Good, his gray Hickey Freeman was here. He'd been looking for it, too. Bet. Crystal had his cornflower blue shirt dry-cleaned and starched. She'd even snuck and purchased a matching tie. The tag hung loosely from the inside stitching in case he didn't like it. Crystal would do shit like that, buy him something and spring it on him when he least expected it. Her thoughtfulness was an endearing quality that caused him to gush with unexpected warm feelings towards her. "You go girl," he whistled softly to himself as he opened his drawer and pulled out some silk boxers and a pair of gray dress socks with blue doo dads. Crystal had picked these out, also. She must have been preparing to take him to one of her endless lawyer functions. Damn. This was so easy. Easier than getting dressed at home, where shit was scattered here and there. He and Crystal had discussed living together several times, but he couldn't bring himself to do it, not yet. For now, Crystal was satisfied with a quasi living arrangement and he still had a place to call home; which was a small, but modern studio on Connecticut Avenue, sparsely decorated, but comfortable. If he played his cards right, he hoped to win a housing lottery the following spring and purchase an old row house near Historic U street, which was experiencing serious gentrification. Damion was rather confident he would get it. The woman heading the lottery liked him. He'd already reconciled that it would be necessary to pull a stunt like Eddie Murphy's character did in *Boomerang* when he got with Eartha Kitt. Shoot, in order to get closer to the American dream, Damion would go ahead and take one for the team. His team, that is, and he'd get that house, too. He was in the position to take a chance in a sketchy neighborhood on the rise. Plus, the old heads were sure that "U" street would return to its former glory the way it was before the riots of 1968.

Damion turned right off Minnesota Avenue into Gary's parking lot. He was 15 minutes late, but he didn't see Gary's Cadillac. Damion flipped aimlessly through an outdated magazine while he waited for Gary and listened to the receptionist talk about Andre this and Andre that. From what he could gather she lived, ate and slept Andre. But when Gary walked in the office 30 minutes later, she was talking about Winston.

"I hope old girl is using condoms," he thought, while he stood up to hi five Gary's ring-laden hands.

"What's up man!" Damion said while slightly turning up his nose at Gary's loud cologne.

"My man D! Looking like a million dollars! How unh, how you like MY threads?"

Gary spun around for Damion to take in the royal blue rayon shirt open at the neck with the fly wide collar. The three gold chains around his neck sparkled radiantly as they played off the gold in his tooth. He sported some tight, black polyester pants with a pair of black and brown driving moccasins that were losing a fight with the white, well almost white, more like dirty gray, sweat socks.

"You got it, player!" Damion smiled tightly, trying not to laugh.

"Look man, sorry I'm a little late, but you know, the Little Lady wouldn't let me get out of bed this morning, you know what I mean?" Gary said, winking a glazed eye.

Damion nodded, wondering how any man could put booty and weed before business? Well, to each his own, as long as he got paid. Last he remembered, Gary's Little Lady wasn't so little. But, maybe in Gary's eyes...

"Come on down to the studio, man so we can knock this thing out. I promised the Little Lady I'd be back before noon." Maybe Little Lady was just a saying, or a nickname.

Damion followed Gary down the hall and marveled at all the shit he had going on. He sold pagers, cell phones, used luggage and took passport pictures. It was almost as if he had a one-stop shop for leaving the country in a hurry.

Gary handed Damion the commercial copy and guided him in the audio booth. Damion placed the headphones over his head, tapped the mike to see if it was on, and began practicing. Gary had turned his back to Damion and was whispering to two of his partners outside the booth.

"Need insurance for your car?
You got so many points
You can't get far?
Don't despair and don't be wary
Buy your insurance from Gary!"

It was all Damion could do to keep from doubling over with laughter. He cleared his throat.

"Yo, man. Do I read this or rap this?"

"Damion," Gary sighed impatiently while bringing up the pot, "Just read normal like. When we lay your voice track we'll have DJ Ateezy come in with his beats. Don't worry about it, we've got it all under control." Gary looked hard at Damion, glanced at his partner and eased the pot back down, but not before Damion heard him say "I told you that nigga was too bourgeois, we shoulda got Black to do it."

A determined Damion finished in two takes. Gary seemed pleased, after all. He came in the sound booth, gave Damion the grip, and handed him a check. Damion watched for a few minutes while the editor skillfully blended Damion's polished standard English voice with the throaty home grown sounds of DJ Ateezy's Go-Go beats.

He had to admit, it sounded good.

No one noticed when he left, they were busy laughing at something. Damion wondered briefly if it was him. Well, whatever, they was bamas anyway.

As soon as he stepped outside, Damion's skin tingled. It was one of those perfect, flawless, humid-free DC days. He had to do something special to match his mood. Immediately he thought of Madison. He'd take her to lunch at Café Zados. It was a moderate, urban and hip establishment, serving traditional soul food dishes, upscale style. Zados was strategically located on the 14th floor of the Calloway Hotel, overlooking the city. Madison worked downtown, Zados was downtown, so she couldn't give an excuse like not being able to go too far due to time and all that shit. This way he had it all covered. While Damion waited for the top to come down in his car, he searched for her card in his wallet.

First he called Crystal and canceled. He felt a twinge of guilt, but it only lasted a minute. He'd make it up to her. He always did. Besides, she was having lunch with her friend Tony, which was alright, for at least he'd keep her entertained. He chuckled softly to himself, recalling how Crystal thought people at her job would think they were a couple. Damion wasn't worried in the least about Tony pulling up on Crystal because he had a feeling Tony played for the other team, anyway, with an invisible girlfriend. No one had seen her and Tony claimed she was in some masters program at a school down south. How convenient. Crystal considered him her best friend, but Damion didn't want to hurt her feelings. He was just screaming to come out of the closet any day now.

Next he called Café Zados and reserved a window table for two. He then dialed Madison's number and wondered briefly if he was doing the right thing. Once he pressed the SEND button, and heard her voice, cheerful, but tired-sounding, doubt flew out the window. She sounded the same over the phone as she did in person, FINE. "Help desk, Madison Robinson." Deciding to get straight to the point, he asked her out. She accepted. His spirits lifted, Damion popped in a Jamiroquai CD at a red light, and headed towards Madison's job.

CHAPTER 8

Madison—Intrigue
September 1999

Madison made it downstairs before Damion arrived. Her smoking buddy, Demetrius was leaning against the rail; listlessly watching the cars drive by. "Hey, Maddy, what's up Damn girl You 'lookin fly Wanna smoke?" He talked so fast it sounded like one sentence. His rhythm didn't match his relaxed-looking body, but that was Demetrius.

"No, thanks Deme. Enough mail for you, today?"

"Man. The Man 'bout to make me quit. He keep changing the delivery policy, confusing a 'brotha!" said Demetrius, waving his arms wildly. "I mean, deliver this to Ms. Badejo, deliver that to Mr....Daaamn! That's a bad ride." Demetrius stopped mid-sentence and ogled a black Saab pulling up in front of the building.

"It's about time," thought Madison. She was getting tired of standing there trying to look sexy, flexing her calf muscles, standing magazine style. She waved and gave Damion the 'I'll be there in one minute sign.'

"Deme, I don't mean to be rude, but I've gotta go."

"Damn, you know dude? You see them 20's?"

Madison didn't respond. She thought his momma should've named him *damn* instead of Demetrius, as much as he overused the word. She walked down the short flight of stairs towards Damion and his 'bad ride.'

Damion jumped from the driver's seat, walked to the passenger side, and opened the door for Madison.

"Hi, Damion. Thanks," she mentioned, slightly planting a kiss on his cheek. Damion thought she kissed him like she owned him. It seemed as if Madison had been kissing on him for a lifetime.

"This might be dangerous," he thought excitingly as a chill traveled down his spine.

Madison settled into the convertible daintily, crossing her long legs for effect. She snuck a peek at Damion's rear as he lithely crossed over to the driver's side. Although he looked good in his suit, she wished he had on some jeans. Damion looked Madison up and down with obvious appreciation. Madison pretended not to notice as she adjusted her seatbelt.

"You look absolutely breathtaking today, Madison. I mean from the hair to the shoes, you are ready for prime time."

"Thank you, Damion. You look nice, too. May I add, you are ready for the Player's Ball."

Damion and Madison laughed easily together as he took the car out of neutral and headed towards the restaurant. Demetrius watched them drive away, cigarette dangling lazily from his partly open jaw.

"I could never pull a honey like that," he said wistfully to no one in particular- thinking about his last run for the day, and pulled out another cigarette.

"How long do you have for lunch, Madison?"

"I have a 2:30 meeting, so…a little over an hour."

"That's too bad. I just want to kidnap you on a day like this, do you golf?"

"No. I never got the hang of it, really. I like to be more active when I play sports."

"Oh, for real?"

"Yeah, you know, like softball, tennis, basketball."

"What? You ball?"

"A 'lil bit, I got some game. I'll take you right down the middle, man."

"Is that a challenge?"

"Name the place, I'm in your face."

"Madison, let me warn you now, I don't care if you're a girl. If you ball, you ball."

"You don't have to care. I'm a woman."

"OK, OK, you win this round," Damion laughed.

He liked the ease in which they played off each other. It took months with a honey to have a rapport like that. He felt comfortable with her already. Or was that lust? Realistically, she'd been in his car less than five minutes.

The leather seats from the unusually warm September sun felt good on Madison's back and legs. Oddly, she felt very much at ease with this stranger. She peeped over at him while pretending to wipe a strand of hair from her face. Damion was handsome, but not fine fine. There was something about him, though. He had sort of a magnetic appeal, which appealed to her. Speaking of peel, she could definitely peel that suit off, not right now of course, she'd probably have to play the booty-waiting game with him like everyone else. *If* it came down to that.

"Too much wind? You want me to put the top up?"

"No thanks. It's too nice out," Madison protested, noting how observant he was. "We won't have many of these days left, so let's take advantage of it. They say it's going to be a cold winter."

"They always say it's going to be a cold winter. I mean, if it's winter, I expect it to be cold. You Washingtonians don't know cold."

"Yeah, then what's cold, Damion?"

"Do you have to ask? Chicago is cold. It's cold from October until May. Worst part is, you never get used to it, no matter what."

"Chicago's home, hunh?"

"Yep. Good 'ol south side. Although my mom lives in the suburbs in a city called Naperville now."

"Hmm...So how do you know so much about DC? I mean you pulled out the red light district from back in the day."

"Well, I used to come down every summer to stay with my nana, excuse me, grandmother, and me and my boy Todd would ride our bikes to 14th street to look at the ho's, the men buying the ho's, and like, whatever."

"I see," said Madison, raising her eyebrows knowingly. "So let me get this straight. You'd stare at the whores, their johns and whatever? That reminds me of the yadda yadda yadda *Seinfeld* episode."

"Ah, the yadda, so you're a *Seinfeld* junkie too?"

"Ha Ha. Yes I am. I thought I was the only black person who watched it, even though they're just reruns now."

"Never think you're the only, Madison," Damion mentioned lightly as he pulled into a parking spot. He reached into his ashtray and pulled out a few quarters.

"Non-smoker," Madison thought, noting she'd have to clean out the ashtray in her modest vehicle, a '95 Acura.

"I wonder if he'll mind if I smoke?" she thought.

She thought briefly of Trey, her last "friend." He smoked. At first, he just smoked cigarettes, to Madison's knowledge. Eventually, it got out of hand. One evening, Madison found some roaches in her bathroom trashcan. She adamantly told Trey not to smoke in her house. High and nonplussed, he didn't give a damn.

"It's alright, girl. Just stick a towel under the door. Your landlord ain't 'gone smell 'nuthin." Madison asked for the joint he'd just lit, he smilingly obliged, and Madison smilingly let him out the door, flushed the joint down the toilet and never spoke to him again. Stacey teased her for months. She called Trey AM/PM because he smoked around the clock, 24-7. When they arranged to meet somewhere, Stacey would say, "When, now? AM or PM?" and let out peals of laughter.

"Here, Madison, let me get that for you," Damion said as he gallantly helped Madison out of the car. They entered the restaurant, arguing about the funniest *Seinfeld* episode.

"Mr. Cross. Good afternoon. Your table is ready. We've chosen a beautiful spot for you and your companion overlooking the federal enclave. Madame."

The black and white clad maitre d showed them to their table. He was gentle and correct, slightly personable and just snobby enough. He promptly returned with two crystal water glasses and two bottles of Voss sparkling water. After placing Madison's napkin in her lap, he lightly stepped away and walked towards the front of the restaurant. Madison absorbed her surroundings, liking what she saw. The room was flooded with light, and the view of the monument and the surrounding landscaping was spectacular, even though the monument was covered with scaffolding while it was being repaired. The tables were small, but sturdy with heavy linen tablecloths and fresh flowers. The walls were painted a pale yellow, creating a perfect backdrop for the vintage French posters. Billie Holiday was plaintively singing "In My Solitude" in the background. Madison waited until the gentleman disappeared from view and craned her neck confidentially towards Damion.

"Mr. Cross? You come here often." It was more a statement than a question, but the possibility of this man coming to this breathtaking restaurant being called out by name, even, excited Madison.

"Naw. I'm just trying to impress you. I slipped a $50 in his hand with a piece of paper that said Mr. Cross and—"

"What? The Sidney Poitier look-alike?"

"Yeah, I paid him to—"

"Bullshit." Madison laughed amiably.

"OK. OK." Damion confessed while pouring Madison's water for her.

"We do a fundraiser for the station twice a year, and we hold it here. Zados gets free pub, and we get props and great food for the day. "

"Station?" Madison raised her eyebrows inquisitively.

"Yes, WJAZ."

"Whaaat? Is that where you work?" Madison inquired, eyeing him curiously.

"Not really. You ever listen to the introduction for the—"

Damion's concentration was broken by a woman with super-sized boobs rushing towards their table.

'Geez Louise, they really do make those things to order,' Madison thought, irritated by the sudden interruption.

"Ummm, excuse me, Mr. Cross, Could you sign this autograph for my girlfriend? She's a fool for WJAZ's Mellow Moods. She'll be so tickled to have your John Hancock," purred large lip-glossed to perfection lips.

Madison did not like the way this underdressed, over-made-up chick emphasized cock. Besides, she was rude, just coming up to somebody while they were talking, mini melon breasts hanging out of her half shirt, nipples hard and batting her eyes all Betty Boop style. She knew those pencil erasers were hard. What a bitch. Madison concentrated on Damion. He looked a little sheepish as he signed his name on a lipstick-covered napkin.

"Here you go," he smiled shyly. "I'm glad your girlfriend likes the show."

"Yeah, said the breasts. "I saw the NEXT newsletter, too, Mr. Bachelor." Her voice oozed with obvious wanton lust.

Madison called on her mama's home training to keep from saying something not so nice. She calmly decided to see how Damion would handle this. Man test number one. It's not as if he was her man, but this woman was unnecessarily inconsiderate. She couldn't wait to tell this story at her next A group meeting. The group was comprised of mildly to 'without a doubt' successful women. They were type A women deemed a success by today's standards; great jobs, cars, homes, even pets; however, they were all single. So they'd meet once a month for wine and cheese and discuss everything from world affairs, politics, family matters, and of course, men, where the ratio of men to women in DC was at least 5 to 1. With that in mind, they supported one another. More often that not, they'd have to sit a member down and remind her she was a classy woman acting like a type C, commonly referred to as either a hoochie mama or basement girl.

"Unh…I'm sorry. I didn't get your name?"

"Debbie," she drooled.

Damion couldn't help but think about *Debbie Does Dallas*. Her nipples were extremely well defined beneath the thin material of her shirt. He wondered if Madison noticed. Her breasts were so large, they hiked up the shirt a bit, exposing her bellybutton, which of course, had a ring in it, and was surrounded by washboard abs.

"Debbie, this is my friend Madison."

Debbie looked at Madison as if seeing her for the first time. She pushed up her breast in that too tight shirt and then extended an acrylic-laden jungle pattern-painted finger nailed hand to Madison.

"How you doing, Macon?"

Madison stared at Debbie for approximately 5 seconds and picked up her water glass, never once taking her eyes, which had turned to flint, off of Debbie.

Debbie withdrew her limp hand and turned to leave; satisfied she'd pissed Madison off enough.

"Bye, Damion. My girlfriend and I be listening. So don't stop what you doing."

Madison knew she wanted to say that to him in bed. She could see Debbie now, wearing red, high-heeled come screw me pumps, tied to a cheap brass bed, flicking her weave from side to side and moaning "...don't stop what you're doing, daddy, ooooh!" Madison rolled her eyes disgustedly.

Debbie walked away, switching like there was no tomorrow. Damion looked directly at Madison, catching Debbie's walk with his peripheral vision, thinking it was the second time that day a woman switched for him. Women were bold creatures, for sure. Madison was calm as a cucumber. He wanted to give her dap for not shaking that woman's hand, because she'd chumped the hell out of Madison. His boy Todd would love this story, also a breast man. Well, Todd was everything, actually. He just loved women.

A petite dread-locked waitress approached the table. Her dress and manner mimicked that of the maitre d.

"Mr. Cross? Are you and your party ready to order?"

"Hello, Mia. If you'll just give us a moment."

"Sure thing, Mr. Cross." She returned immediately with two new bottles of sparkling water.

"I'm sorry about that, Madison. I know she heard me say your name."

"Damion. There's no reason for you to apologize for someone you don't know. I don't care. I'll probably never see her again, unless it's on a street corner."

Damion laughed aloud.

"You handled it well, though."

Madison needed to put that ugly scene behind her.

"So finish telling me, what do you do? Or are you like Tommy on Martin?"

"I unh, well my voice is the introduction for WJAZ's nightly slow jam show, and occasionally I'll sit in for the dee jay when he has other engagements."

So that's why his voice sounded so familiar at Home Depot, she thought.

"Are you familiar with WJAZ Madison?"

"Yes. Yes I am Damion. Um, Hermond White and Angela Gains have that relationship program, what is it?"

"Gender Crosstalk"

Yes. That's a great show, because it gives black men and women a chance to hear one another. Plus the hosts are like, real. Their chemistry is great; they interact really well with each other, you know?"

"Their chemistry should be great. They're fucking. "

"What? Madison asked, not sure she'd heard correctly. He couldn't have dropped the "F" bomb so casually.

"They're fucking." Madison gulped her water.

"But Hermond is always talking about his wife and the baby and—"

"Madison. Let me explain something to you," Damion interrupted gently.

"It's work dynamics. Nine times out of ten someone in any office is doing it to somebody else, even if their home life is all that."

Madison was visibly disturbed. Damion hoped she wasn't one of those naïve, the world is a great place type chick. He abruptly changed the subject.

"What do you have a taste for, Madison?"

"Whatever you suggest, I trust you."

Naïve, thought Damion. She must be one of the good girls. He figured at that moment he'd have to play the not pressed for booty game with her. Todd taught him that one. The strategy was to never touch the girl, no matter how sexy or willing she seemed. After 5 or 6 dates, she'd be clawing all over you, begging you for it. Damion signaled for Mia, who appeared instantly. She gave Madison a sideways glance and turned towards Damion. Madison wondered briefly how many women he may have entertained here. She observed Damion as he ordered, the same for both of them; a lobster bisque, a mixed green salad with balsamic vinaigrette and angel hair pasta with grilled chicken, mushrooms and artichokes. The tub scene flashed in Madison's mind again; this time, Damion was reading *Black Enterprise* and drinking a glass of Chianti.

As if reading her mind, Damion asked Madison if she'd ever found her ceramic tub. She apprised him of her mental house furnishing theory and learned that he was in a housing lottery, and if he won, would acquire a fixer upper in Columbia Heights by next spring. Madison couldn't help but watch Damion's lips. They were sexy to death, as well as his teeth, which were like, too perfect. Damion was a great conversationalist, charming, engaging. Madison shifted rather uncomfortably. His lips were so hypnotizing. She was trying not to stare and at the same time, starting to moisten. To her right, the monument became the most fascinating object to

Madison. Damion, noticing her distraction, switched gears to discuss the view of the Federal Enclave, which was breathtaking.

"DC is a great city, don't you think, Madison?" With those large eyes staring into his soul, Damion wasn't quite sure how to read Madison. "I mean it's a place where you can actualize your dreams, with a bunch of other black folk doing the same, don't you agree?"

Suddenly self-conscious, Damion watched Madison closely while she squirmed and looked away. After a slight pause, Madison answered him carefully.

"Yes, if you're persistent enough, all your dreams can come true," she said dreamily as their salads arrived. She spoke as if she'd been thinking of a particular conversation in her head and finished her thought out loud. All Madison could think about was Savannah when she first met Lionel on the dance floor in "Waiting to Exhale." Should she exhale? Naw, too soon. So she took a few quick breaths and concentrated on looking into his eyes instead of those juicy lips.

Damion observed that whatever had gotten into Madison was definitely gone, and now she was extremely responsive and upbeat. She hungrily tore into her salad and made light conversation, the picture of perfection. He liked what he saw, for sure. Her manners were feminine, her appetite was healthy, 'cause she gave the bisque a run for the money, her humor was timely, she was all that.

The rest of lunch went smoothly, and before long, Madison looked at her watch and reminded Damion about her 2:30 meeting. It was ten minutes until two. Damion asked Madison if she wanted any dessert. She declined due to the lack of time. Although Madison didn't know how much the meal cost, she laid a $10 on the table for the tip. Madison knew Stacey would have something to say about that.

"Girl, if the 'brotha asked you out, he pays for everything. Tip my ass!"

'Shuttup, Gazoo!' she thought humorously, and giggled mentally thinking about that little green pain in the butt martian that clowned Fred on the *Flintstones*. Stacey was kinda like Gazoo, she'd have to remember to tell her that next time they spoke. Madison had a mouthful to tell, now, and it definitely wasn't boring, by any stretch of the imagination!

Damion told Madison to put her money back in her handbag. After she protested, he told her he could write it off. She gingerly placed the currency back in her wallet. Damion paid the bill with a gold Amex and they walked out into the sunny afternoon, discussing the black exodus and white influx in the District.

CHAPTER 9

Madison—Love Is...
September 1999

Damion dropped Madison off without much fanfare. He'd given her a kiss on the cheek and told her what a wonderful time he had, and tried to kidnap her one more time, trying to tempt her with an invitation to play one on one, up to 11. He even said he'd give her 3 points to start. Madison told him they'd play soon, because she couldn't say no to a good challenge.

When she got to her desk, Madison immediately checked her e-mail. She had 7 messages. The first message informed her that the meeting was canceled. Her first thought was to call Damion back and tell him she was free, but she didn't have his cell number. Damn, he didn't even have her home number. She berated herself for not catching that one sooner. The second e-mail was from her girl Barbara. They were going to hook up for a minute after work for happy hour at the Hibiscus Café. Happy hour on Monday? There must have been some serious drama this past weekend. Madison checked the rest of her messages, none of which were terribly exciting. She checked her voicemail; Mrs. Portal had called three times. That woman had issues. Madison would deal would her after she returned from the restroom. Madison was euphoric after the date, and she wanted that warm and fuzzy feeling to last just a little longer.

When Madison returned to her desk, she realized her handbag was sitting on the counter in the restroom. She rushed back exasperated, a sick feeling gathering in the pit of her stomach. The last thing she needed was to have her handbag stolen. Her relief was barely audible when she noticed her handbag in the same place she'd left it. Madison checked to make sure nothing was missing. Thank God everything was intact.

Suddenly she heard this moan and then "Bernard!" in a hushed, yet intense whisper. Immediately thereafter, the person began to cry. More nosy than concerned, Madison peeked under the stall and recognized Pilar's shoes. They were distinct and stylish, Pilar's without a doubt. Madison remembered when she bought them, after a weekend trip to NY. Just then the stall door opened with a slam, and Pilar rushed toward the sink and begin to splash cold water over her flushed face.

"Pilar, Pilar, what's wrong?"

Obviously surprised, Pilar looked up with tear-stained eyes.

"Madi."

"Pilar. What is going on? Is it the kids?"

Pilar looked at Madison for a long time. She then looked at the mirror, patted her swollen face and breathed a long, defeated, sigh.

"How much time do you have, Madi?"

"As much time as you need, Pilar."

They were startled as two women walked into the restroom, gossiping about the soaps.

"Let's go to my office," Pilar suggested.

Madison felt weird as they walked in silence. She felt disconnected, somehow, as if the office was displaced in a surrealistic background, like a Dali painting, and she was just a visitor; a head without a body.

Pilar closed the door unceremoniously once they reached her office. She solemnly gestured toward the leather sofa for Madison to sit down. Madison's stomach was full of flurries by this time.

Pilar walked nervously back and forth while she told Madison this incredible, unbelievable tale.

"Madison, if I don't tell someone, I'm going to explode."

Pilar took a deep breath, exhaled and slowly began.

"In high school I met the love of my life. We dated for two years, then he moved to NY with his parents. At first we wrote each other everyday, but as time progressed, I'd hear from him less and less. I went to school at Pepperdine and he traveled throughout Europe, Africa, Canada and South America to 'broaden his perspective' as he would say. I'd get these exotic looking postcards from all over the world. Meanwhile, after I graduated, I focused solely on my career. I spent the next 10 years building what I thought was so important, even going back to school and getting my masters. This guy, Bernard, was bent on starting his own business. I asked him to move back to DC, but he wouldn't have it. He said he would not raise his children in pretentious ass color-struck DC. I wasn't even thinking of kids, and I knew for sure I didn't want them growing up in NYC. Plus, I thought he was silly, chasing this dream of his. After I got the position I have now, I decided it was time for me to get married. I'd dated several men, but none of them made the grade. When I met Mitchell, I knew he would suffice. He was honest, hard-working, church going and wanted a family. His job was steady and reliable. He also put me first, which I appreciated. He wasn't terribly exciting and there were no bells and whistles, but I knew it would work; that is, until Bernard showed back up. I ran into him six months ago outside of the Convention Center, and Madison, it was if a day hadn't passed. He is extremely successful, never married, no kids, and was in town for a convention. He skipped that afternoon's seminar and I didn't come back to work. We went to the Willard and that was all she wrote. I've been sneaking to the city once a month ever since. I'd tell Mitchell my territory expanded, and these trips were necessary. Madison, I am so in love with Bernard, and I'm out of control. I just want to drop everything to go and be with him. Mitchell and I haven't made love for weeks. I'm almost out of excuses. He's so understanding and sweet. But you know, Madison, I was crying because I don't feel guilty. This just feels so right."

Madison watched Pilar pace frantically, back and forth, steadily gaining speed, her face radiating with excitement. It was if Pilar herself were in another world, forgetting Madison entirely. Madison was dumbfounded to say the least. Perfect Pilar, doing the diggety with her old sweetheart. At a loss for what to say, Madison stood up as Pilar's phone rang. A double ring indicated an outside call. Pilar shook her head twice as if to escape from her trance, glanced at her watch, and hastily picked up the phone. Immediately recognizing the voice on the other end, she sat on the edge of her desk, crossed her legs and began giggling like a schoolgirl. Madison slipped out the door as she heard Pilar say "I miss you, too, baby."

As she walked back towards her desk, Madison realized Pilar must have been with this Bernard character when she got those shoes.

"What a Monday," she whistled softly to herself, thinking about how crazy love is.

CHAPTER 10

Madison—Your Voice
September 1999

Madison was so worked up from her visit with Pilar she figured she'd go home and cool out before the happy hour if she decided to go at all. All those folk who were PC-challenged would have to wait until tomorrow. She just wanted to tell Stacey about Damion. She shut down her computer and checked her supervisor's office to see if he was there. Nope. Madison swore Mr. Carothers thought he was in the banking business. He was gone most days by three o'clock.

The red indicator light on her phone glared incessantly at Madison, daring her to check her messages before she left. Madison sighed impatiently as she dialed her password. One message. Whoop de do. Probably her mom wondering when she was going to stop by. As far as her mom was concerned, Madison owed her visiting time for being raised properly. Madison obliged mainly because her mother was an excellent cook, and she wasn't very motivated in the kitchen. Cooking is no fun when you are alone. Her mom still served her father everyday, and was the epitome of the perfect wife and mother; albeit a little obsessive. She kept Madison and her brother's room exactly the way it was before she left for college. Her parents experienced the true meaning of an empty nest, for neither she nor her brother Paul had returned home since they left for college. He was in Seattle with his white wife and their two kids. Her mom never really warmed up to Cynthia, who insisted on being called Cindy, but loved her grandkids.

"From Washington to Washington," her mom would say, marveling on the ironies of the two cities, one primarily white, one mostly black. "...from hippies to the Hill." Madison figured her flair for writing came from her mom.

"Hey. Madison. I'm going to be at the station this evening." The voice brought Madison from her reverie. "Listen up if you get a chance. Oh, this is Damion. I had a really nice time at lunch, and I'd like to try and hook up with you sometime this weekend, and oh, could you leave your home number on my voicemail? I'm on (202) 555-1908. That's (202) 555-1908." Madison placed the cradle on the receiver, and breathed deeply, trying to calm her wildly beating heart. She didn't even know this guy, yet the effect his voice had on her was unreal. Madison changed into her sneakers and was on her way out the door when Demetrius dropped a package on her desk, bobbing his head to a Sony Discman.

When he spotted her he pulled his headphones from over his ears and placed his hand on his stomach, laughing uncontrollably. Madison didn't have to ask what was so funny, he volunteered soon enough.

"Damn, girl, I ain't know you was so funny. You make a 'brotha laugh, girl."

He picked up the packet and walked towards Madison.

"Wait a minute, girl. Damn, you said

'I drove a 1976 Plymouth Volare station wagon, orange with wood paneling on the side, with one headlight, and the inability to make sharp left turns due to a bent tire rod.' I'm feeling you," Demetrius finished, still laughing, handing Madison the packet. It was a copy of her article "Hoopdies Keep You Humble" in *The Chocolate City Voice*, a local black-owned publication Madison sometimes freelanced for.

She took the paper from Demetrius, stuffed it in her subway bag, and walked towards the elevator. Demetrius didn't need to be in the mailroom with his nosy ass. Not that she minded him reading it, but he was just irritating sometimes. Once outside, she inhaled the fresh September air, lit a cigarette, and walked to the subway.

When she got home, Madison opened her windows to let some fresh air in her stuffy apartment, checked her messages and called Damion and Stacey, leaving a message for both of them. She lay on her sofa and flicked on the TV, drifting off into a deep sleep.

The shrill ring of her phone awakened her a few hours later. She could barely hear for all the noise in the background.

"Hello. Hello?"

"Trick, why the hell aren't you here?"

"Stacey, I had a long day and—"

"Long day my ass. You left a message on my machine at 5 o'clock. It couldn't have been that long. All the girls are here except for you. What's up? You pregnant or something?"

"Stacey, I'm good girl, just emotionally drained."

"You get some and didn't tell me about it? I know, it was the weed man, and you're too embarrassed to tell me."

"Stacey, I said emotionally, not physically drained."

"And that's why I asked if you were emotionally drained. Wait. Hold on...."

Madison heard her in the background explaining to Nikki, Barbara and Tracy why she wasn't there.

"Ok, Madi? Yeah, do you need me to come get you or...Wow! That mofo is FINE!!" Madison heard the phone drop.

"Hello? Hello? Stacey?" Madison heard a lot of shuffling and giggling and peals of laughter. Finally Stacey picked up the phone.

"Madison, you are really missing the honeys, dude was a gift from the heavens. He goes in the MG. Aimee just got here, why did that crazy girl stop a metro bus in the middle of Wisconsin Avenue and give the bus driver her card? She's crazy, but she says he was an MG, too." The MG was Stacey's term for the memory gallery. It was her mental honey gallery, which she called upon on many a lonely night for pleasuring purposes. Madison heard more squeals and shuffling, then finally a squeaky voice screamed into the line.

"Madison? Madison?"

"Yes", said Madison impatiently.

"Hey girl, this is Aimee. I haven't seen you in forever, what time are you coming down?"

"Hi, Aimee. I'm kinda tired. I'll catch up with y'all next time."

"Oh, what you get some?"

"Aimee, I tell you, I don't even have the energy to do anything right now, so I'm just gonna chill, right here on my comfy sofa." If the 'brothas only knew how horny her girlfriends were...but everybody's got to play the game.

"Alright, there'll be more fyne men for me, then. 'Cuz you know we got the same taste in men, right?"

"Right, so what's up with Metro man?"

"Don't sleep, Madison. He seems like he might be a nice brother. At least I know he's got a j-o-b."

"Alright, girl. Don't let me find out you're making like Jada Pinkett in *Jason's Lyric* riding off in the sunset with your Metro man."

"Alright Madison. I'd rather ride off in the sunset with a man than be on the sofa alone."

Stacey apparently snatched the phone from Aimee.

"Both ya'll need to quit. You wouldn't be so petty if you had someone to occupy your time. So what's the deal, trick? You coming or what?"

"No, Stacey. I'm tired."

"Alright, tramp, I gotta go. I'll call you, later."

Stacey hung up before Madison got a chance to say goodbye.

Madison yawned, stretched and tried to resume her nap, but it was too late, she was awake. The sparring with Aimee forced her to get out of robot mode. Although they played with each other all the time, Madison wondered if Aimee wasn't the least bit serious. She still had a bitter taste in her mouth from the last time they went out. Madison, Aimee and Anna had gone to happy hour at Heart & Soul Café. They'd worked the room on both sides and met back at the table after a half hour or so. They leaned towards the middle of the table to compare fine notes. When Aimee found out she and Madison had the same number from this guy named Jayson, Aimee snatched the number from Madison, and tore it up, laughing. Madison didn't think it was too funny, and made a mental note to cut Aimee back.

It was chilly, now that the sun had gone down. Madison closed the windows, prepared a quick snack and ran water for a bubble bath. It was 8:30, Damion should be on now. Madison brought her radio into the bathroom and turned the dial to 96.7. A commercial was on. She took advantage of ad time and pulled a large fluffy purple towel and matching washcloth from her wicker hamper and placed them on the toilet seat. As she toe-tested the water, Damion's voice filled the small, but immaculate area, distracting Madison momentarily, causing her to scald the top of her foot. She turned the COLD faucet as far as it would go and sat on the edge of the tub, swirling the water until it reached the right temperature. Although it hadn't been proved medically, Madison was convinced that the hand could withstand greater heat than a foot, that's why she toe-tested. The water had to be just right, too, or else her privates had a hard time forgiving her for just jumping in a tub of hot water without first taking the proper precautions. Madison lit a few candles and stepped into the inviting bubbles. Damion's voice was too much, it was smooth as butter and slick as oil, just the right combination to make a girl improve her fantasy life tenfold. She looked around the tiny space and wondered how she and Damion would fit in here. She felt her color scheme made the room look larger than it really was. She'd decorated the bathroom tuxedo style, white and black, with a splash of color. The white tile with the stark black trim practically begged her to keep it simple when she first moved in four years ago. "Ah well," she reasoned, if she and a 6'9 brother could fit on her twin bed and do it when she was in college, then Damion could certainly make do in here. Madison sunk down until just her head was visible and let Damion's voice relax her. Now he was giving the breakdown of the songs she'd missed by artists who transcended decades: Minnie Riperton, Earth Wind & Fire, The Isleys. Brother was jamming. Madison almost pulled the radio in the tub when Damion mentioned her name. She saw the glaring headlines announcing her unnecessary death, blinking, neon-style; "Help-Desk Girl Electrocutes Herself."

"...And this goes out to Madison, the Home Depot lady, get that tub, girl."

He chuckled softly as he played Roberta Flack's "The First Time Ever I Saw Your Face." Madison melted, enjoying the melody more than she ever had in her life. He followed that with "There'll Never Be," by Switch and then the long version of "Moments in Love." She felt as if Damion were speaking directly to her. What a man. She was hooked, hooked on that voice. Madison sunk deeper in the tub, exposing only her head and allowed the music and the voice to envelop her. She constructed a tribute in her head as the songs invaded her soul and her fingers delved in a place soft and dark and deep.

From Madison's Journal

September 13, 1999

I met this honey named Damion at Home Depot, can you believe it? I'm obsessed with his voice. It's hypnotic. He's cute. I think I might like him. We'll see. I thought of this one in the tub after he dedicated a song to me on the radio.

Your Voice
Your
Voice is warmed hot fudge
Pouring
Over frozen vanilla ice cream
Melting
It's hard surface and
Canvassing the sides
Making craters racing towards the
Center
Resembling valleys and mountains

Your
Voice gently massages my soul
Like a professional masseur
Kneading
The knots of tension from my
Muscular frame
Sliding over my impenetrable skin
Working
Up a rich later like your favorite bar of soap

Your
Voice challenges the air waves
Flows
Freely with the wind and lands
Gently
In the stamen of my open ears and
Drips
Nectar throughout my essence

CHAPTER 11

Damion—Big Surprises Come In Small Packages
September 1999

Crystal strutted into the radio station, overcoat buttoned to the neck, backpack filled with wine, cheese, and crackers for the impromptu picnic she planned for Damion. He would be shocked when he unbuttoned her coat to find her butterball naked. She squealed with anticipation while Chuck, the night duty guard, rang Damion's extension. After a few seconds, Chuck grinned heavily into the phone when he announced Crystal.

"Yo, man, inspector gadget's down here for you. Should I send her up? Man, it's Crystal man. Alright, she's on her way. Be careful, she packing a Uzi!"

"Chuck, you're too funny."

"Aw, go head, girl, you know I just be playing 'wit you."

"I've got your inspector gadget alright," she thought naughtily, fingering the nylons in her right pocket she planned to use to restrain Damion. When Crystal stepped out off the elevator, Damion was waiting for her, smiling broadly, arms outstretched. Crystal jumped into his arms and almost cried from joy. He felt and smelled so good.

"Ow! That backpack is dangerous." Damion removed the bag from her shoulders. "What do you have in here? I hope it's some food, 'cuz a brotha's hungry." Damion sniffed the bag.

"It's just my stuff from the gym, D."

"Oh, so those are your socks smelling like cheese, then?"

"Alright, Alright, Get those tapes off this table and I'll show you."

Damion cleaned the psa cartridges off the small table immediately, wondering what Crystal was up to. Crystal hummed to "The First Time Ever I Saw Your Face" while she set the table. Damion watched her, thinking if she'd come up two minutes earlier, she would have heard him dedicating that song to Madison. The way he did it was smooth, though, because he didn't say whom the dedication was from. A twinge of guilt shot through his gut while he watched Crystal scurry to make something special for him. Within minutes, Crystal had transformed a small rusty table to a romantic setting for two by setting up candles, cheese, crackers and wine, all on a white linen tablecloth. How she fit it all in that gymbag, he never knew. Her movements turned Damion on, even though she was wearing that silly overcoat.

"What's wrong with you, Crystal? Give me your coat."

"Why don't you take it off me?" teased Crystal, who by this time was ready to explode with excitement.

When Damion realized she was wearing her birthday suit, he took off her coat, whistled loud and long, while turning her around slowly, taking in every inch of her tight little body. Damion sat her on his stool, and rushed to an old gray file cabinet full of old albums, miscellaneous items and dust, and unrolled a life-sized poster of El Debarge. He turned and faced Crystal, singing "Oooh, and I Like It."

"Keep your day job, baby" said Crystal laughing. "Oh, but then again, you're like Tommy on Martin, so you don't really have a job."

"Girl, you stupid" Damion chuckled, spinning her around on the stool.

"D—speaking of Debarge, please play my favorite Switch song."

"Sure, baby." Damion stood up at the control board and loaded the CD. Before Crystal knew it, "There'll Never Be" was blasting throughout the studio. Damion turned around and watched her for a moment. He sat on the stool and softly called Crystal's name, who'd left her stool and began fussing with the arrangement.

She obediently went and sat in his lap. Damion rubbed her tiny shoulders and began massaging the nape of her neck.

"I'm sorry I couldn't take you to lunch, but I had a good meeting with a prospect. How was your day?"

Crystal, totally relaxed, tensed momentarily at the mention of the word prospect, but immediately shrugged it off. It didn't mean anything. Her girlfriend Jill told her she looked way far into things, creating scenarios that didn't even exist. Jill was a diehard self-fulfilling prophecy guru. She truly believed that what you claimed, became.

So she always stayed elevated, positive, even when things didn't go her way. It was difficult for Crystal, though, after catching Damion cheating twice before. Not once, but twice. She'd caught him once with some chick named Junie, walked in on them while they were watching a porno, but there was a time he didn't know about, when she called this girl named Chaka, whose number kept popping up on his Caller ID and told her to stop calling her man. She'd agonized over that phone call for weeks, but the calling became more intense and at late times too, like booty calls. Crystal would check Damion's Caller ID and he didn't seem to notice. Anyway, 'ol girl tried to pretend like she didn't know what Crystal was talking about at first, then Crystal called her out and told her to stop playing and acting stupid because there was only one Chaka Jones in DC. Crystal had no way of knowing that, but she decided to play Chaka and see if she'd fall for it. She did. Crystal figured Damion was probably tripping wondering why Chaka never called anymore. So after nipping *that* in the bud, Crystal began to pay Damion a lot more attention, figuring he wouldn't want to go anywhere else if he had it all at home.

She thought of the nylons, and ruled against them. God forbid she wrap them around his neck and get a Junie flashback and choke the shit out of him. She vowed to make this a great session. If she kept her mind blank and only concentrated on his presence here and now, it would be alright. Sex was so mental.

"Baby? I asked you how your day was?"

"Ooh, I'm sorry. I was so caught up in the music and that massage, I just zoned out. My day was ok, but some real dramatic shit happened to Tony."

Damion placed a finger over Crystal's lips and grabbed her soft neck. He traced a path with his lips where his fingers had already traveled. The small hairs on Crystal's neck stood up like a razzed porcupine, and goose bumps popped over her upper body like Braille. She craned her neck upwards to meet Damion's inviting lips. He kissed her long, and slow and deep. Crystal didn't know what had gotten into Damion lately, but she liked it. He stopped kissing her long enough to change the record, and take off his clothes. Crystal poured a glass of wine for Damion and herself. They nibbled on the cheese, crunched on the crackers and toasted to future success.

"This is some really good cheese, baby, where'd you get it?"

Damion helped himself to the last of a cheese he didn't recognize, but found delicious.

"I picked it up from a little shop in Georgetown. It's a goat cheese made at Firefly farms. It's called Meadow Chevre."

Crystal poured the last of the wine, given to her by her friend Brenda from the VinoLovers club. Brenda was bold, beautiful and extra fabulous, and she knew wines like nobody's business.

"Goat cheese? Made in a Chevrolet?"

Crystal smirked and twisted her lips, wondering if Damion was teasing or if he was for real. She decided he was teasing, so she responded in kind.

"Don't arch your eyebrows like that; you could do with a little exposure. It doesn't have to be American cheese to be good cheese."

Damion licked his fingers and laughed.

"Why I oughta...you're going to the moon!" Damion mimicked a poor imitation of Ralph Kramden from the *Honeymooners*.

Ignoring him and changing the mood, Crystal poured a little wine from her glass on Damion's chest and slurped loudly, while massaging what she considered to be her special friend. Damion grunted with pleasure and passionately grabbed her hair from the back, lifting it hard from the roots. He kissed her again, passionately, and quickly stepped away to put on the long version of "Moments In Love." Crystal followed Damion and stood on top of the stool. He turned around, wrapped his hands around her bottom, and snuggled his face in the place he called his. She arched her back and moaned with delight as Damion lifted her off the stool. He gently lowered her until she joined with her special friend. She grabbed the back of his neck and squeezed her legs tight around his body while he moved his hips in motion with the song. The seductive music, the flickering candles, the atmosphere, and the danger of maybe getting caught bombarded Crystal's senses, causing her to climax within minutes. Damion eased back down on the stool and turned Crystal in the opposite direction. He licked her back and grabbed her waist, moving effortlessly in seductive circles until he couldn't take it anymore, climaxing seconds before the song ended. Crystal clung heavily to Damion, grinning with satiated exhaustion. Meanwhile, in another part of Washington, Madison cried out Damion's name, seconds before the song ended, as the warmth from her body blended into the lukewarm water and the dissipating suds.

#Place the numeral 1 by the CD to indicate song #1.

CHAPTER 12

Madison—The Game
September 1999

The rest of the week proved to be anti-climactic for Madison. She couldn't find Stacey to tell her about Damion, and speaking of Damion, he hadn't called. It was Thursday and she was beginning to wonder if their meeting was legitimate. She'd thought about him quite often, and listened to WJAZ nightly, hoping to catch him. She didn't. Even her bi-monthly visit to her manicurist, Maisie, was marred when she peeled the dreaded pink DC parking ticket off her windshield. It was raining, and some of the ticket stuck to her freshly painted nails, ruining her index finger. Well, Madison wouldn't give the District her money this pay period. Her check was spoken for almost down to the penny. She hadn't planned for a ticket; she wouldn't pay for a ticket. Not now.

To make matters worse, Pilar asked a huge favor of Madison when they went to lunch on Thursday. They sat in Negril's brightly painted interior and discussed Bernard over jerk chicken drummettes, rice and peas, salad, cocoa bread and ginger beer. Pilar's face was flushed with excitement. Madison wondered if it was the spicy food or her obvious lust for this Bernard character. Pilar wiped her mouth, sipped the ginger beer, and went for the kill.

"Madison, Mitch and I are having a small get together at my house this weekend. Most folks were on the Vineyard for Labor Day, so we decided to break out the grill and set up those card tables one last time and just, kick back. My mother's going to have the kids, so we plan to do it up. Madison was nodding her head and smiling in agreement, having no idea what was going to come next.

"That sounds like a lot of fun, Pilar. May I bring a guest?" Madison immediately thought of Damion. It would give her an excuse to call him. Howard would be her backup plan. Howard was this guy who worshipped the ground Madison walked on, even though she never gave him anything. He was a nice guy; Madison just didn't have bells and whistles with him. She always kept him in the back of her mind, though, as an alternate. No matter if Madison asked him for something in the eleventh hour, Howard would adjust his schedule if he had to, and oblige.

Pilar interrupted Madison's thoughts completely.

"Uh, well, Bernard will be here tomorrow for a one-day seminar on Small Businesses and Electronic Commerce, and I asked him to come by for a minute. I told him a friend of mine would probably accompany him, but I'd have to ask her first. Pilar was giving Madison the "pretty please" look.

A clumped up ball of nerves gathered in Madison's stomach like rolling tumbleweed in a hot Arizona desert. Pilar had definitely banged her head against something.

She stared at Pilar in disbelief, dropping the half-eaten cocoa bread on her plate. Madison's facial expression gave her away completely.

"Madison, I *have* to see him, it'll just be a couple of hours, because his plane leaves at 4:00. I swear I wouldn't ask if this didn't mean so much to me. And if Mitch thinks that he's with you, there wouldn't be the slightest suspicion. Plus, once my husband gets downstairs at the card table, that'll be it. He won't budge. You know how those men folks do." Pilar never spoke this fast and frenzied. Madison continued to stare at Pilar with disbelief. She figured Pilar's heart was beating at warp hummingbird speed, while she felt a flat line coming on.

"Madison, it won't be long, I promise, just a couple of hours."

Deep down inside, Madison knew it was wrong and deep down inside she wanted to scream "Hell No!" But somewhere, very much on the outside, her defeated lips mouthed "OK, just this once," like that would ever happen again. Madison took a sip of the now watered-down pink lemonade and whispered a quick prayer, hoping God wouldn't strike her dead on the spot.

"Thank God!" Pilar exclaimed. "Let me give you details. I know you'll like him, Madison, he's a Libra just like you are."

'Libra, chibra, the man is still a cheat,' Madison thought bitterly. Another half-hour ticked by as Pilar outlined detail after detail of her outrageous plot. She reminded Madison of the Mad Hatter from *Alice in Wonderland*. Seemingly alright on the surface, like mad dapper, but loony as a cuckoo bird underneath his little suit. Not that Pilar was crazy, she was just caught up, apparently with that stupid love. That kind of love scared Madison. Her ex-boyfriend had stupid love. Carlos was extremely possessive. Stacey blamed it on the Latin blood running through his veins. Madison didn't care what kind of blood he had, she only cared about her life when he experienced jealous rampages and would kidnap her, drive his Mercury Cougar like it was a Formula 1 race car and try and run them off the road. That's when she started smoking. She never knew when Carlos would go off, and her paranoid nerves couldn't take it, so she turned to Virginia Slims. It took her two years to break up with Carlos, although her relationship with Virginia Slims remained intact. Madison loved Carlos, but she was scared of him. The dynamics of fear, uncertainty and doubt just didn't blend. Unfortunately, she hadn't met a brother yet who treated her like Carlos, although his possessive antics lived on. For years, Stacey referred to him as Fatal.

"Girl, where's Fatal? What's up with Fatal? What walls has Fatal knocked holes into today? Shit like that. Madison hated for Stacey to see a movie with an unforgettable line or scene, she'd play it to death. A couple of years back Madison wanted to scream every time Stacey said, "You can't handle the truth!"

When they finally left Negril, Madison wasn't the least bit surprised to find a ticket on her windshield; it's just the way her week was going. She would even venture to believe that Damion would call her tonight and make a date for Saturday, of course. Pilar was so ecstatic about Madison's decision, she flipped out a $20 and told her to take care of the ticket. Madison would take care of more immediate needs first, like her gas tank, and deal with the ticket later, with the other one. She knew the PC-challenged world had blown her phone up, and truth be told, Madison just didn't want to be bothered.

This would be a great night to meet with a couple of the girls at Utopia to get her drink on for free. Her boy Philip sponsored Thursday's there, and Madison took full advantage of their friendship; with one stipulation, that she not have more than three drinks. Philip was an excellent musician, and was waiting for his big break. Meanwhile, his days consisted of band practice, kicking it with Madison's cousin Nancy, tying to get his nephew Mitch Gunz signed to a music deal, and hanging out at Utopia, a well-decorated thirty-something type spot with good food and good music.

The rest of the afternoon went by swiftly as Madison had many calls to return. She was starting to worry about Stacey. They talked every day almost, and Madison hadn't heard so much as a peep out of her.

Madison arranged to meet Six, Gail and Diana at Utopia.

Six lived down the street from her, practically guaranteeing Madison a ride home, if she decided not to drive or wanted to really get her drink on. Gail, a petite doe-eyed beauty whose looks defied her age, was always up for a good glass of wine and good dialogue. Diana just liked to hang. Stacey nicknamed Diana 'Maxwell,' because she'd meet you "Whatever, Whenever, Wherever." Stacey had a nickname for everything and everybody, no doubt.

Jamal, Utopia's Moroccan owner, met Madison at the door with a warm hug and double cheek kiss. As usual, he was dressed in all black with his jet-black hair slicked back in a ponytail that fell in sexy curls. Madison remembered when Utopia first opened, and so did Jamal. Madison and her friends quickly became regulars, and Jamal made it a point to take care of her whenever he was at the restaurant, personally preparing Madison's favorite, "Jamal's Chicken."

Madison walked to the back of the restaurant towards their table. The crew was already assembled. Gail was politely fighting off some stranger, who'd obviously approached her with his best mack game. Diana, Philip, his drummer Kevin, their actor friend Victor, Gail and Six were deeply involved in a controversial conversation. Six, so-called because she truly exemplified the theory of six degrees of separation, was the type of person that knew everyone and everything on the political scene. She caught the bug by working as an assistant to Kweisi Mfume, and wore that as a badge of honor, stating her political views loudly and confidently.

Poor Kevin was on the defensive. He sat straight as a board with his arms crossed. Usually Kevin's hands were very active; it was if he were always playing the drums, real or invisible. Victor, a lithe, reserved Prince look-alike, kept sucking his teeth saying, "Nah man, that ain't true, nah man."

Diana, an attractive Korean-Black woman, had her lips pursed and her eyes narrowed with disagreement, highlighting her Asian features. Philip was steadily puffing on his benchmark cigarette and rolling his eyes, signaling impatience with the entire scene. Six was animated to the point of agitation. Her eyes were brilliant and her hands seemed a well-rehearsed scene of choreographed expression.

"...and that's why Georgetown is all white now. Considered a swampland, white folks knew the value, and we sold our homes and our souls, breaking our necks to move out of there, and look at it now. It's only a matter of time before "U" street is like that. Mark my words, people. Buy your property NOW, or else, come the millennium, DC won't be called chocolate city, it'll be dubbed vanilla heaven. You can disagree with me if you want to, but I've been watching this trend for the past ten years."

"Six. You don't know shit. You got a crystal ball in front of you?"

Victor arched, suddenly coming alive. "I mean, if that was the case, then how come a white person can't get elected Mayor?"

"Excuse me, Madison said dramatically in an effort to break the tension, I understand they're shooting *Love Jones II* in this spot. You guys must be the extras."

"What?" Diana, mightily peeved, snapped her neck towards Madison.

"Man, I ain't really like that movie too much" said Victor, who'd served as the body double for Larenz Tate in *Why Do Fools Fall in Love?*

"What's up, Madi?" Philip said, standing to give her a hug, glad that someone broke the tedious conversation.

"Diana, if you ever got out to the movies, you'd know what Madison was referring to in *Love Jones*."

"Right, there's a couple of scenes where friends dialog over music, good poetry, mother wit, just enjoying each other's company and reveling in their friendship," Kevin stated.

"Damn, the nigga used the word reveling." Philip lit another cigarette.

"I really liked the film, the soundtrack is like that." Kevin chose to ignore Philip and gestured to the waitress.

"Ok, I get the point! Thank you for your black brothers film review, Kevin."

"RRRRaarw," laughed Six, clawing the air with an invisible scratch. Everyone laughed at Six's antics, and Madison took her place at the table next to Gail, causing the wannabe pimp to excuse himself. Gail hugged her thankfully, and promised her a drink. The rest of the evening brought more spirted laughter and jokes. Before the girls left, Philip made everyone promise to come and support his young nephew when he performed at the upcoming Black Family Reunion. Even the plea produced more jokes. Victor vied for the last word. "I don't know man, you want me to come see some brother named Mitch Gunz, should I bring my AK? "Man, you can kiss my ass-ay," laughed Philip, who could always hold his own.

Madison was so tired when she got home, she had just enough energy to take off her clothes, brush her teeth and go to bed. She fell asleep thinking about Damion's soothing, velvety smooth fondue-dipping finger-licking voice.

Friday arrived just in time. It had been a tough week, and Madison couldn't wait to chill this weekend. Damion called her at work around 11:00 a.m.

"You so busy you can't even return a brother's phone call?"

He must have called last night, Madison figured quickly. She hadn't checked her messages. Madison, delighted to hear his voice, but determined to make him pay for not calling sooner, responded glibly.

"Excuse me. With whom am I speaking?"

"Madison, hey, it's Damion."

"Oh, ok. Hi, Damion, how are you?"

"Ah, come on girl, you know you happy to hear my voice. Did you hear my dedication to you on Monday night?"

He sounded as if he smiled when he spoke.

"Dedication? Dedication, how?"

Damion's instinct told him that Madison had indeed heard him on Monday evening, but if he knew women, she was probably salty that he hadn't called her all week. Women's time and men's time were at least a week apart. He remembered when he started dating Crystal. He might not call for two weeks and she'd have a fit. It was no big deal to him, he was thinking about her, but he didn't feel the need to "check in" everyday. He supposed he would have to play the phone game with Madison as well. Females were a trip, boy.

"It was no big deal, Madison. I just dedicated this Roberta Flack song to you."

"That was nice, Damion. I'm sorry I missed it. I love that song, you're a sweetheart."

The proof was in the pudding. If Madison hadn't heard it, she would have asked which Roberta Flack song. Damion decided to take a different approach.

"Madison. I love your name. It is so thorough. Mmmm."

It sounded to Madison like he was licking his lips.

"Well, I called to see if you wanted to meet me and my boys at The Basement tonight."

"The Basement? You're a house head, hunh?"

"Love it. Got to. I'm from Chi-Town."

"That's cool. You and your boys? How many of my girls would you like me to bring, at the last minute, Cupid?"

This girl needs to be spanked, Damion thought amusedly.

"Madison, it's up to you. My boys and I try and hit the spot like once a month, and I thought you might enjoy it."

Madison felt like Damion was going for the triple threat. First, he wanted to run her by his boys to see if she was enuf. Fine enuf, paid enuf and cool enuf. Second, he probably wanted to see her in a different type of environment, and thirdly, Madison was sure he wanted to gauge what type of person she might be through her friends.

"What time are you going to be there, Damion?" Madison inquired, deciding to get to the point.

"Around 12:30."

"I'll see you there, then."

"See you there, then. Enjoy the rest of your day."

"You, too."

Madison called Stacey. No answer. She tried Six. No answer. A light bulb went off. Madison called the Beautiful ones, Bibi and Jai. To Madison, they were two of the most beautiful women in DC. She only hung with them on special occasions. They weren't that tight, but socially they fit like strawberries and shortcake. Madison enjoyed the attention and all the free stuff they got. Bibi was 5'9 and shaped like Barbie. She was jet black with hazel eyes. Go figure. Jai was 5'8, and was the spitting image of Sally Richardson. Madison was 5'7 and held her own. No matter where they went, they got f.r.e.e. Free fries from McDonald's, Free drinks, Extra chicken from Popeyes, etc. Damion and his boys would lose their minds. Hopefully Damion wouldn't be attracted to either of them. But, that was the chance she'd have to take.

From Madison's Journal

September 16, 1999

Are there any sane people left in this world? I'm not trying to be dramatic, but I just found out today that Pilar, whom I admire very much, is NUTS. She is happily married, or so I thought, and is screwing her high school sweetheart. And now she wants me to come to a cookout at her house and pose with this dude as my boyfriend. And I agreed. I can't believe it. And, I can't believe I couldn't say no. I would have liked to have brought Damion, to get Pilar's opinion on him, but the bigger picture is for me to try and reconcile bad intentions with good deeds.

Good Deeds

I am about to explode
Saying Yes Saying Yes
When I really want to say Hell No

Maybe I'll put my real feelings in a letter
And stick it in a drawer
Wishing I was a kid and didn't know any better
Say, when I was around four

I said what came in my heart
took place in my mind
and flew out my mouth
Wasn't worried about playing the part
Getting stuck in a bind
Causing someone's feelings to travel south

Ah well, such is the price you pay for being grown
Following the status quo of good manners
It's what the old folks call "being raised"
But it's hard trying to balance what the truth doesn't condone
Struggling to carry the "Not a problem, banner"
Hoping God notices the price I paid
For doing

Good Deeds

CHAPTER 13

Madison—The Test
September 1999

Both Bibi and Jai were excited about going out. Madison arranged to scoop them by 11:30. That way they'd get to The Basement around midnight so Madison could get the lay of the land before Damion came. When they got to the club, the music was thumping and the drinks were flowing. Madison politely accepted a drink from some chiropractor and was attempting to make a quick getaway when she bumped into a guy with his back to her. Some of her drink sloshed on his shirt and she began to stammer an abrupt apology when he turned around and lit up the dark room with his smile. She sheepishly checked her watch, which, after squinting to see the small roman numerals, showed 12:20 am

"I see you getting your drink on," Damion teased. Madison bit her bottom lip in embarrassment and swiftly took in the boots, jeans and black tee he wore. Madison wished she could have been that t-shirt. It was hugging him all comfortably, and those jeans showed the promise of a greater tomorrow.

Damion broke the ice by asking if he could get a dance at 12:30. Madison grinned and nodded yes. By this time Mike had caught up with her and by his mere presence demanded an introduction. Madison dryly introduced the doctor to the disc jockey/voice man, then Mike possessively escorted her away, discussing pressure points. An excruciating eight minutes passed before Madison excused herself to go to the ladies room. On the way back, she looked for Damion, and had no trouble spotting him, well the jeans, actually. True to his word, he grabbed her hand, and navigated his way through the throng of bodies to the middle of the dance floor.

The rest of the evening just flowed. Madison and Damion danced well together. He was easy to follow, his moves effortless and carefree to the thunderous melodic bass of house. The music transported Madison to another world, where only they existed against a backdrop of black bliss. Periodically she would hear Damion saying "Go head, girl."

At one point, during "Follow Me," a crowd gathered around Madison and Damion, clapping wildly after their impromptu performance.

Todd and Rod gladly accompanied Bibi and Jai most of the evening with drinks and jokes. Madison rarely sat down, and when she did it was most entertaining. Rod just kind of stared and drooled at Bibi. His sole occupation appeared to be keeping Bibi's glass full. Todd seemed to be the most gregarious, discussing push-button topics, particularly how all black women in DC were attitudinal and hard to get along with. Madison took a sip of her drink and left the table before Jai jumped in his behind. That was one of her pet peeves, and she would intelligently break him down, then make him buy her a drink. That was just Jai. She was a psychologist.

Around 3:30, Damion asked Madison if she wanted to go to breakfast. Madison really wanted to go, but understood full well the power of intrigue. She declined, using Bibi and Jai as an excuse. As if on cue, Jai walked up and said she was ready to go. Damion and Todd agreed to walk the ladies to their car. Rod had disappeared somewhere in the club.

As they walked to the car, Damion placed his arm around Madison's shoulder. Bibi gave Madison the look, like "Don't let that brother get too close. He don't know you." Madison ignored her. Even after all that dancing, Damion still smelled fresh. He was so manly. He whispered in her ear.

"Madison, why don't we do something tomorrow? Well, actually, technically today."

Madison was glad to have the opportunity to say she had something to do. Thinking about Pilar, Bernard and the cookout gave her a sick feeling, but she quickly shoved it off, lest Damion sense her mood swing and begin questioning. Plus, the moisture from his breath stimulated her inner ear. Dangerous.

"Damion. "I wish I could, but I'm busy tomorrow. I mean today."

"Well, how about Sunday, then?"

"My family and I have Soul Food Sundays, so…"

"*Soul Food?* Like the movie?"

"Yeah, sorta. My parents are from the south and they still believe in everybody sitting at the table together and bonding, if you will. Even though I'm grown, my parents still expect me to come to dinner on Sundays."

Damion felt a deep sense of respect for Madison and her family values. That was refreshing. He found himself studying Madison intently. Her inquisitive glance shook him out of the family reverie. "Ok, Madison. I'll just give you a holla."

Damion bent down and kissed her lightly on the lips.

Bibi and Jai started giggling and cooing like pigeons. They were more than a little nice from the cascade of free drinks, and it seemed as if Todd was trying to get his mack on big time.

Damion looked at them briefly and snorted with amusement. He then turned back to Madison and cupped her chin in the palm of his hand. The movement was tender and scared Madison to death. She felt like a trembling bird with a bruised wing who just happened to fall in someone else's nest, in this instance, chest. She cocked her head and squinted her eyes and stared deeply into Damion's eyes. There was a pregnant pause, so Madison felt compelled to break the ice.

"So did I pass the test or not?" she teased, eyes sparkling with admiration and infatuation. Damion's blazing eyes returned Madison's stare boldly and unflinchingly.

"We haven't had a chance to talk about y'all yet. I'll let you know, though."

Madison was surprised at his bluntness, and awkwardly said goodbye. She needed a cigarette, bad. Plus she was afraid to open her car door, in case her car smelled like cigarettes. She, Bibi and Jai were puffing away before they got to The Basement.

Fortunately, Damion walked over to Todd and attempted to pry him loose from Jai. "Come on, man! Leave her alone. She don't want your skinny ass."

By this time, Madison had jumped in her car, turned on the ignition and opened the door for the girls. Damion and Todd walked away slowly, laughing as Todd flashed him a napkin with Jai's number. As Madison changed gears, Damion turned around, waved, and shouted, "Madison! You got an A++!"

Madison managed to spin off in a fishtail, leaving dust, leaves and fliers twirling aimlessly in her wake.

As they were walking back to the club, Damion spotted a couple of guys coming out of the gay club next to the Basement.

Damion creased his eyebrows and his jaw dropped at least three inches once he recognized one of the men. He hit Todd hard in the ribs, and speeded his pace.

"Man, that's Crystal's boy Tony."

He works down at the Dept. of Adjudication with Crystal. They been friends for damn near ten years, and I *bet* you she doesn't know he's gay."

"Man, they could just be 'chillin. The music might be good in there. You don't know if they like that."

"Todd. It's almost 4:00 in the 'mornin, and two men are leaving a gay club, together. You don't have to be a detective to figure that shit out. Dude is definitely a pillow biter."

Todd shrugged his shoulders. He couldn't care less, one way or another. Damion's mood had changed from sugar to shit in a matter of seconds.

"Whatever, man, let's go get Rod and get our grubb on at Ben's Chili Bowl."

"Nah, man—you go find that bama. I'll stay out here in the semi-fresh air," Damion joked weakly. As Todd jogged back towards the club, Damion walked to his car, leaned his long body on it, and looked up at the stars, boldly dotting pitch black night, challenging the imagination while triggering lost memories. "These are the same stars that taunted me 21 years ago," Damion remembered like it was yesterday. Indeed, these stars lit his shame as he lay on his back gasping for breath. He was nine. He was at a two-week camp in North Carolina. His sole enemy was this oversized kid named Big Turk. No one believed he was 10. He couldn't be. Damion was convinced, Big Turk's sole purpose on this earth was to make him miserable. One afternoon, the team leader paired Big Turk with Damion for a navigation exercise in the woods, of which Turk naturally dominated. What did Damion know? He was a city kid from the South side of Chicago. Turk was a bigh country boy from planet asshole. Turk threatened to lose Damion on purpose, taunted him with the map and controlled the compass. The dread Damion felt weighed his shoes down like bricks, which caused him to walk slowly. Soon dusk fell. And after what seemed like an eternity, an irritated Turk began to chat nervously. Every time he heard a noise, he'd grab Damion and look around.

"D, you hear that?"

"Hear what?"

"Hear that!"

After a while, Damion's responses became static.

"It's probably a deer."

Damion's only thoughts centered on escape—from the woods, and Big Turk's musty ass arms.

Even at that age, Damion was astute enough to recognize a crazy person. He felt as if he needed to tread lightly with Big Turk, not just because of his size and bullish ways, Turk didn't seem to have it all together. What was it his mother called it? Oh yeah, "his screws were loose," Damion remembered. By this time, Damion recognized they were truly lost, and suggested he take a look at the compass and map. Big Turk didn't take kindly to the idea. He snarled at Damion, and threw the compass like a professional shot putter, tore the map in quarters, and stuck it down his pants.

"Maybe your lost ass can find the way back when you find that compass, bitch!"

Damion stood there, arms hanging loosely at his sides, and wondered what he had done to deserve this. He promised God right then and there if he got out of this, he wouldn't take loose change from his grandmother's purse anymore. Big Turk grabbed his crotch. "You can find your way to these nuts, though!"

Damion turned in the general direction of the compass, and dropped to his knees on soft, moist soil. The fading light made it difficult to see very well, so he'd have to try and feel for the compass. He took in the smell of pine and rotting branches, inhaling deeply. Damion said a quick prayer asking God to get him out of the woods and away from Turk, who, without warning, jumped on top of Damion, putting his puffy, sweaty palm over his mouth, while attempting to snatch Damion's sweat pants down with his free hand. The soil fought to make a permanent imprint underneath Damion's fingernails as he jockeyed for a better position. Suddenly the world became a muffled haze—squirrels scattering, the scratching of cricket's legs singing their raucous love song, the caw cawing of unidentified birds—sounded cavernous and far away. Damion forced his nine year-old brain to think of the best defense to keep from getting hurt. The only weapon he could think of was his mouth. He bit Turk's hand so hard he drew blood. It worked. Turk hurled a blood-curdling scream into the darkness while he pressed Damion's face in the leaves and dirt. But he let up enough for Damion to turn onto his back. That's when he noticed the young stars trying to squeeze their way into the black night. He kicked and swung his arms as anyone whose life depended on it would. Thump thump thump. Turk felt like a wet, lumpy sand bag. Turk jumped up and ran off cursing and yelling. Damion sat up slowly, the reality of what had almost happened beginning to sink in like sugar cubes in the hottest of coffee. At that point, the beams from several search lights bounced playfully off the trees and Damion heard the camp counselor calling his and Turk's name. He wanted to scream, but with his cracked lips and dry mouth he couldn't utter a sound. From afar, Damion heard screaming that seemed to get closer and closer. Only when the search party shined their light on a dirt-covered, tear-stained Damion, did he realize that he was screaming.

When all was said and done, Damion and Turk were less than two miles from camp. After the incident, Damion adopted the name Brown Bag, because the camp counselor said he couldn't find his way out of a paper bag. Big Turk never messed with him again, though.

"Damion! Man, you 'drivin or what?" Damion was shaken from his reverie by Todd.

"Man, I got it," Damion reluctantly agreed, because Todd and Rod were more than a little tipsy from entertaining Bibi, Jai and a host of other honeys.

Not surprisingly, Damion had lost his appetite. But his boys would probably trip if he tried to go home, now.

"Come on, man, get the lead out of 'yo ass. I'm fucking starving!" That would be Rod, who used fucking as an adverb whenever he could.

"Alright, bamas, get in the car!" Damion barked. He tried to shake himself from his melancholy state, and was glad Madison didn't agree to go with him after all. Her girls probably thought Todd and Rod were asses. They were, but they were his boys.

CHAPTER 14

**Madison—Bonding
September 1999**

T he sun straining to penetrate Madison's blinds was like a laser burning through her eyelids. She flipped on her other side trying to escape the rays, too lazy to get up and shut her blinds. The moment she thwarted the sun, as if on cue, birds began to happily chirp the "you better get your butt up" song. Madison grabbed a pillow and smothered her head with it. The phone rang. Madison gritted her teeth and gruffly answered.

"Yes!"

"Madison?"

"Yes."

"Are you asleep? You sound muffled."

"Yes."

"Wake up."

"No."

"I want to take you to breakfast. This is Damion."

Madison shifted and pulled the pillow from over her head and thought about breakfast for a minute, trying to recall whether or not she'd told Damion that she had plans this morning.

"Madison?"

"What, Damion?"

"Madison. You've got morning breath. Get up and brush your teeth. I'll be there in half an hour."

Madison was slowly coming alive. She pushed the covers back and tentatively stepped out of bed. Sometimes her wooden floors could be cold. Madison semi-hopped a few short steps to the window and peeped hesitantly through the blinds. It was going to be another beautiful day.

"Madison? Wake up. My day won't be complete unless I take you to breakfast."

"Damion. You'll be where in half an hour?" Madison's grumbling stomach betrayed her tough girl act.

"And how do YOU know my breath stinks? You psychic or something?"

"Madison. Look. I know it takes girls a long time to get ready, so I'll go wash my car and pick you up in an hour ok? Anywhere you want to go."

Madison's stomach and ego pleaded with her to stop the game playing for now. Didn't she tell him she was busy?

"Damion, you drive a hahd bargain" Madison chided in her best Boston accent. I live in a small three-story brick apartment building near the Rittenhouse on 16th street. I'm in unit 301. When you get here, honk your horn, and I'll come downstairs, alright?"

"Alright, ghetto fabulous. I'll honk my horn nice and loud so your neighbors can see who is taking you to breakfast. Why don't you meet me downstairs in an hour?"

Madison paused momentarily. Damion was sure a take-charge kind of guy, in a common sense type of way. He seemed to joke a lot, but so far, most of what he said made perfect sense.

"One hour it is. I've gotta go, my line is ringing."

"Madison."

"Yes, Damion."

"Madison, you know I've got a lot of sisters. Please get ready. Please get ready."

Madison's response was to click over to the next caller. When she heard Pilar's hushed, but excited voice, she wished she hadn't answered the call. She vowed to get a Caller ID box in her bedroom, it was rapidly becoming apparent the box in the living room wasn't enough. Pilar whispered about five minutes nonstop, reiterating the plan for Madison and Bernard. Finally, Madison cut her off.

"Pilar. I'll be there. Excuse me. We'll be there. You've given me a description a blind man could see from, and I have his cell number. I gotta go, now, my phone is ringing. See you there. Smooches."

Madison was going to kiss whomever this was who saved her from Pilar.

"Good Morning!" she chirped merrily into the receiver.

"Madison. Please get ready."

Madison laughed heartily while opening her blinds.

"Damion. Really. I've got one foot in the shower, honest. So your car *and* me will be clean."

"Ummm," Damion muttered, wondering why, why in the hell did Madison tell him she was getting in the shower? Why? He was trying not to envision her butt naked, but the visual picture he got was so strong, all he could do was say "Ummm."

"Don't believe me then, Damion. Believe this. I gotta go." Click.

Madison couldn't stop smiling as she got in the shower. She washed everything extremely well. She wanted to smell so good to Damion that he would want her for breakfast instead. Whew. Just thinking about him made her all goosepimply. "I need to stop," she said aloud. Madison thought about what her grandma would say for a quick remedy to her horniness. Her grandma was a southern matriarch who took her role of being a grandma seriously, including rendering unforgettable life lessons. She could hear her now, Southern dialect strong and caring. "Madison. That's de problem 'wit you young people today. You just jump inna things. You don't give no time for nuthin. You don't know each other. Nuthin. Just hops into the bed like yous a bitch in heat."

As Madison stepped out of the shower, she heard the last two rings of her phone.

'Damn,' she wondered. It couldn't be Damion already. Heart pounding, she checked the clock. It had only been 20 minutes. Too lazy to walk to the Caller ID box, Madison listened to her voicemail. It was Six, asking if she was going to attend the A group meeting. The topic was "Starting an Investment Club" and afterwards they were all going to brunch at Montgomery's Grill. Madison had never really been good with numbers and was glad to be going out with a honey as opposed to starting her day looking in a bunch of women's faces talking junk, after the business of course.

Madison got dressed quickly enough, however, her hair was not behaving. It was too curly. Exasperated, Madison yanked and pulled and brushed until her hair was too straight. She growled a frustrated, throaty sound and plugged in her curling iron in when she heard an aggressive knock on her door.

'This is how high blood pressure begins,' she thought and stormed towards the door.

The peephole never lies, and the peephole told Madison that Damion was at the door. She exhaled, opened the door, and before she could say anything, Damion thrust a beautiful arrangement towards her.

'This brotha is too smooth,' she thought.

Madison flashed one of her best smiles, usually reserved for taking pictures.

"Thanks, Damion. These are very pretty. Smell good, too. Let me take care of these and I promise I'll be ready soon." 'What happened to me meeting him downstairs?' Madison wondered. He was trying to be slick.

She walked to the kitchen to put the flowers in water.

"Care for something to drink?"

"Madison, I'll be fine. I have a couple of calls to make, but I only have three words for you."

Madison beat him to the punch.

"Please get ready," and ran towards her bathroom. Too excited to concentrate on her hair, Madison brushed her thick disobedient hair into a ponytail and put on a little more makeup than usual to atone for the snatch back. She lengthened her lashes, plucked a few eyebrows that were struggling to grow past her bi-weekly wax, and darkened her lip liner. She listened intently to see if she could hear what Damion was doing, which seemed to be speaking with someone. His voice was barely audible, but that didn't stop the hairs from rising on the back of Madison's neck. She wondered if she should throw on a baseball cap. Her brother's best friend Terrence had told her once there was nothing sexier than woman with a baseball cap and her ponytail hanging out of it. She would handle this mini crisis with one intelligent question. Sticking her head out of her door, Madison cleared her throat lightly trying to catch Damion's attention. He had on a light wool sweater, which hinted at the taut muscles underneath, some jeans (Thank God) and a nice looking pair of driving mocs, Prada by the looks of them. The way he was arched on her straight-backed chair, elbows resting comfortably but alert and the curve of his strong hands as he cupped the phone to his ear almost took Madison's breath away. Her first throat clearing was barely audible. She tried again. This time Damion spun around in the chair to face her. A smile curved around his full lips as he lifted his head and arched his eyebrows in a "yes" gesture.

"Damion, do you have the top down today?"

"Alright man. Get up 'wit me. I'm out." Damion hung up the phone and stood up to stretch. He looked like a panther ready to pounce.

"It's a bit cool right now Madison, but I'll take it down after brunch if that's what you want," Damion offered. He briefly studied her. "Is that why you put your hair up?"

"Yeah, Yes. That's why." Madison lied, twirling her ponytail nervously.

"You sure you don't want any coffee or anything? Cappucino? Espresso?"

"Look Madison Starbucks," Damion teased while walking around her apartment, "I only want you to do one thing."

"I know, I know!" Madison yelled as she popped back in her bedroom.

"Please get ready."

"It's not please anymore, Madison. It's get ready, now."

Madison figured she'd carry the baseball cap and grabbed her backpack when the phone rang. She hoped it was Pilar calling to say she'd temporarily lost her mind, and to scrap that crazy plan, but instead she answered to some loud giggles and guffawing.

"Hello?"

"Tramp! Where you been?"

"Stacey? Where have YOU been? I've been trying to reach you all week. And where are you now?"

"Girl, I'm at Maisie's, getting some new acrylic."

"Stacey. You just had your nails done, why in the world are you back? Believe me, I can find better things for you to do with your money."

"Look, tramp. One of my nails came off in David's back, and I had to get it fixed."

"Stacey, that's TMI, but who the hell is David?"

"I'll tell you about him later, girl. Right now, you think I'm giving up too much information, your whorish behind ain't giving up none at all. Who is Damion and why are you tripping over him already?"

"First of all, tell Maisie she's in trouble, and second of all, I'm about to walk out the door, so I can't talk either."

"Oh, I forgot, you going to sit up under those bourgie Greek chicks in the A group meeting? I mean asshole group meeting? What's the topic this week? 'Why do I make 120K and How Come I Ain't Got No Man?'"

"Stace—Come on girl. Why don't you come over to moms' tomorrow and have dinner with us? You know she loves some Stacey. You always make her laugh."

"Nah, Mama likes those deep discounts I give her at the store." Stacey laughed while Maisie said something in the background. Just then Damion's voice boomed,

"Oh, shit! Not my favorite!"

It was open season for Stacey.

"Wait wait, Maisie, be quiet."

"Madison. I can't believe you've got all three *Godfather's* AND *Scarface*, AND

Goodfellas AND *Once Upon A Time in America*. Damn girl. You alright."

"Uhp. Don't let me find out you got some dude over there!" Stacey squealed. This was just the sort of thing that would keep her juiced for hours.

"Stacey. I really gotta go, I'll see you tomorrow at 1:00 at mom and dad's ok?"

"Girl, I ain't hanging up this phone until you tell me who you got over there?"

"I'll give you a hint. His name rhymes with ...click"

Madison hung up and dashed out of her room. Damion was squatting and running his fingers over the movies in her entertainment center. There were a couple of videos sitting near his feet. He heard her approaching and grinned up at her like a little boy.

"I'm impressed, Madison. A true mafia diehard. And, all your movies are in alphabetical order, too."

Madison noticed he had a couple of movies on the floor beside him.

"Well, what is that beside you, young man?

She stood over Damion with her hand on her hips.

"Oh, I picked up *She's Gotta Have It* and *Jason's Lyric*. See, my boy Todd and I have an ongoing bet. First, we need to compare Tracy Camilla Johns in this movie and *New Jack City*. Madison looked confused. "What we're comparing is a guy thing. And secondly, I've got to convince Todd that ain't Jada Pinkett's booty in *Jason's Lyric*.

"Damion, I don't mean to disappoint you, but I don't lend out my movies, I never get them back. It's not personal."

Damion stood up. Madison didn't realize how tall he really was, but she'd had on heels when they went to lunch and at the club.

"Oh, you've got that friends and family policy. I understand. Sometimes the people closest to us can be so trifling. But technically, since we're just getting to know each other, I don't fall into either category, really, and I have some collateral."

"Oh yeah, and what's that?"

"That's this."

Damion gently grabbed Madison and kissed her. On the lips. His lips were softer than a Krispy Kreme 'Hot Doughnuts Now' right out of the oven. His breath was fresh and his tongue tasted like Crest's cool mint gel. Madison kept her composure on the outside, but on the inside, she was a newly erupted volcano, lava burning the earth and anything else that got in its way. Damion stepped back and Madison swayed momentarily. She had to shake it off like a dog shakes off water after he accidentally gets wet.

"You're a trip, Damion. You think you can just give me that good morning breakfast kiss and you get whatever you want?"

"I'm not getting what I want, yet. I just wanted to make you an offer you couldn't refuse."

"That's it. You're out of line," said Madison jokingly. "...and you better have my movies back by next Saturday or I'm coming after you." What did he mean, he wasn't getting what he wanted, yet? Things were happening entirely too fast, and Madison meant to slow them down.

"Thanks, now where do you want to eat?" Damion asked while reading her plaques and various writing awards.

"How about the Front Page?"

"How about Parkway Deli, since it's right around the corner? Then we'll be able to make more of our day, and we don't spend a lot of time waiting in line."

"That's fine, because I have something to do this afternoon for a friend of mine."

'He probably wanted Parkway the whole time,' thought Madison. But that was fine by her.

"Ok, let's go then. Oh, I forgot to unplug my curling iron. I'll be right back." Madison had to write down some key words of a poem that was building itself in her head. She'd get to it later, but it would address those softer than soft lips of Damion's.

When Madison returned, Damion was reading through a stack of papers and laughing heartily.

"Madison. You are just full of surprises, what's this all about?" Damion queried while he held up the front page of *The Chocolate City Voice*.

Madison sighed while forcing a smile. Damion was rather nosy and now he was REALLY into her personal stuff. She didn't want him to critique her writing style or topics as she was rather sensitive to feedback from non-professionals.

"I freelance occasionally for *The Chocolate City Voice,* and headlined for a columnist who took a 6 week sabbatical."

"Hoopdies Keep You Humble: How My Hoopdie Kept Me From Being Hincty.

Aging Grace—Weight Redistribution, the Transformation of Toenails into Claws and Dimples In A Place That Ain't On Your Face." Creative and funny, I like it. Madison? Damion looked squarely into her large doe-like eyes. "You corny, ain't you?"

Madison simply shifted her feet and said "Let's go." How dare he call her corny! How dare he? Since high school, Madison tried to shake the "white girl" stigmatism from her beloved sisters and brothers. Just because she grew up in a white neighborhood and attended predominantly white schools did not mean she wasn't a true sister. She never failed to wonder why speaking the King's English worked against her. White people felt extremely comfortable with her, and would say things like, "You're not really one of them," whereas her brown counterparts would always view her with suspicion until they got to know her. Then they'd tease her about the way she spoke and her bourgie habits. Madison clearly remembered her brief stint with an all black insurance firm and bristled at the thought. On her first day, a contemporary asked Madison to walk to the store with her. As soon as they entered the little hole in the wall, Madison wrinkled her nose in curiosity. It was a little bodega and the smell of dried fish and plantain was overwhelming. Besides, the fact that it was 90 degrees and the place had no air conditioning didn't help either. When she looked in the freezer that held ice cream and empanadas, she asked Karen where the Hagendaas was. Karen belted out a refreshing laugh and said "Hagendaas? Hagendaas? At a 'corna store? Girl, you must be crazy. You better get an ice cream sandwich and call it a day." When Madison complained about the bullet proof glass, Karen laughed again. "Madison, you alright with me, but where you from?"

She and Karen were still friends, but several people in the office ostracized her; she never felt completely comfortable. And now Damion was pushing her sore spot. He motioned as if to walk towards the door, but stopped, looked around the entire apartment and shook his head affirmatively. "You know Madison, you've got a really nice place. Perhaps you'll help me decorate mine when I move. I like your style. It fits your personality."

'He must have sensed the doghouse coming,' Madison thought as she grabbed her fitted black leather jacket and opened the door. But, he was already talking about the future. That was a good sign. She felt much better once they hit the fresh, cool air. The morning passed so swiftly that she almost missed her rendezvous with Bernard. She was supposed to pick him up at the New Carrollton metro station at 2:00, then they would head on out to Upper Marlboro.

After looking at antiques in Kensington, Damion asked Madison if she wanted to go for coffee or ice cream. They seemed to have a lot in common. By the time Damion told Madison he liked go to Starbucks, buy a large latte, come home, throw a scoop of vanilla Haagendas in a huge mug and add a dash, well, a tablespoon of Amaretto, it was all over, they were definitely kindred spirits. Madison did the same thing, but added a pinch of Bailey's Irish Creme liquor instead. Damion was alright, after all. Brunch was perfect, and now it had to end and hell had to begin. All for Pilar's crazy ass. Ah well, what are friends for?

Madison's Journal

Saturday, September 18th.

Dear Journal, I gotta make this quick. Damion and I are going to breakfast. But I've got to share. This man just kissed me. I swear it's the best kiss I've ever had. His lips are soft as butter, and his tongue explored me like Matthew Henson explored Alaska. I couldn't resist. If his tongue is that warm and sensual in my mouth, I can only imagine...I think I'm in trouble.

Butterfly Effect
You kissed me on a Saturday
Melted straight through my center
Massaged my soul like hot rocks
From molten lava warming ice cold winter

Beautiful from the inside out
Compassionate, kind and giving
Slowly erasing any doubt
That Love belongs in the land of the living

You kissed me on a Saturday
And turned my world upside down
Made me think it was a Friday
Spinning in a theme park teacup—twirling round and round

Dazed and confused—I wonder
Could this be real?
Maybe it's an emotional blunder
No—my heart knows what it feels

You kissed me on a Saturday
Suddenly the world stood still
Renewing my faith in the unexpected
With respect for your core and your strong will
Removing old feelings of being used and rejected

Took me totally by surprise
Gave me hope for the future
A lifetime of sunsets and sunrises
You zipped up past wounds with a perfect suture

You kissed me on a Saturday
Euphoria my natural happy pill
Rocked me like a baseball
Hit to a wide open left field

You came at a time when I thought I needed rest
God placed you here and told me "Try this one on for size"
I hope this is true and genuine and not just a test
Damion—you give me butterflies

CHAPTER 15

Madison—Deception
September 1999

Madison knew from the jump that Bernard was an asshole. She had no problem spotting the overdressed gentlemen reading the *Wall Street Journal*. She pulled in front of him and rolled down the window.

"Bernard?"

"Madison?"

"Who else would be calling his name? She thought irritably.

As soon as he got in the car, he asked her not to smoke. In her own car. He then asked in a snide tone why she was 15 minutes late. Madison rolled her eyes and systematically tuned him out as he explained why his time was so important. He was a businessman, and he was on a tight schedule, and he was going to have to rearrange things and…

Madison, who had been biting her lip, one because she needed a cigarette, no, actually one, because she wanted to be with Damion right about now and two, she needed that cigarette, lost most of her cool.

"Bernard. I don't know you, but, first of all, relax, it's Saturday. Second of all, if you weren't so busy trying to get some ass then maybe you wouldn't have so many issues."

Bernard didn't skip a beat.

"Ms. Madison, he said acidly, between clinched teeth, clinched crooked teeth,

"It seems as if you corporate brainwashed negro's don't understand free enterprise and entrepreneurism. It doesn't matter if it's Sunday, New Year's or Mother's Day. I have my OWN business and if I don't work, I starve. Capiche?" Bernard sat back in the seat and went for the kill.

"Also, I thought Pilar would have more class than to associate with someone so uncouth, *and* a smoker. "

Madison stopped the car, looked hard at Bernard, and just started laughing. She couldn't believe this MF. It was so unbelievable it was funny. His response was to look at his watch and huff impatiently. Madison lit a cigarette and didn't say a word to him during the rest of what seemed like an interminable 20-minute ride.

When they finally got to Pilar's, she was waiting anxiously at the fence looking up and down the street like a pressed schoolgirl. Madison pulled out her last cigarette and promised to think happy thoughts. So, she began to think of Damion, that electrifying kiss, those sculpted arms, those perfect teeth, and put a smile on her face.

However, the Oscar winner was Bernard. As soon as they got out of the car, he put his arm around Madison and performed a true meet and greet with everyone at the cookout. He even went downstairs, to forbidden land, to speak to Mitch and his boys, who barely looked up when he spoke. Pilar was right behind them, pointing and cooing and making Madison sick. She thought Pilar was a little too obvious, but then again, she knew. Also, if everyone thought she and Bernard were a couple, why would they ever think Pilar would be attracted to him? It was a good plan, Madison had to admit.

The cookout was very nice. Under one tent, one could choose from traditional bar-b-que foods. Beef hamburgers and hot dogs, ribs, potato salad, baked beans, smoked sausage, and coleslaw. Madison dubbed the other tent, the healthy wealthy tent. There was grilled salmon, shrimp, lobster tails, grilled turkey breast, zucchini, squash, broccoli, corn, red peppers, mesclun salad, beef kabobs, hummus and pita chips. Finally, for those who didn't mind getting a little dirty, there was a small table covered with brown paper, a roll of paper towels, a bowl of wet naps, and a huge bucket of male crabs. A smaller bucket held the female crabs. The desserts were inside, prepared and chilled just so. Pilar had gone all out, and it showed.

Too bad she wasn't hungry. The food was nice to look at, but Madison couldn't touch it. The incurred stress of having to play "pretend" with Bernard and the burden of her secret proved to be too much. Just too much. Besides, everyone just *loved* Bernard. He was a golf player, aggressive, outspoken, well rounded, handsome and worked for himself. Oh yeah, and vacationed at the Hamptons. At least that's what he said. Bernard answered all the questions directed towards Madison, solidifying his position as the man, including the "how long have you two been dating, to where did you find him, to ah, do you know what kind of potential a good-looking couple like you two have?" Bernard ate it up, as well as a respectable amount of food from the healthy wealthy tent. Madison figured a brotha like that wouldn't be caught dead in public eating a hot dog and some baked beans, but she bet 10 to one that his freezer and cabinets at home told a different story.

Pilar executed her plan with precision. At the appointed time, she tiptoed downstairs with a cold six-pack and announced, a little too loudly, that she had to run to Fresh Fields to pick up some ingredients she'd forgotten for the creme brulee. This ploy was to keep any of the card players from coming upstairs. Sam, one of Mitch's oldest friends yelled, "Crim Broolay? Pilar, please, why can't you just hook a brother up with some peach cobbler? Mitch, man, I told you marrying somebody named Pilar was going to be trouble." The basement erupted with raucous laughter. Madison and Bernard were standing by a group of Trivial Pursuit enthusiasts at the head of the stairs when she heard the laughter coming from downstairs. In seconds, she spotted Pilar's head ascending the stairs.

"That's right. I'm 'bout to run a Boston on yo ass!" That would be the rowdy spades table in the basement, which always drew a crowd. Everyone was so happy. Madison would have really enjoyed it herself had she been with Damion, she was sure of it. The plan now called for Madison to excuse herself, powder her nose, and detach herself from Bernard, freeing him to go to the store with Pilar. While in the bathroom, Madison looked in the mirror and wondered how Pilar could look at herself daily, knowing she was dogging a good man. She splashed some cold water on her face and took deep breaths to steel herself to continue the charade. Next time, common sense and her gut would supersede good deeds. As Madison came out of the bathroom, she could hear her heart beating through her ears. She had the distinct feeling that something was about to go very wrong.

Mitch had come upstairs. He'd pushed back part of the curtain with his hand, and was looking out the window facing the front. Madison's heart caught in her throat. He NEVER left his chair when he was playing cards.

"The year Jackie Robinson broke the baseball color barrier?!" some trivial pursuiter screamed.

Mitch turned around and looked at Pilar with an indescribable look.

"Right you are kiddo. Wow, you sure know your sports!" More laughter. More clapping. The gamers seemed far away.

"Madison. Aren't you going to the store with Pilar and your boyfriend?" Mitch asked with a polite smile, if you could call the contorted twist a smile.

"Mmm hmmm," Madison nodded quickly, as she couldn't pay herself to speak at the moment.

"Oooh! That's my song! I luuuv "Me and Mrs. Jones" That DJ is jamming!" An enthusiastic gray-haired guy stood up and pretended he was slow dancing with a partner. He was immediately checked by his wife, a striking woman with silver hair, lots of noisy jewelry and a great sense of humor.

"Not enough for you to leave this game to do the two step with your 'ol ass. Now sit back down."

Looking much older than his years, Mitch slowly turned towards the basement as Madison found her voice.

"Did you want us to pick up something for you, Mitch?"

Clack Clack Clack as the triumphant trivia buff moved his piece forward three times.

"I forgot to tell Pilar to pick up some ice for the downstairs cooler, but don't worry about it. As long as the boys are drinking, they don't really care."

Rumble Bumble Tumble went the dice as another player rolled.

"Ok, see 'ya, then."

Madison tried to appear nonchalant, but her knees were shaking.

"I'll take Science and Nature."

"…we got a thang going on!"

"Fool, let Billy Paul sing his own song. Puhleeze!"

Madison rushed outside and placed her hands on her temple in an attempt to alleviate the stubborn headache that stuck to her like stink on a skunk. When she finally stopped rubbing her temples, Pilar's car could not be found. Neither could Bernard, Pilar, or their collective conscious be found, while a truck driver grinned deviously to himself thinking how lucky he was as he stared down on the crown of Pilar's head, bobbing rhythmically up and down as Bernard drove recklessly, zig zagging towards nowhere.

CHAPTER 16

Madison—A Family Reunion
September 1999

After the cookout, Madison struggled to make sense of the whole Pilar thing, but to no avail. Filled with nervous energy, she began to write frantically about what she later titled, "Stupid Love." It would make a great op/ed somewhere or other. Madison finally went to bed at approximately 3:30 am, with visions of Mitch kicking Pilar's butt dancing in her head.

Madison's mom woke her the following morning and asked her to come over earlier to help cut the strips for the peach cobbler. Madison sleepily grumbled her acknowledgement. She knew it was no use fighting with her mother, who never really asked for her help. But it was odd that she called last minute like this.

"Oh, mom, by the way, Stacey is coming by for brunch, ok?"

"Sure, thing, hon. But hurry up and get your tail over here. I need all the help I can get, 'cause you know your daddy ain't too useful in the kitchen."

'...in the kitchen, in the yard, around the house, and feeding the dog,' Madison thought. Her dad wasn't too useful in a lot of places, but he was such a loving person with such an infectious laugh, there was nothing Madison's mom could do when it came to fixing things, but call a professional. Professional landscaper, home improvement person, electrician, you name it, her mom had an envelope stuck in the yellow pages for a specific service.

"Alright, Ma. I'm jumping in the shower now."

After hanging up the receiver, Madison pulled the covers over her head to snag

15 more minutes of sleep. She woke up an hour later. Giggling, she got up and rushed to get ready. Her mom probably knew she was lying about jumping in the shower. She tried to think of a viable excuse as to why she was late, but nothing seemed to work. Her mom would poke holes in all her sorry excuses. She was still thinking of a "good one" as she walked in the door of her parent's tidy Silver Spring, MD home. After hearing a confident male voice, she stopped dead in her tracks.

"Come on, Ma. Let me lick the bowl, please. Madison won't get mad, in fact she won't even know. Just let me—"

"Let you what, boy! There will be a rumble in the jungle if you try and steal what's in my bowl!" Madison ran and jumped in her brother's outstretched arms.

"Ms. Madison doesn't deserve to lick the bowl, Ms. Madison has a time discrepancy," teased her mom.

"Ma, why can't you just say I'm late, why 'time discrepancy'? Madison chuckled, straining her neck to see her mom in her brother's vice-like grasp. Madison now twisted back towards Paul. She gave him a sloppy kiss on the cheek and sucked his skin until she looked like a fish. It was a game they played when Madison was younger. She thought that's how kissing was done, so big brother Paul just played along with her. Seeing Paul's apparent strain, she slid out of his arms, snatched the mixing bowl off the counter and greedily began to devour the tasty mix her mom used to make coconut cake.

"Paul. What the heck are you doing here? I would say what the *hell* are you doing here, but ma might have a conniption."

"Madison, you aren't too old to have your little nasty mouth washed out with soap."

"Alright, Ma. I was just kidding. Paul. Why are you here? Where are the kids? Where is Cynthia? Excuse me, Cindy? Are you moving back home?"

"Madison. Slow down. You remind me of that cartoon character, uh, what's his name, he's always talking, non-stop, run-on sentences, umm ummm, you know, that little mouse…"

"They say the first thing that goes is the memory bruh." Madison wiped cake mix off the bridge of her nose.

"Sniffles! That's it, Madi. You're just like Sniffles!" Paul harrumphed triumphantly. All three Robinsons laughed easily and comfortably with one another.

Madison took a moment to look at her brother. He was really good-looking. He was 6'3, 220 and looked like he was in the best shape of his adult life. Cyndi liked to hike and bike, so they did plenty of it, there being no shortage of trails and mountains in the outskirts of Seattle, Washington. A deep brown, Paul had dimples that would make a cashew jealous. His hands were well-shaped and his nails were neat and trimmed perfectly. His baby-face easily belied his 37 years.

"I flew in for the weekend for a small business conference held at Howard University. I served on one of the panels."

"What panel was that, Paul?" Mrs. Robinson asked as she briskly washed the used pots and pans. "I was a panelist for a plenary session about how to cash in on start-up companies, from setting precedence to preparing for IPO's. There's a lot of money to be made out there, Ma. You just gotta know where to find it. Robert Louis and Chaz Washington, the primary organizers, wanted to stress career independence and entrepreneurial strategies. Overall, I think they pulled it off."

Madison immediately thought of Bernard and got a bad taste in her mouth. She walked towards the refrigerator, plucked a glass from the cabinet and poured some water. The cake mix was too sweet anyway.

She scowled at her mom, who was eating Paul's words up. She probably had no idea what an IPO was, but he sounded smart, and Madison's mom loved her male child.

"So how are my favorite niece and nephew?"

"Madison. The only reason they're your favorite is because there aren't any more little Robinsons running around. Speaking of which, Madi. You will be 30 soon. What's up with that?"

Madison put on spoiled pout number one. This gesture involved thrusting the lower lip slightly above the upper lip, widening the eyes and holding the head down in a pitiful stance.

"Paul Robinson. What are you saying? Just because I'll be thirty doesn't mean I need to be barefoot and pregnant."

"Madi Mae, you know ma wants some more grandbabies." He knew he'd pushed a button, and was steadily gaining ground.

Madison was gearing up for spoiled pout number two, which usually led to kick in the butt number one.

"Paul. You need to stop worrying about when I'm going to get married. Just because you married to that white woman doesn't mean you have to adopt all their beliefs. Just because white folks get married before they're like, 23, doesn't mean everyone should."

Sensing sibling tension and perhaps trouble, Madison's mom interjected.

"Ya'll get on outta here and let me finish, please. It's been very quiet around here, and that's how I like it. Quiet."

"Speaking of quiet, where's Dad?" Madison didn't want to discuss marriage or babies anymore.

"You know your daddy. He's downstairs in the basement watching that *SPEN*."

"*SPEN*?" Madison and Paul asked at the same time.

"Yeah. That sports channel."

"Ma, that's *ESPN*," laughed Paul. "I think I'll go down and join him, since I'm not wanted here," Paul teased.

"Alright ma, I'll help you with the cobbler, now." Madison butterfly-punched Paul in the stomach and whispered in his ear, "Ma saved your ass."

"Madison. There is no cobbler. I just wanted to surprise you like your brother surprised us."

"Ma...Paul always get what he wants. I bet you made sweet potatoes." Mrs. Robinson nodded affirmatively. "I bet you made macaroni and cheese." Minnie Robinson nodded again. "I bet you made corn pudding."

"Yes, Maam, Madison. Just look in the oven and see. Cooked perfectly, with no burnt edges."

Madison rolled her eyes and walked over to the stove and opened the oven door. She closed it, turned around and watched her mother and Paul hold their stomachs they were laughing so hard. The peach cobbler was beautifully brown, and baked. Been baked.

"What's so funny in here? Ya'll left the door open." Stacey's voice preceded her. She almost ran into Paul, who was on his way downstairs.

"Uhhhp. Don't let me find out Paul is home!" Stacey squealed. She had always liked Paul. But he told Madison confidentially that she was just a little too rough around the edges. Stacey shrugged off Paul's disinterest in her by convincing herself he only liked white women. Madison didn't have the heart to tell her, but Paul didn't have a preference per se, he just liked good-hearted women.

"Stacey! How are you, and how's your mother?" asked my mom while Stacey gave her a big bear hug.

"Moms is fine, I'm even better" Stacey sang as she opened pots and poked her nose in the oven. "Especially after Harley man."

"Harley man?" Mrs. Robinson inquired.

Madison figured it was time to grab Stacey and get her out of the kitchen. She thought her mom was their age, and would tell her anything.

"Stace, let's go sit on the deck, and you can tell me why you were at Maisie's, ok?"

"Girl, I had to get new nails. I broke three of them in Harley man's back."

Madison's mother visibly frowned. Although she was cool on the outside, she was 'ol school on the inside, and what she just heard was a little too much information. Back in the day, Mrs. Robinson would have told Madison to be careful hanging around a woman so fast.

"That's it. Stacey! Deck! Now!"

"Ok, ok," Stacey laughed and then mouthed "ok, ho," pursing her mouth perfect "o" style. She grabbed some nuts from the snack bowl and followed Madison outside.

"Everything looks real good, Mrs. Robinson. I can't wait to get my grub on."

Mrs. Robinson frowned slightly. Madison knew why. Stacey hadn't washed her hands before she dug in the nut bowl. Madison's mom was a stickler for clean hands. Madison would bet her left pinky the bowl would be gone when they came back to the kitchen, washed and nuts in the trash. That's just the way her mom rolled.

Once Madison and Stacey were comfortably seated in body length lawn chairs, the catching up began fast and furious. Madison told Stacey all about Damion and their dates. Stacey wasn't thrilled a bit. "He seem slick. I don't trust him."

"Stacey. You don't even know him."

"I don't care. Who was he talking to while you were curling your hair?"

"I don't know. I mean it's none of my business. He was in my place."

"Exactly. Does he have a girlfriend?"

"I don't know, I don't think so."

"So, how you 'gone let him kiss on you and you don't even know if he got somebody?"

"Well, Stacey. I guess I'm a bit old fashioned. I figured if a guy is sweating me as hard as Damion is, then he can't have a girlfriend."

"Dear Madison, you know what assuming does. So assume he does have a woman until you have more information. And if you want this one, keep your legs closed, please. We don't want him to get to know you, before he gets to know you, if you know what I mean."

"Well, Ms. Break-A-Nail. Apparently you didn't keep your legs closed for the Harley Man."

"You can't compare that."

"Why not?"

"Because that's all it was, and all it will be. I went into it knowing the deal and I escape unscathed. See how it works?"

"I gotcha. Now will you tell me about Harley man?"

"Madi! Stacey! 5 minutes girls and brunch will be served."

"Girl. Why is your mother the black June Cleaver?"

"Yeah, but her name would have been Junette or some shit like that."

Stacey almost choked, she laughed so hard.

"Girl. You stupid. Ok. In a nutshell, I left Nordstrom's early last Monday, because they were doing a major floor change and preparing for a huge sale. And I'm like, shoot, how much changing do I have to do for fragrances? None. And you know it was real nice out. So, on my way home, I pull up to this red light and looked to my right. You know how people always look around them when they drive?"

"Stace, c'mon! Get back to the story!"

"This is the story. So girl, I looked to my right and saw this HONEY on a Hog."

"A hog?"

"A Harley, Madison. Girl, he had on some blue jeans, some biker boots, his helmet and some black shades. He didn't have on a shirt, and his skin just glistened girl. His back was so tight, he looked like a king cobra arched over the handle bars. So, I leaned over and said loudly, 'cause you know Harleys have those throaty engines, and said, "Excuse me, but you're going to get a ticket if you don't put a shirt on."

He looked right through me and said, 'Why?' Girl, between him looking like Karl Malone and sounding like Barry White, I messed up my thong. So I responded with, "Cause you look so good, you 'gone cause a woman like me to have an accident." After which, he smiled, and said, "I'll put on a shirt only if you give me yours."

"No he didn't!" Madison interrupted.

"Yes he did, and yes I did!"

"Stacey!"

"What?!"

"Stacey!! That's IT for you."

"I had my oversized OLD NAVY tee on and a tube underneath. So when I took off the shirt, my boobs stuck out to never never land, which was a good thing, 'cause Harley man is a tittie man."

By this time Madison was sitting on the edge of her chair, greedily devouring Stacey's story.

"Madison, Stacey! Are you going to eat outside?"

"Ma, we're coming. Just a second! Stacey, HURRY UP! You know we can't continue this conversation at the dinner table."

"So as I was saying, I know that light. It's damn near 3 minutes. You know the one at Connecticut and East-West?"

"Yes. Continue," Madison stressed impatiently, stamping her foot.

"Ok, so I got out the car, walked around and gave it to him."

"Gave him what?"

"The t-shirt, stupid."

"So did he put it on?"

"After he stared at my titties for a second, he said 'thanks' and took off his helmet to wipe his head, and why did I die? Why is he butterball bald? Whoo hoo! He put on my shirt and said 'Where can I return this?' Girl, I said 'Follow Me', and switched back to my car like Loretta Devine did in "Waiting to Exhale" when Gregory Hines was watching her walk to her house, and made him follow me home."

"No! Then what happened?"

"THEN we didn't leave my house for a week, and role played every imaginable character, from Cleopatra, Jones that is, to Dolemite, to just everybody."

"Did you go to work?"

"Girl, I couldn't leave David. His sexiness was addicting. I told my manager I had to leave town on an emergency for at least a week because my favorite grandmother wasn't well, and my family needed me."

"You are so trifling. Did you get enough of that adDICTing thing?"

"Plenty. And then some."

"So where is he now?"

"I don't know. After we couldn't think of any more interesting roles, he rolled. He kissed me and left the same way he came. With my tee shirt and his jeans and boots."

"Stacey. I'm sorry. That's just not believable."

"And sometimes, Madison, neither is your naïve and self-righteous ass. Let's go eat."

Brunch was spirited to say the least. Mr. Robinson stayed long enough for two helpings and a few jokes and went back downstairs to join *ESPN*, again. Stacey and Paul continued to rankle one another. Between the two of them, it was hard to get a word in edgewise, they were born to contradict one another. After listening to their rhetoric for some time, Mrs. Robinson decided to nip their lively conversation in the bud.

"Stacey and Paul. You two sound like an old married couple." That did it. Stacey immediately clammed up, while Paul laughed and joked, "Well, Ma, one out of two ain't bad."

Stacey stuffed cobbler in her mouth while Paul discussed dates for Kelly and Scott to visit their grandparents for two weeks the following summer. Once Madison cleared the table, Madison's mom announced that in fifteen minutes, everyone was going to go to the Black Family Reunion. No questions asked.

"Mrs. Robinson, I'm going to have to uh—"

"Stacey. You are just like family. You are going with us." Mrs. Robinson had spoken. She stood glaring at Stacey defiantly, arms akimbo. That was the stance she took before she spoke about one of her more passionate topics, civil rights. She was a 60's baby. "Do you know what it took for Dr. Dorothy Height to pull off such a magnificent undertaking? Not only here in our nation's capitol, but in cities throughout the U.S.?"

Stacey took a step back.

"Alright Mrs. R. I'm going. I'm going."

Stacey lifted her hands in defeat. She really just wanted to get home and soak her tired, oversexed body. But she would do it for Mrs. Robinson. The last time she got fussed at like that is when she told Mrs. R. that she wasn't going to vote because the people running for office were clowns and couldn't be trusted anyway. She received the dogs, hoses and Pettus Bridge lecture then. She'd also voted ever since.

"Now I'm going to get your daddy out of his chair. When I get back, you guys better be ready."

"Yes, Maam!" Paul answered with a salute. He then looked at Madison and Stacey. "Who's driving?"

"You are!" they chimed in unison.

"Whatever happened to being independent women?"

Paul shook his head as he grabbed the morning's trash. Their mom hated trash stinking up the house, and would be late for an event until he or Madison tied it up and took it outside. Even though they were both out of their parent's house, the trash thing was automatic.

The family reunion was truly an outstanding event. The National Council of Negro Women made sure there were activities for the entire family, from toddler to elder. As soon as they approached the monument grounds, Mr. Robinson took off towards the *ESPN* sports tent. Mrs. Robinson followed right on his heels. Donna Richardson was leading a fitness routine, and there were Nike and Reebok sponsors peddling their wares, giving away associated ancillary products.

On the small stage to their left, they heard powerful, sultry singing from a male performer. Madison, Paul and Stacey couldn't get too close, as there was a large crowd around him.

"Who is that?" Stacey asked, touching a youthful looking older woman.

"Oh, that's my son! That's Raheem DeVaughn, hon. He is going to blow up one day!" The mother was beaming. She was a beautiful Hershey brown, teeny, stock full of energy with huge presence, and a long bundle of locs that inched past her waste. Her sole job for the moment seemed to be focused on working the crowd and bringing in onlookers. The guy did sound good, though, and he was a cutie. He would be fine. Another gorgeous woman with natural hair was selling his CD's to the right of the stage. She must have been a friend of Raheem's mom. Madison made a mental note to come back before they left and buy his CD to support him.

The group walked on. They ran into Paul's ex-girlfriend Yvette. She was a beautiful voluptuous brown woman with super deep dimples, just like Paul's. Out of all Paul's girl friends, Madison liked her best. She was really sweet, and into her brother big-time. But once Paul met Cindy, it was pretty much all over. Yvette was hurt, but she and Paul were great friends. He was honest and upfront with her from the beginning. He'd told her,

"You're my best friend. I couldn't think of anyone else to tell." Yvette handled it with grace. Madison didn't know if she would have been as cool. Stacey definitely wouldn't have handled it well. Heck, with Stacey, there would have been a fight.

Bored with the small talk and "What have you been up to's," Stacey actively surveyed the grounds and tilted her head towards a brother near the face-painting tent.

"Madi—I'll be right back. Girl, if I don't see you in twenty, meet me at the food tents. I want a funnel cake."

Instantly suspicious, Madison looked towards where Stacey's eyes focused. Of course. It was a tall, brown-skinned bald guy with a wife beater, some jeans and some Tim boots. Of course, vintage Stacey.

"Stacey. He probably has 5 children and three 'baby mommas,' you need to stop."

"Look Ms. Prude. At least I'll find out what the deal is, unlike you and Damion." She strolled off.

"Damion. Who's Damion?" asked Paul, breaking away from his conversation with Yvette.

Madison hesitated, and Yvette turned in the direction her name was called. Her twin sister, Peachezz, and their best friend Nichelle were less than 10 feet away but wouldn't come any closer. Unlike Yvette, they never forgave Paul for breaking her heart. They all stood there, hands on hips, head turtling, and shouting.

"Yvette. Let's go. Now! Derric is waiting on Independence, holding up traffic for you. Derric was Peachezz's husband, and had the patience of Job, so Madison was sure that was a lie. She observed the women more closely. None of them seemed to have aged in the past several years. Even though Nichelle was a friend, they could have all been sisters, honey-brown with fly hairdos and attitudes specially cultivated in the District of Columbia. Yvette looked longingly at Paul and mumbled an apology.

Paul opened his arms for a famous bear hug.

"Baby don't worry about it."

Yvette grinned like a Cheshire cat while they hugged amidst the groans of the hissing women. Madison started. She could have sworn Yvette was smelling her brother's underarms. Ah well, maybe she was seeing things. It was hot.

"I wonder what life would have been like if I'd married her?" Paul said, as he watched her walk away. She still looked good to him after 10 years. Fuller. More settled. Paul turned towards his sister.

"Baby sis, who is Stacey talking about?" Madison looked at her watch and attempted a diversion. "Oh, Paul. I told Philip I'd come check out his new act, his nephew Mitch Gunz will be performing soon." Paul didn't miss a beat. "Madi, what does Mitch Gunz guy have to do with what Stacey said?" Madison sighed.

It might be a good to get a male perspective. They walked and talked. Surprisingly, Paul wasn't overly protective or judgmental. He just told Madison to be careful and take things slow. Feeling a bit more comfortable, she told him about the lunch incident with the chicken head.

"Well, Sis. This brother seems as if he's on the up and up, but if people feel free to approach him like that, then perhaps he's giving something out you don't know about. I mean, if he's a dee jay and all—"

"He's not really a dee jay, Paul. He's a voice talent and on occasion he dee jays for WJAZ, with like, just slow, jazzy stuff."

"Still Sis, if 'ol boy is in the public eye, there is a certain amount of prestige and power associated with that, which is hard for many women to resist. So you need to think about that."

It was a beautiful day, and the brother and sister duo were truly enjoying themselves. There were several vendors hawking their many wares, including imported African goods such as wooden fertility carvings, kente, ivory, mudcloth and jewelry, to vendors selling original black dolls, artwork and black memorabilia.

"This was a good idea mom had. I'm glad she made us come."

"Yep. me too, Paul."

As Madison and Paul walked towards the Karibu Books tent, Paul spotted a tent with a colorful flag flapping softly in the slight breeze. The flag read "Catering a la Carte" and had an image of a steaming cobbler bubbling over with juicy goodness. The line outside the tent was doubled with patrons. Paul lost it.

"Madi, look, it's Mr. Larrry! Mr. Larry! I can't believe he's here!"

Madison tugged on her big brother's shirt and figured she'd ask the obvious.

"Unh, Paul, uh, who is Mr. Larry?"

"Mr. Larry is a homegrown DC legend! He used to sell dinners out of his home in NE. Fried catfish, ribs, collards, cornbread. Mr. Larry is the bomb, Madi!"

Paul was so excited he was actually shaking. Men and food, boy. He and Madison grew up in the same place, but hung in different circles. So while he was out eating Mr. Larry's food, Madison's mom was making sure she knew how to cook so she could "keep a man." Funny. Gender socialization.

Paul was still carrying on.

"And his cobbler? His peach cobbler? Everybody loves Mr. Larry's peach cobbler. He gives ma a run for the money, Madi. I hate to say it but it's true. They are the *absolute* in pies, succulent, bursting with flavor and the crust; the crust is so tender it just dissolves in your mouth."

Without so much as a 'come on,' Paul made a bee line towards Mr. Larry's tent.

"Oh, I see. Mr. Larry. Madison whispered as she limply followed her brother.

While they were waiting in line, which wrapped twice around, Madison filled Paul in on more Damion details. He seemed distracted and droned on about Mr. Larry's catfish and fried Whiting. Usually, Paul would take a situation and turn it over, providing a logical and detailed common sense resolution. More often than not, he was right, and Madison respected him for that. But today, he was so caught up in getting a piece of fish and cobbler, he couldn't concentrate. All he offered was "Madison. Be careful, 'lil sis. I know you're a big girl now, but take it slow. Stop letting him kiss on you, too. That's giving him a green light to go to the next level. So have some pride and respect about yourself." Paul then proceeded to count the people in line ahead of him and calculate the amount of time it was going to take him to get to the front of the line.

A frustrated Madison told Paul she'd be waiting for him outside of the tent. She reminded him about Mitch's performance. He barely acknowledged her. As soon as she stepped into the sunlight, she noticed Six coming her way, with a short, red-headed girl in tow. Six approached Madison and gave her the usual cheek to cheek kiss and introduced her to her associate. Six could never just introduce a person with simplicity, like, Madison, this is Jane Doe, Jane this is Madison Robinson. She had to take it a step further.

"Madison, this is Crystal Leonard. She came to the A group meeting on Saturday. You know the day you played hooky?"

Madison shook Crystal's hand while Six continued the biography.

"Madison, Crystal is a hearing examiner for the Bureau of Traffic Adjudication on "K" street."

"Crystal, Madison works for an Information Technology company downtown."

"Nice to meet you, Madison." Madison was amazed at the power in the voice of such a tiny person.

"Likewise," Madison smiled, made a mental note regarding Crystal and her recent DC parking tickets, and turned her attention to Six.

"Six, shouldn't you be with the council member? I thought this would be more work than pleasure for you."

"Not when Amber is around."

"Who's Amber?"

"His wife."

"Oh, I see. So who else is here?"

"Anaya and the girls, Jean, Marissa, Angie and Jill."

"Six seems to know everyone," Crystal said gaily.

"Yeah, she should run for an at-large seat," Madison joked.

"Madison, you just missed Crystal's boyfriend, D. He emceed for the WJAZ tent. He's pretty good if I may say so myself."

The mention of WJAZ caught Madison's attention. Perhaps Crystal's boyfriend knew Damion. She looked at Crystal closely for the first time as Six droned on about who's who and wondered briefly what kind of person she was. She was extremely petite, and well-built. She appeared confident with just the right amount of feminine edge. Soft, but not to be reckoned with. She was dressed rather conservatively, with a hint of a wild side with the lipstick she wore. Once Six paused long enough to take a breath, Madison was going to ask Crystal about her boyfriend possibly knowing Damion.

At that moment, Paul exited the tent with a huge smile on his face and BBQ rib juice on his cheek, and a plastic bag bursting at the seams with Mr. Larry's cobbler.

"Madison, I got enough for you, Ma and Mrs. Jahmal." Mrs. Roblin Jahmal was her parent's next door neighbor, and she practically raised Madison and Paul until they reached middle school. Her parents treated Mrs. Jahmal like a member of the family. Many Sundays the widow would join the Robinsons for dinner and entertain them all afterwards with like renditions of Motown songs. The Supremes and the Marvellettes were her specialty.

Six hugged Paul and spent several minutes on the Crystal—Paul introduction. By the time she finished, Stacey walked up to the group and Leo that she is, took full command of the conversation and changed the energy of the entire group. Before long, Six spotted Tanya and JoAnn, a couple of her sorority sisters. Six responded with their signature call. She did that to irritate Madison, who was in a rival sorority. Crystal muttered her good-byes and hastened to keep up with Six, who turned around once to blow a kiss to Paul and say "smooches." Stacey, who'd tasted a piece of Mr. Larry's cobbler, decided she didn't want a funnel cake, but soul food instead. Paul and Stacey linked arms and disappeared into the tent. He was determined to get her hooked on Mr. Larry's food.

Crystal looked at her watch, excused herself from the gregarious Six, walked towards 17th and Constitution, and climbed into a black convertible Saab, top down.

Madison looked up at the clear turquoise sky and daydreamed about Damion. He was definitely someone she could fall in love with. She made a mental note to ask Crystal if she knew him when she saw her at the next A group meeting.

Had she been a little more observant, and watched Crystal hop into Damion's car, instead of looking into the sky, she wouldn't have to ask, and the story would end here.

Madison's Journal:

Late Saturday, early Sunday, September 18/19, 1999

Dear Journal: what makes a person lose their natural mind? A man for a woman? A woman for a man? It's a phenomenon. Pilar has it. It's called Stupid Love. I don't have to tell you; the cookout was a disaster. I can't sleep for thinking about it. I can't really explain what happened, I don't have all the facts, yet, but bottom line, only stupid love would make someone act like they don't have a brain. This poem is for Pilar.

Stupid Love

Forrest Gump said "Stupid is as stupid does"
But can a phrase so simple explain stupid love?
Simply put, stupid love makes you do stupid things
It clouds the senses from distinguishing between wants and needs
Even if the affected wears a wedding ring
The laws and expectations of society you fail to heed

You don't think about reaping the seeds you sow
At the time for the now you're just a bundle of feelings
For common sense and logic has flown out the window
And the heights you reach with this person has no ceiling

Because you're caught up in a swirl of passion and emotion
And the only thing that matters is the now
You live for the moment and pledge your love and devotion
Knowing the high will end but you don't care and you don't know how

Stupid love is a rollercoaster ride on a finite track
Taking you on the highest of highs and the lowest of lows
Common sense disappears and you're a slave to pheromones
Stupid love may be just as addictive as crack
Some actually lose a job a car a home
And where you'll end up nobody knows

Stupid love leaves you wanting more
For the first time in years months or ever your heart goes pitter patter
Like Stephanie Mills singing "I never knew love like this before"
What other people think or perceive doesn't even matter

Stupid love rarely ends in a civilized way
Because it begins under predetermined circumstances
Admittedly you owe Karma a debt
But you know it has to end some day
Regardless of risk you jumped right in and took your chances
Understanding full well that what you do is what you get

If stupid is as stupid does
You may slip on more than one occasion
If a phrase so simple explains stupid love
Beware the "stupid" powers of persuasion

CHAPTER 17

Madison—More Hot Water?
June 2000

The stinging, slightly soapy taste of bath water rudely awakened me from an apparently deep sleep. The water was cold. "What is Damion up to?" I wondered. Maybe he's preparing breakfast, in the best way he knows how. Microwave the bacon, pop the waffles in the toaster and throw some cheese in a skillet and scramble some eggs. Well, I should have time to soak a little more. It feels so good to relax.

I flipped the lever to add more hot water, and added more good smelling bath gel.

If we play "Crocodile Dundee" this morning, Damion will certainly be going down under... to explore and claim new terrain. Ladies, I know you can relate.

While the water heated, I grabbed the remote to relax even more with my favorite Maxwell CD, Urban Hang Suite. Although Embrya was growing on me, it was something about Urban Hang Suite. Something about words that weren't said, emotions experienced which only music could comprehend.

I slipped back into the water's arms as Maxwell's "Til the Cops Come Knocking" made me think back to last October, when things really heated up with Damion and me.

CHAPTER 18

Madison—Happy Birthday, Madison
October 1999

When Madison returned to work on Monday, she headed straight for Pilar's office to find out what happened with she, Bernard, and Mitch. Pilar's office was closed and locked. Slightly worried, Madison returned to her desk and attempted to send Pilar an e-mail, but the return message stated she would be out of town on business for three weeks. Madison couldn't get over how bold Pilar was.

"She must really be in love to have lost her head like that," she whispered softly to herself, while responding to her e-mail messages.

Stacey helped to break the monotony of Madison's day. She stopped by and surprised Madison with some food from the Islander restaurant. Stacey knew that Madison loved Ms. Addie's cod cakes with mango chutney. The two friends walked outside to an open-seated area to catch up with one another. The weather was still unusually warm, but had a faint scent of the fall to come in the air.

"Madison Robinson. I'm not giving you these cod cakes until you tell me what you're planning for your 30th?"

"Stacey. I should be asking you. But then again, maybe I shouldn't," Madison said sarcastically. Stacey held her 30th at Ozio's cigar bar and lounge. All the girls were smoking stogies, trying to look slick in some tight all-black get-ups. The photos made it look as if the party was a dance ensemble or a chic clique. Stacey thought it was the coolest, but Madison's throat hurt for a week, and it was hard to get the cigar smoke out of her clothes.

"B* please. Let me find out you still holding Ozio's against me, and you'll never get these cod cakes. Hey, what about dinner and drinks at MXXIII? That would be real cool. You could have a table upstairs with all your real friends, and when those A group ho's come, we won't let them past the rope, and they'll just have to wait downstairs."

"Stacey, please," Madison laughed. "Don't playa hate, girl, participaaaate!"

The rest of Madison's lunch hour flew by quickly while she and Stacey planned different 30th birthday scenarios. They never came to a conclusion, however, and agreed to play it by ear.

Later that evening, as Madison recounted her day for Damion, she told him about Stacey and their grandiose plans. She actually wanted to see if he would volunteer to do something for her, even though they'd just met. He didn't say much of anything, just asked her to lunch on Tuesday.

October 15th, which fell on a Friday, turned out to be a beautiful crisp fall day, just right for a birthday. Since Madison considered her birthday a holiday, she'd arranged to take off work and have a long weekend. She and the girls decided to have brunch at Woodside Deli in Silver Spring on Saturday, and then she could have the rest of the day to herself. She planned it that way, hoping that Damion would want to do something special. It had been two weeks since she mentioned her birthday and she wondered if he was going to remember. He had been such a sweetheart, though. He called everyday, so she rarely called him, in fact, she didn't even know his numbers by heart. They'd spent another Saturday together antique shopping in Frederick. She was reprimanded by Six for missing another A group meeting, but Madison didn't care. Damion was better than any A group meeting. Fleetingly she made a mental note of asking that red-headed girl if she knew Damion when she went to another meeting; whenever that would be.

After preparing a light breakfast for herself, Madison made a cup of tea and sat down Indian style in her leather chair to write. Every year at this time, she looked at her short/long term goals and accomplishments from the previous year. This was one of Madison's ways to measure her growth, and tenacity. She had several checks, however, there were a few projects that were put on the back burner never to resurface again. She looked long and hard at "Meet the Right Man" on her list and wondered if she'd met the right man. Ever since he snuck a kiss that Saturday morning, Damion had been a perfect gentleman. After several moments of deep thought, she placed a check mark by "right man."

At that moment, Madison heard a loud, persistent knock on her door. She jumped up and peeked through the peephole. It was Damion.

"What in the world is he doing here?" she wondered.

When she opened the door, he rushed in and gave her a big bear hug.

"Pack your bags, Madison. We're going away for your birthday."

Madison stood there, mouth ajar, door ajar and stared at this crazed man in front of her. Damion was looking exceptionally well. The cool air smacked him faintly on the cheeks, giving him a slight blush. His energy was infectious and Madison had no choice but to share his enthusiasm.

"But Damion, I -"

"But nothing Madison, just pack your bags, beautiful. You don't turn 30 everyday, and besides, I'm sick of hearing about you chained to that desk and those pc-challenged co-workers of yours. Don't you deserve a bit of R&R?"

Madison poked out her lower jaw and said in her best Marlon Brando, "Listen, you've made me an offer I can't refuse. I'll be ready inside of 30 minutes."

Still smiling, Damion asked her if she had a weekend bag to pack her things.

"I have a suitcase, Damion. Is that not good enough?"

"Well I have a little better, Madison. This is a casual weekend, so you should be comfortable and travel as such." With that, Damion reached outside the still open door, and pulled in a large green duffel bag with a bright pink ribbon covering the handle.

An impressed Madison took the bag from him and was surprised at how heavy it was. Interpreting Madison's perplexed look, Damion insisted she open the bag. Inside, Madison found a complete gift bag from Bath & Body Works, with soap, exfoliating gel, shower gel and lotion. He'd even included a matching loofah and a couple of pink candles. Underneath the gift bag was a plush white towel set by Ralph Lauren. Sitting next to the towel were a pair of Esprit shower shoes, white with a pink stripe. Madison was overwhelmed. She'd been spoiled in relationships before, but this, this was truly a first. Fighting tears, she reached up to give Damion a hug, who was looking extremely proud of himself.

"Boy, by looking at this, you must want me to be squeaky clean and butt naked at all times," Madison flirted openly.

"Madison, please," Damion smirked. "You're making me feel cheap," he clowned, covering his heart with his perfectly sculpted hands.

"It shouldn't take you so long to pack, now that you have some of the basics, oh and, look in the front flap for the bonus."

Madison's heart fluttered uncontrollably as she sat down and unzipped the front flap. He'd made her a really big birthday card on the computer. The front cover had a pretty rose on it, and the text read—Happy 30th Birthday, Madison. The inside inscription read "To the most intelligent and creative being I've ever met, I look forward to getting caught in your love net... if you're fishing." On the right side of the card, he'd taped Maxwell's Urban Hang Suite CD. Madison played her old one so much, the CD was scratched in several places. After reading this, Madison could no longer hold back the tears.

"Thanks, Damion," she mumbled. "You are so sweet." Damion helped her to her feet, and wiped her tears away with the back of his middle finger. While she looked at him, he licked her tears from his finger and smiled seductively. Madison melted. He cupped her face in his warm hands and kissed her, sending little electric shocks through her entire body until she trembled slightly. She melded the front of her body closer to his, but he gently pushed her away while the goose bumps ran frantically up and down her arms and legs. Mentally shaking herself back to reality, Madison took a step back and attempted to focus through hazy, lust covered pupils, and wondered where he was taking her.

"Damion, where are we going?"

"That's a loaded question, Madison," he joked. "Just pack outdoorsy clothes and a nice dress for dinner, or something."

"Ok, well let me pack, and I'll have to call my mom and dad and Stacey and…"

"You can call them from the road, he interrupted lightly, yet firmly. "We really have to get going before afternoon traffic, so if you could shoot for 20 minutes."

"Ok—I'll be out shortly," Madison chirped, as she ran in her room to pack, shower and dress, wondering how she was going to be ready in 20 minutes. Realistically, she knew it wouldn't happen. Damion probably knew, too, Ah well, he was such a sweetie, and so thoughtful. Once Madison got out of the shower, she added a few more panties to her birthday bag. She reasoned that if Damion pulled the kissing number that he did this morning, she would need a fresh change of underwear. She couldn't stand that 'ol wet and nasty feeling of pre-soaked undies. Madison wondered briefly about standing the girls up on Saturday. She'd probably be called out for this one. Stacey wouldn't give a damn, but Six, Bobette and at least three other A group members would probably be really concerned. Bobette was the appointed "girl, we have to have a talk," leader in the A group. As an attorney barred in 4 states, she could litigate her tail off, and was an excellent mediator. Members knew they didn't have a chance against her when she came for you. Those green eyes of hers could look right through you. Currently she had a US Attorney chasing her, and she could care less. Said he was too busy to give her the attention she needed. After Madison told Stacey, Stacey was like "Shit, attention, who needs it with all the dollars he could drop her way?! She stupid. Attention, she could go to a day spa for all that. I tell 'ya, Madison, you know some strange birds."

At any rate, Madison would be prepared if she got a call from Bobette.

The trip to nowhere was extremely pleasant. Damion was in such a wonderful mood, looking at him, Madison sensed that she could really fall in love with him. The feeling intimidated yet excited and subdued her. Riding up I270, then coasting up the National Highway, 68, was breathtakingly beautiful. The mountains arose stately and proud, the trees were competing for attention in all their glorious fall beauty—the hues were exceptionally deep this year, golds and auburns and deep reds.

Madison felt a serenity that was almost tangible. The peace enveloped her like an electric blanket. Damion was reflective. On occasion he'd point out something to Madison that captured his attention, he particularly liked silos and the jagged red rocks on the side of the mountains—nature's natural pumice. Madison was more than curious about their destination. They passed Polish mountain, which she thought a rather odd name for a mountain, but when they approached Negro mountain, Madison wondered if it were a conspiracy. And could she really trust the Negro next to her driving her to God knows where? They still didn't know one another too well. But for the most part, there existed the kind of comfortable silence between them that two people share who've known each other for a long time.

They stopped for a restroom break once. Damion joked incessantly about the old rickety wooden general store and raggedy gas pumps. They didn't even know it was a gas station at first. Damion teased the owner, who had to be at least 80 years old, and his handy dandy tobacco chewing, overall wearing, bi-focaled assistant in a good-natured way, who had to be at least 80, all the while affectionately hugging and planting kisses on Madison's forehead and cheeks as if she were truly his. Madison can't remember when she sanctioned this, but it felt good, so she embraced his affections. It's funny how we act when we like someone, she pondered, knowing damn well that if this brother didn't touch her soul like he did, she wouldn't allow him to command her personal space like that.

"Whar y'all newlyweds headed up to?" the assistant asked, tobacco spittle staining his fuzzy chin.

"Up nawth and west a bit," Damion answered cheerfully. Madison punched him in the ribs, because she was sure he'd give away the secret location, plus the country accent was a bit forced. She didn't want the old dude to think Damion was making fun of him; but the guy was very good natured. He was probably like, screw it.

I've lived long and hard, I'm just happy to be alive.

"Well, ya'll be careful up there nah, headin towards them mountains. Hear tell we's gonna get hit mighty hard with a rainstorm tonight."

"Sure thing, old-timer", Damion said, while tipping his baseball cap off to the assistant.

The old guy smiled a toothless grin and winked at Damion.

"And take care of dat purty woman you got there. She's a keeper!"

"I sure will, and do plan to keep her," Damion smiled as they drove off. Madison looked back at the two men, who stood still like statues in time. She watched until they became barely discernible dots. If one hadn't swatted a fly, and the other hadn't spit tobacco, she'd have wondered if they really had that experience. Madison was in seventh heaven. Here she was, having the best memorable time of her life with this gift of a man—people thought they were newlyweds and they were on their way to have fun, just for her. Okay, well two people so far, but they were just the beginning. What in the world had she done to deserve this? Well, one thing was for sure. She wasn't going to mess this up. Never ever. In the back of her mind a small voice questioned the "never ever" part of her thoughts. She quickly brushed that aside and turned towards Damion.

"How much farther do we have to go, Damion?"

"'Jus hold on to 'yur britches," he said, imitating the old gas station guy.

Madison just rolled her eyes, conceded defeat and relaxed completely.

Two hours later, Madison began to see signs for Deep Creek Lake. She could barely contain her excitement as they drove past nature's children. Madison rolled down her window to absorb the aura. The lakes were sparkling, the air smelled deeply of pine and the sun poked laser beams through the dense and shaded foliage. Closing her eyes, Madison could hear the slight clanking of docked boats as the light wind swayed them to and fro.

Damion took advantage of Madison's closed eyes and pulled over to blindfold her. Much to his surprise, she didn't resist. She was playing along with the game, what a good girl. Damion could not wait to make love to her. He would wait, as that was part of the plan, but she was so willing to please, he knew it would be a more than pleasurable experience. He'd been quiet most of the trip thinking of Crystal. He'd been neglecting her emotionally although he'd made it a point to be there for her physically. He thought of the first two years of their relationship she reminded him of her birthday and they'd do something static, like dinner and a movie. However, Madison mentioned her birthday once, and he began planning what would make her happy over two weeks ago. Thank God Crystal had a business trip this week. She had to fly to Phoenix for some specialized training that would enable her to skip a grade step when it was time for her review. Her favorite cousin lived there, so she planned to stay the weekend and wouldn't be back until Sunday evening.

Within five minutes of the blindfold tie, they pulled up in front of Damion's friend Michael's A-frame wooden cabin. Michael and his wife Niger had the cabin built from the ground up just last year, so there was still a lot of cleared land around the house perimeter, but 3,500 square feet of living space did not a small cabin make. Although the outside had an old, rustic quaint look, the inside was super modern. Michael and his wife fought about whether to make the property a "smart house" or not, but Niger won that battle by letting him think about how "smart" that would be while he spent three weeks on the sofa. She played dirty, but he loved her with his whole being, and her happiness and overall well-being came first. Michael teased Damion constantly about settling down, and was all too happy to hand over the keys when Damion told him he wanted to do something special for a friend's birthday.

Damion turned off the ignition and gently untied the blindfold. Madison's already large eyes doubled when she saw the house.

"Oh my God. Damion. What? This is sooo cute!" Madison jumped out of the car and spread her arms wide, sharing her joy and passion with the world. She ran up to the porch and plopped in one of the wooden rocking chairs and squealed with childish delight.

"These are just like at Cracker Barrell! Oh my God, I looooove it Damion." I could love you, she thought. Take a deep breath, Madi girl, she chided herself. Baby steps. Just remember to take baby steps with this one.

"Damion. You didn't have to do all this for me, why did—"

Damion cut her off by placing his forefinger over his lips, giving her the "shhh" sign. Madison promptly quieted and watched Damion unload the car. She watched him lovingly, wondering why and how no woman had snagged him, yet. Ah well. Madison heard Stacey's voice asking her if he had a woman. Madison still hadn't asked Damion. He simply couldn't have a girlfriend. He was just so giving and open. Madison couldn't imagine how one man could give so much to more than one woman. Well, she was going to thoroughly enjoy herself this weekend, and she would even give him some. With pleasure, she thought, as a dull, longing ache swept through her entire lower region.

Damion dangled the keys temptingly in front of Madison. Since his hands were tied with their luggage, he'd placed the house keys between his teeth. Madison jumped up from the rocker, snatched the keys from his mouth, replaced them with a quick kiss, and went through 4 different keys before she hit the jackpot.

"I thought my arms were going to fall off, girl, you so slow."

"Damion—you need to quit. You mandingo nubian black man prince you."

"Madison, you real funny. Hurry up and open the door, so I can show you what a mandingo I really am."

With that, Madison opened the door wide and gasped with exhilaration. The house was absolutely beautiful. It was open and airy, windows were everywhere and the light overwhelmed the first floor and loft. Madison didn't know black folks lived in Deep Creek Lake, most of her friends went to the Caribbean or Hilton Head. African sculptures decorated either end of the fireplace, filled with dried timber begging to be lit. The furniture was classy, yet comfortable with throws and settees accenting the Persians dotting the perfectly stained wooden floors. The house still smelled of cedar, emitting a warm and inviting sentiment throughout.

"Well, what's wrong with you, girl? You wearing bricks instead of shoes? Look around. I'm going to turn on the hot water so the hot tub can be warmed for later."

Damion disappeared while she explored the house. It was so spacious and beautiful. The windows greedily lapped up the light. Madison didn't know any black folks who didn't believe in curtains. Definitely a first. There were four bedrooms, each carrying its own particular theme, three full baths, one half bath, and closets for days. The kitchen could have been taken directly from the pages of *Home Beautiful*. Glass doors led to a large, wraparound deck. Madison stepped onto the deck and drunkenly absorbed the exquisite beauty. The land sat on a half acre, at least. A tiny gazebo with lattice and ivy graced the right of the deck, while brilliant Japanese maples circled the round edifice. The tall pines, birch and oak trees resembled brothers and sisters holding hands in perfect harmony, surrounding the property in a protective circle. Where the front of the cabin was lacking with landscaping, the back made up for it tenfold. A bright flash caught Madison's eye. She followed a short, worn path through the woods and spotted what appeared to be a private lake. There were approximately 5 homes that she could see surrounding the lake, and small, brightly-painted boats dotted the water, bobbing in unison with the subtle current.

The view was breathtaking. Madison closed her eyes and breathed deeply of the pungent fall air. She started when she felt a hand cover her eyes, then her waist. Damion whispered sexily,

"It's just me. Happy Birthday." The moisture from his breath tickled her ear seductively. Damion squeezed Madison like a roll of Charmin. A volt shot through her body, she had to really concentrate to keep from buckling.

"Thank you, Damion. This is so nice," Madison said, turning to face him. She struggled to regain composure.

"Everything is really beautiful."

"Well, you know you fit right in with all the beautiful things, Madison, but there's one thing that's even better. You're warm and soft and pretty and you smell good."

"Playa. You're good!" Madison chided.

"Hey, you want to go out on the boat before sunset?"

"Damion, the old man said it was going to rain."

"Madison. You believe that old man? He's probably talking about a newscast he heard last month. Look at the sky. Does it look like it's going to rain?"

Madison looked at the clear skies and non-threatening clouds and chuckled softly to herself.

"Ok, you've got a point, Damion. I need to change, though."

"Alright. I'm going to run up the street and grab some sandwiches for us, what would you like?"

"Turkey is good. Lettuce, no mayonnaise. Tomatoes, no onions, barbecue chips, and root beer."

"Root beer?"

"Yeah. Being out here makes me want to drink root beer for some reason."

"Ok, Madison. I'll be *right* back," Damion eyed her suspiciously, backing away from her like she was crazy, and laughing all the while. Madison watched him walk, then sprint away, and hugged herself, still smelling his cologne on her sweater.

Within an hour the couple were on the lake, which wasn't very large, but rather wide. The boat was small, but sturdy. The owners probably used it for crabbing, Madison reasoned. Once they got to the center, Damion stopped the motor and they rocked idly until the boat was almost steady. Madison complimented Damion on his steering ability and they began to talk. He talked about the owners, he talked about the property, how he helped with the layout, referred the builders, so on and so forth. Whatever conversation he'd bottled on the way to the lake, he uncorked. As the afternoon turned to a hazy purple-covered dusk, a lightening bolt appeared out of nowhere. Damion looked up, looked at Madison, and continued to talk. 60 seconds later, craaaack. This bolt was ear-splitting.

Madison jumped.

"Damion—I don't know much about lightening, but I don't know if we're in the safest place or not. This has been real, but it's time to go."

"You scared, Madison?" Damion asked, peering around the lake perimeter, as darkness was dropping fast.

"You right, Madison. I was just playing with you. We'll be back in a flash."

Craaack ziiip crrrracccckkkkk. The crackling lightening snarled in unison with Damion as he said "flash." Madison never heard it. She was ducking the huge raindrops that silently and persistently began to fall. Damion, however, had his own set of problems. The motor would not catch. He cursed softly under his breath at first, then vehemently as the rain drenched his clothes, making them cold and heavy. He stopped for a moment to offer Madison his sweatshirt, but she refused. He looked so pitiful. As the rain beat him down, Damion seemed to shrink. He vigorously fought the motor until it finally, coughed, sputtered and, revved.

"I'm sorry, Madison. I'm not trying to ruin your day. I should have listened to you!" Damion shouted as they sped towards the shoreline.

Madison was slightly teed off because NOW she had a hair issue. A big one. Her thick hair swelled like a water-drenched chia pet when it got wet, making it extremely difficult to manage. However, Damion's gallantry and immediate apology was rather charming. Once they reached land, Damion helped Madison out of the boat and they scampered up the embankment, soggy, waterlogged and punchy. They laughed all the way to the house. Madison went to take a shower and noticed both their bags were in the master bedroom. 'He ain't slick,' she thought, and lost herself in a long, hot shower. The wife, Niger, and Madison must have been cut from the same cloth. She stocked the same shampoo Madison used, and lotion and light styling gel. Madison was able to brush her hair back and stick it in a ponytail. It would dry naturally, and she'd work with the crinkles later on. When Madison walked downstairs, Damion was sitting in front of a blazing fireplace on a thick, pleated rug. Maxwell was playing softly in the background.

"Hi, there."

"Hi, there. Did you have a good shower?"

"Did YOU have a good shower?"

"Mine was very relaxing," Madison said.

"Mine was quick. I wanted to get this fire going so you wouldn't be cold."

"Thanks, Damion." Madison said appreciatively as she sat down next to Damion. He looked at her, touched her hair and asked,

"Why didn't you keep it loose, let it dry faster?"

Madison was moved by his tenderness, and promptly removed the scrungee. Damion rubbed his hands through her hair and stopped short at the nape of her neck. Madison was like puddy in his hands. He brought her willing face close to his and instead of kissing her immediately on the lips, he softly planted kisses on her cheeks, her eyelids, her chin, her forehead, her ears, the base of her throat, and finally, her lips. Madison closed her eyes as his tongue explored, conquered and dominated her soul. After such an earth-shattering kiss, Damion gently helped Madison to her feet, as Maxwell beckoned them to dance in his atmosphere. '…Til the Cops Come Knockin' seemed to speak directly to Madison, but Damion remained the perfect gentleman, that night, the night after, and the night after. He cradled her at night, and spoiled her during the day, but he never let his hands slide below her waist. Even when things got hot and heavy in the hot tub, he only lovingly caressed her face and traced his finger along the outline of her breasts. Madison was almost driven to a frenzy, but she was too proud to ask him to just take her wild style… so she waited.

CHAPTER 19

Damion—Damion's Resolve
November 1999

Reflecting on Madison's birthday weekend, Damion just had to give himself playa points for not having sex with Madison. Todd called him Iron Man for having such a strong will. When Damion first told Todd, he didn't believe him. They met at Takoma Station three weeks after Damion returned from the lake. The Station was small, but quaint, and had some of the best jazz in Washington; plus no other establishment made Long Island Iced Teas like the Station.

"Man you was up in the woods with that honey for four days and Three LONG ass nights, and you ain't hit it?" Todd asked in disbelief. "What's wrong with you man, didn't I teach you better than that?" He shook his head, sat back in his seat, and sipped his drink.

"Yo, man. It was all I could do. Madison is just so sexy." Damion explained, "And the best part is, she doesn't know it, man."

"Brother, sounds like you whipped." Todd observed.

Damion took a big swallow of his drink and looked around. There were all types of honeys swarming around the bar, but Damion wasn't thinking about them. His mind was preoccupied.

"I ain't think you was into 'ol girl like that. I mean you just met her, when?"

"September, man."

"And you haven't had sex with her, yet? Man, she 'gone think you a bitch. It's November!" Todd exclaimed. "Man, I'm going to get me another drink—I'ma get you one, too, cause your ass is slipping." Todd got up from the table and disappeared into the crowd. Damion turned towards the stage and tuned into the band. They sounded good. Their jazz was nouveau, yet had a hint of old school, like some Miles Davis with Coltrane backing him up. Each member of the group played off each other in a seamless syncopated harmony. The pianist, the bass guitarist, the saxophonist, the drummer, the woman playing the cello—were like one unit—perfect. That's how Damion felt when he was with Madison, like a unit. She fit into his arms, perfectly. When he stood in back of her and squeezed her tight, her behind snuggled just right against him. It was if his pants came equipped with an invisible mold made with the specifications of Madison's behind. He really couldn't explain why he didn't make love to her at the cabin. The setting was right, Madison seemed more than ready, but, something held him back. Before he could really analyze what that something was, Todd came back with two voluptuous, top heavy women. He introduced them, and whispered into Damion's ear,

"It's time for you to get your *man* card, back. You can have the one with the smaller titties, which seem to be a size D from where I sit, and the big ass. I'll take the one with the dimples, the DD's and the bigger ass. Thank you."

Todd then sat down and apologized for whispering.

"I'm sorry, ladies. I just had to let my dog know that I told y'all you could have ANYthing you wanted tonight, he just has to pay."

They giggled while Todd signaled a waitress. Damion took a deep breath, and girded himself for the dog and pony that was to come. Turning back to the band, he tuned out once he heard Todd explaining to D cup that Damion was a disc jockey. Focusing on the band and his inner thoughts, Damion barely spoke to the women, whom Todd kept entertained with stories from he and Damion's childhood and continuous drinks. They hung onto every syllable. He'd probably end up with both of them, Damion was sure. At 1:30 am, Damion excused himself to call Crystal. Even though it was late, she told him to come on over, anyway.

Damion left Todd, Twiddle dee dee and Twiddle dee dum in their perceived drunken glory, competing to see who could drink the most shots. For sure, Todd would have a story in the morning.

Damion arrived at Crystal's a half hour later. He threw his jacket over the sofa, climbed up the stairs, threw off his clothes and fell into bed with Crystal. She turned around to give him kiss.

"Damn, baby. You must have been drinking those iced teas again, I can smell it. That and cigarette smoke, you sure you don't want to shower, first?"

Annoyed, Damion thought he was going to find peace, here. He forced himself to get out of bed.

"Crystal. You can ruin a wet dream, you know that?"

"Forget you, Damion. Sleep your drunk ass on the sofa, then."

Crystal didn't mean to respond like that. In fact, she just wanted him to be close to her, but he did stink.

Damion snatched a pillow, stormed to the closet, grabbed a blanket, and stomped downstairs and plopped on the sofa. He picked up Crystal's phone and dialed Madison's number. After one ring, he hung up. It was 2:00 am, he wouldn't dare disrespect her like that, calling this late. He'd call her in the morning, then. Maybe they could do the museums or something. Damion curled up on the sofa, fetus style and fell asleep with a smile on his face.

Crystal, who was wide awake by now, lay on her back and pummeled her fists against the bed. She heard him slam the phone down, he must have checked his messages. A small voice prompted her to hit the redial button, but she didn't. They'd just had a stupid fight, over nothing, really. She berated herself for just not keeping her mouth shut. But Damion should have known better. He did that all the time. Whenever he went out with his boys, he'd come over there, toasted and horny, looking to have sex. That just didn't sit right with Crystal. He'd just started that in the last year of their relationship and she was determined to put her foot down and stop the madness. She fought the urge to go downstairs until she heard the steady, even breathing of his sleep, interrupted occasionally by an irritated snore.

The next morning, Damion awoke to the smell of fresh coffee. He groggily climbed off the sofa and arched his back. He must have slept wrong, because he was stiff. Maybe he and Madison could go shoot some hoops or something. This Saturday was Crystal's sorority grad chapter meeting. He walked to the kitchen and poured a cup of coffee. He must have just missed Crystal because the area still smelled like her perfume. She'd left a note on the refrigerator.

"Baby, your breakfast is in the microwave. When you finish, just leave the dishes in the sink, and I'll take care of it after the meeting. Don't go too far, I wanna do a movie tonight. Love ya. C."

Damion opened the microwave door to a stack of pancakes and maple cured bacon. "Damn!" he thought. Why did she have to be so damn cool like that? More importantly, how did he sleep through her preparing this? She wouldn't, no couldn't do anything that would make him want to leave her for someone else. He thought of Madison. Maybe he would cool out for a minute, lay low. He found out during her birthday weekend that she smoked. That shit wasn't cool at all.

As Damion greedily devoured the pancakes, he thought of all the reasons he shouldn't call Madison. There was only one. Crystal. But WHAT if, he missed this opportunity and it turned out that Madison was the ONE? What if? Didn't he owe it to himself, Crystal, even, to find out? It would not be fair to Crystal if they got married, and a few months or years later, boop, he was having an affair. It could happen. Only time would tell. Maybe after the physical with Madison, he wouldn't be so pressed. "That's what it is," thought Damion. "I need to have sex with her. Just go ahead and get it over with."

Damion called Madison from his cell and left a message for her. He counted the Saturdays on his finger to verify it wasn't A group Saturday. Crystal had taken a real liking to her new peers and Damion made it a point to keep Madison away if he knew Crystal was going. The juggling wasn't cool. Wasn't cool at all. It was a little too close for comfort.

Damion turned on the water for his shower. He looked in the mirror at his tired-looking eyes and five o'clock shadow. He looked like shit. Acted like one, too, last night. He'd make his behavior up to Crystal, soon. After an unsuccessful attempt to locate his razor, Damion began to look in Crystal's toiletry drawer. As he rooted through the piles of girly stuff looking for a razor, a brightly-colored envelope caught Damion's attention. The return address was from her OB/GYN. He raised his eyebrows curiously and picked up the envelope. Damion's heart began to race as he read the letter:

> "Dear Ms. Leonard, our records indicated that you have not renewed your birth-control prescription. If you are dissatisfied, please apprise us so that we may suggest another product. If you would like to set up an appointment for alternative methods of birth control, we will be happy to assist you. You may call the appointment desk at 202-555-7455. Thank you and happy holidays. Nurse Amari."

The correspondence was dated October 20th. "Shit! Shit! That bitch!" Damion shouted. "I can't believe this shit!"

By this time, steam was escaping from the bathroom door. Damion couldn't believe Crystal was trying to get pregnant. That was the oldest trick in the books. He ran to the cabinet where she usually kept her pills and opened the door. Ibuprofin, Theraflu, Vicks VapoRub, Vaseline, but no pills.

Damion was furious. "Never again," he murmured between grinding teeth and a clenched jaw. He turned off the water to the shower, threw on his clothes, grabbed his jacket and left.

CHAPTER 20

Madison—Let The Games Begin
November 1999

November started off super busy for Madison for some strange reason. R. Payton, editor of *The Chocolate City Voice* called Madison and asked her to work there part time as a proofreader and copyeditor through January. Madison agreed, however it took her nearly an hour to convince Mr. Payton she could do most of the work on-line, from her virtual office. Madison tried every logical argument she could think of; including the difficulties of finding her a desk, office supplies, a computer, a printer and access to the Internet. The *Voice* was a small black-owned paper that hadn't fully embraced the power of technology and the economic value of e-commerce. Finally, Madison pulled her trump card.

"Mr. Payton, if you let me work from home," she wheedled slyly, "you won't have to pay for my parking, my mileage, or the added electricity expense of having me there late nights." Mr. Payton operated from an old, renovated house in NE Washington. An independent entity, Mr. Payton paid for a lot of the operating expenses himself. He began to listen to Madison once she appealed to his wallet.

"Alright, Ms. Robinson. You win," he said wearily. "Just don't let me have to chase you down for no deadlines."

"No problem, Mr. Payton," Madison said victoriously. She thought it odd that he never called her Madison, only Ms. Robinson. But then again, she never know what the R. stood for. He was, Mr. Payton. A true veteran of the old school, Madison would have to bring him into modern times slowly.

Speaking of slowly, Damion had yet to make his move. They had been seeing one another for two months and the only love they'd made was with their eyes and tongues. Stacey pissed Madison off one day with her unsolicited mother wit. They were speed walking through Haines Point. More like tourist walking to Madison. Stacey liked to stop for anything. She wanted to stop and look at the boats docked on the marina. She wanted to stop to see who was playing tennis on the courts, she wanted to see if the young people camped out in the parking lot were smoking weed. She wanted to look at the ducks paddling in the Potomac. She wanted to cradle her body in the hand of the famous sculpture, "The Awakening." It took them nearly two hours to walk 4 miles. Stacey called it exercise. Madison called it socialize. She did it just to spend some quiet time with her friend, who usually talked the entire time, but that was Stacey. This particular brisk November morning, Stacey decided she wanted to Damion bash. Since she hadn't met him, she didn't like him.

"Madi, what's up with you and that boy?" she snorted sarcastically.

"Stacey, nothing is official yet with Damion and I, yet." Madison said hesitatingly, knowing Stacey was about to start. She hadn't really forgiven her since Damion had whisked her away for Madison's birthday.

"What you mean, ain't nothing official? He takes you away for a romantic weekend, wines and dines you, calls you every day, takes you a lot of places, and you ain't official? What's up with that? And you ain't even told me how the diggity is, what's up with that? What, you embarrassed?" Stacey's tirade lasted all of 15 seconds she was talking so fast, Madison wasn't quite sure if she was in rhetorical mode or what.

"Well?" Stacy stopped, turned towards Madison with her hands on her hips and looked squarely at Madison.

"Well, what?"

"B*, don't play games with me," Stacey snarled. "How is he in bed?"

"I don't know," Madison responded softly, and tried to take a step forward.

"You don't know? You don't know? What do you mean you don't know?" Stacey said, not moving an inch.

"Stacey, you've been married twice, and if you don't know the answer to that one, I don't know what to tell you." Madison chided, and walked forward.

"Listen, smart-ass, you mean to tell me you and devil-boy haven't done it, at all?" Stacey caught up to Madison and stopped, again.

"No."

"No licky licky?"

"No."
"No sucky sucky?"
"No."
"No nada?"
"We kiss."
"You kiss?"
"Yes."
"He is screwing somebody else."
"Excuse me?"
"He's having sex with somebody else, Madison," Stacey said, pretending to do sign language. "Don't be so naïve, all the time."
"Stacey, why couldn't he just be respectful of me?"
"Respectful? Have you told him you felt uncomfortable doing it, or that he was going too far?"
"No,"
"So what makes you think he's thinking about being disrespectful towards you?"
"He's a gentleman, Stacey."
"He's a cheat. Did you ask him if he had a woman?"
"Stacey."
"Ok, you just haven't gotten around to that yet. Who does most of the calling?"
"He does."
"Right." Stacey started walking this time.
"What do you mean, RIGHT?"
"Madison. Don't you get it? He maintains control like that. Where is he, now?"
"I don't know. Home, probably."
"Home. Have you been there?"
"Yes."
"Have you spent the night?"
"No."
"Like I said, right. It makes perfect sense. Madison, listen to me, I know a playa when I see one."
"Well, you haven't seen Damion, and I really don't appreciate you making such negative assumptions about someone I really like, Stacey. So stop."
"What kind of duck is that?" Stacey said suddenly, pointing through the guard

rails at a family of ducks.

Madison, surprised that Stacey would drop the subject so easily, looked, and told her it was a Mallard.

"So, if it looks like a duck, sounds like a duck and walks like a duck, then… it's a duck, right?" Stacey harrumphed triumphantly.

"So if it rhymes with duck, then it must be fuck… you, right?"

"Madison Danielle Robinson. I'm just trying to keep you from being so caught up in some dude you really don't even know. Be careful, girl, that's all I'm saying. Be careful."

Shortly thereafter, Stacey dropped Madison off at her apartment. Madison spotted what looked like Pilar's car parked in a crooked, hurried fashion. Madison checked her mailbox and climbed the few flights of stairs trying to get in the last bit of exercise. Walking down the long hallway, she saw a stooped figure near the elevator. As she got closer, she could see clearly who it was. Pilar was camped in front of her door sitting on several pieces of luggage. Madison let out a deep sigh. Pilar snapped her neck in the direction of the sigh.

"Oh, hi, Madi. I saw your car out front, and figured I'd stop by for a minute." Pilar said sheepishly.

"How long is a minute, girl?" Madison asked, suspiciously eyeing the luggage.

"Let's go in your place so we can talk, ok?"

Madison turned her key in the lock and regretfully said ok. Pilar was her girl and all, but she was pushing the envelope. Pilar followed behind her, taking two trips to bring in all her baggage, not including the baggage in her heart or the monkey on her back.

Madison told Pilar to make herself comfortable, went to her room to change and check her messages. Damion had called twice. Six, Diana and Bobette had called. Great. She was hotline city when she had something to do, but the minute she was home alone, the phone didn't ring. Go figure.

After three cups of tea and one box of Kleenex, Pilar asked Madison if she wouldn't mind her camping out at her place until things were situated. Madison felt her gut churning, again, but felt obligated to help out a sister in need; although Pilar could really afford to stay in a hotel, perhaps she was looking for female companionship or something. Apparently Mitch wasn't speaking to her. According to Pilar, after her disappearing act at the cookout, Mitch acted rather strangely once she returned home about three hours later. She told Mitch that the only reason she went to the store without Madison was because she knew that Madison was the second best hostess besides herself and would keep things running smoothly until she returned.

But, on the way back from the store, which just took a few minutes, there was a horrible accident, and traffic was backed up for miles. By the time traffic cleared, Madison's boyfriend Bernard had to catch a plane, so Pilar just swung him by the airport. Mitch didn't bother to ask Pilar about Bernard's bags. If the brother had any, they would have been in Madison's car. However, he held his peace.

Pilar talked in bed that night to Mitch about how nice Bernard was and how everyone at the cookout felt that he and Madison were a perfect couple and that this guy might be "the one." Pilar told Madison she felt kind of weird because Mitch was eerily quiet. She told him on Sunday she would have to go to NY for at least three weeks to jumpstart this new project. She spent mostly all day Sunday with the kids and promised they could go to the city this winter to see the lighting of the Christmas tree. She tried to make love to her husband to "store up" as he was fond of saying; however, Mitch wasn't feeling too well. So, Pilar took three weeks vacation from work, left strict instructions with her assistant to inform anyone and everyone she was out of pocket in preparation for a new project, and high-tailed it to NY and Bernard.

"The first two weeks were like a dream, Madi." Pilar said wistfully. She was balled up on Madison's sofa with a hot cup of tea and Madison's throw comfortably placed from the waist down.

"We were like newlyweds. We rode the surry and experienced the city at midnight under a full moon. We went to Rockefeller Center and ice-skated. We dined at Tavern on the Green and were lucky enough to catch *The Lion King* on Broadway. We even made the big screen on David Letterman. You know how they have that roving camera in midtown?" Madison didn't know what she was talking about, but shook her head in the affirmative.

"Anyway, we shopped in the Village, and of course, he took me to the shoe district. We played tag in Battery Park. We crossed the bridge and went to Queens, Richmond Hills for some real West Indian food and then we crossed the Indies and had an East Indian dinner in Jackson Heights. We walked from Columbus Circle to Harlem and jogged in Central Park. We held hands walking down the Avenue of the Americas like high school sweethearts, oh, we were weren't we?" Pilar giggled.

Again Madison just nodded. Truth be told, she was itching to call Damion back.

Pilar reminded her of the adults on the Peanuts cartoons. You never saw them, but all you heard was "wanh wah wanh wah."

"So, to make a long story short, we made love in every nook and cranny in his apartment and in the stairwell of his apartment and on the fire escape. Until the third Tuesday, that's when things got all messed up."

"What happened, Pilar?"

"His fiancee came back early from Europe."

"Fiancee?" Madison asked incredulously.

"Yeah. She's a makeup artist, freelancing for top designers around the world."

"Did you know he had a fiancee?"

"Uh, yeah. But he said he only asked her to marry him because I was married and he thought it was too late for us."

"So, what were you doing, Pilar? Trying to prove to him that if wasn't?"

"We were just having fun."

"Pilar, married women don't just have fun. This is some serious shit. You've taken a childhood fantasy too far, Pilar. Do you hear me?!" All Madison could think about were Pilar's kids and good 'ol Mitch.

"Madison. Maybe you don't understand, yet. Bernard is my soulmate."

"Pilar. Bernard is an asshole, and he's playing you!"

"You poor thing, you've never really known love, have you?"

"If it makes me stupid then I don't want it. So why are you just coming to me, today? It's Saturday?"

"Well…"

"Well, what? When did you leave NY, Pilar?"

"Yesterday."

"Yesterday? Where did you stay?"

"With Bernard."

"With Bernard? Where was his fiancee?"

"With Bernard. She's a really lovely girl."

"Pilar. I don't understand." Suddenly Madison began to feel really sick.

"Pilar. Where did you sleep?"

"Madison. That really doesn't matter. Bernard truly loves me, and he has an extremely open-minded and well-rounded fiancee. I think they'll be good for one another, she's very independent, you know."

Exasperated, Madison didn't want to hear anymore.

"So why are you here, Pilar?"

The river of tears began.

"I called Mitch to ask him to meet me outside so he could help me with my bags. He came out of the house and hopped in the passenger seat and told me to drive. I asked him where, and he said he didn't care, he just wanted me to drive."

"Where were the kids?"

"Mitch told me they were at a basketball game."

"Ok, so then what?"

Madison could barely understand Pilar through the tears. She gave her a new cup of hot tea and let her cry herself out.

"Then he told me he saw Bernard tap me on the butt before he got in the car at the cookout. He said he didn't quite believe it. So he tried to put it out of his mind."

Madison remembered the odd look Mitch had at the cookout when he turned away from the window. She couldn't believe how bold and stupid Bernard was to try that crap, but then again, thinking about Bernard, and the rush he must have gotten being in forbidden territory, she could believe it.

"But, Madison. Mitch has to this date, been a creature of habit. He goes to bed every night at ten, is up at 4:30 and out of the house by 5:30 am. One particular night, he said he couldn't sleep and was channel surfing, when he passed by David Letterman, and for a split second, he saw me and Bernard out on the NY streets, waving to David's stupid ass cameras."

"He saw you and Bernard, what were you all doing?"

"He had his arm around me."

"Oh, Pilar. Oh, I'm soooo sorry." Madison couldn't help but think she should not have brought that jerk to her house, her husband's house, because she might have gotten away with it.

"I never should have tried the cookout thing," Pilar stumbled.

"Hmmmph," was all Madison could manage.

"Mitch then gave me his "I'm a man" speech and went on and on how real men feel and real men think and real this and that. He told me to drop him off and keep on driving, and to think about what I'd done to him and his kids."

Madison was stunned. This was like a nightmare. And the sad thing about it was that Pilar didn't seem to be bothered about her failing marriage, she seemed more upset that she got caught. Well, she would do what she could to help Pilar, but mentally and emotionally, she was long gone.

The tea rushed straight through Madison. On her way back from her 3rd bathroom trip in an hour, the phone rang. It was Damion. This was his third call. Something must be up. Madison briefly told him about Pilar and the freelance stint. Unexpectedly, Damion asked her to pack her duffel and stay with him for the weekend, one to give Pilar some think time, two, since Madison was going to be so busy with *The Chocolate City Voice*, he wanted to spend some quality time together. He asked if she wanted to check out an exhibit at the Corcoran that afternoon and then they'd have a nice dinner to celebrate her gig. Before he could finish his sentence, Madison had begun to pack her stuff. The knots in her stomach began to dissolve, Damion could really make this weekend 'mo better. She chose some sexy new lingerie that sat in her drawer untouched for the past six months. She liked to stock up on new lingerie after an old relationship ended. Madison didn't feel right wearing the same lingerie for a different guy. As she caressed a smooth, pink silk nightie, Stacey's words rang in her head like an incessant school bell.

"He's screwing somebody else, Madi. Don't be so naïve."

"We'll see about that, Ms. Stacey." Madison mouthed silently and pulled two pairs of thongs from the bottom of her underwear drawer.

"Madison?"

Madison spun around. She was so caught up in her thoughts about Damion she momentarily forgot about Pilar.

"Yes, Pilar. How are you feeling?"

"Unh, I'm ok, where are you going?"

"I'm uh, going to spend the weekend with Damion. Give you a little quiet time, you know?"

"Me? Quiet time? I could have checked into a hotel for that."

"Oh, I see." Madison's voice waned.

"Girl, I'm sorry. Selfish me. I didn't even think to ask if you had plans. Go ahead. I'll be alright. I wish Montana were here."

Montana was Pilar's yellow lab, and she hoped Pilar hadn't flipped to the point where she would try and bring her dog into a "no pets" property.

"Is it ok if I look at one of your movies?"

"Sure, Pilar. Whatever you need." Madison said sympathetically while zipping her duffel. "Listen, I'm going to take a quick shower. Why don't you familiarize yourself with my place, and if you have any questions, you can ask me before I go."

"I'll be alright, Madi. Your place is only so big."

'It's more than what she has right now,' Madison thought as she smiled and turned to go into the bathroom. People are a trip, she mused.

While Madison was preparing to visit Damion, he had some housecleaning to do himself. After he'd calmed down enough to talk to Crystal without yelling—he called her cellular. She answered in a hushed voice.

"Hi."

"We need to talk."

"D, you know I'm in the middle of my sorority meeting. Can't this wait, and did you find your breakfast, ok?"

"Crystal. Excuse yourself right now."

"Alright, baby. Hold on a second."

Damion heard muted voices, then gradual silence as Crystal walked out of earshot of curious sorors.

"Yeah, baby."

"Let's talk about that."

"Excuse me?"

"Let's talk about a baby."

"D—What on earth are you talking about? Do we need to talk about this in person?"

"Hell, no!"

"D—I'm sorry. I just don't get it."

"Neither do I, Crystal. I don't get why you stopped taking your pills. What the fuck is up with that shit, Crystal?"

All Damion heard was silence.

Then soft sobbing.

"Crystal. I'm waiting for you to answer my question. What is wrong with you, girl? I thought you were smarter than that."

"D. I was going to tell you when—"

"When what, Crystal? Damn! You were going to tell me I was caught in a trap once my fucking foot was cut off? Hell, no. I'm not going for that shit."

"D. I'm really sorry."

"Crystal. I really don't want to talk to you right now. Do not call me until I call you. I don't want to hear your voice or see your yellow, freckled face. You need time to think about what you've done. Peace."

"D, wait, please. I can explain."

"Later."

CHAPTER 21

Madison—Unexpectations
November 1999

When Damion opened the door, Madison could sense something was horribly wrong. His eyes were red-rimmed and he looked disheveled, although he smelled as if he'd just showered. Maybe it was the five o'clock shadow. Or maybe it was the crumpled way he stood in the doorway. Damion's carriage was usually very erect. He seemed to force a smile and gave Madison one of his famous bear hugs. Even though he hugged her a long time, it felt empty to Madison. She strolled in the hallway and plopped her duffel on the floor.

"You hungry?" Damion politely mustered.

"No." Madison was too full of tea to be hungry.

"I'll be ready soon, ok?" Damion turned and walked toward his bedroom. He was wearing a faded forest green Polo robe.

"No." Madison said again, only this time more firmly.

Damion stopped. He turned to face her. Madison felt as if he was just looking at her for the first time.

"No!" she said loudly, while taking off her jacket and throwing it over a chair.

Damion just stood and stared at her.

"Come here now, Damion!"

Looking like a little boy whose toy cars were just run over by a real truck, Damion walked to where she was standing. Madison rubbed his stubbled chin, stood on her tippy toes, grabbed him around his neck and squeezed with all her might. At first Damion didn't respond. When he did, he hugged her as if she were a life preserver thrown to save him from drowning. He seemed so vulnerable, so shaken.

"What's the matter?" Madison asked after wrenching herself from his embrace long enough to stare into his troubled eyes. Damion looked at her with his head cocked to one side, obviously weighing whether or not he should say anything. After a long pause, he offered a pebble of an explanation.

"A good friend of mine just betrayed me."

"Oh," was all Madison could manage to say. His pain was so heavy. Damion really needed her. Now. Not really understanding what came over her, Madison firmly placed her hands on either side of Damion's neck and pulled him to her lips. She aggressively kissed him until he began to respond. Madison pressed her pelvis against his robe and began to grind as if not only her life, but his, depended on this one, desperate act. Madison had been waiting forever for this. This moment in time, suspended in her fantasies, living and growing in her imagination. She needed Damion as much, if not more, than he needed her. Right now. She moaned in spite of herself. She put her hands inside Damion's robe and gently rubbed his torso, scratching his back seductively with the tips of her nails. Without missing a beat, Damion greedily planted kisses on her face and neck. He dropped to his knees and lifted her shirt, kissing and licking her belly button while unbuttoning her jeans. Madison groaned with intense pleasure that came from somewhere deep inside her. Damion traced his finger along the soft hairs that led to her aching warmth. She grabbed the base of his neck and threw her head back, squeezing her eyes tightly. Damion slowly pulled off her jeans and snuggled his face where the zipper once was, deeply breathing her sweetness. He tenderly held her legs as she stepped out of her jeans, one unsteady, impatient, unbalanced leg at a time. He ran his tongue up and down her trembling thighs and intimately cupped her behind. He licked her and blew hot breath through her already moist panties. Madison began to shake so badly she almost collapsed. Damion stood up, cradled her and headed towards the bedroom. She fell hard on his bed. Damion looked at her so hard, his eyes burned.

"You are so beautiful," he repeated over and over again. Madison's eyes were locked on his. They were red and fiery and watery all at the same time. He took off his robe and Madison gasped inaudibly when she saw how perfect his body was. He looked like a bronzed statue with the sun filtering off his v-shaped back. She wiggled heatedly with anticipation. Damion paused long enough to dim the intense sunshine flooding the room by shutting the blinds. He reached in his nightstand and

#Place the numeral 2 by the CD to indicate song #2.

pulled out a condom. He then turned his attention back to Madison.

"Funny," she thought momentarily. She imagined their first time would have been after a romantic dinner or during another getaway weekend, but not like this, unplanned, unexpected.

"Are you ready for this?" Damion's voice was hoarse.

Madison could only nod her head. Bad enough she was groaning like some sick bear a moment ago.

"Madison. I've been wanting to make love to you since Deep Creek," Damion said lovingly as he touched her soft, brown skin in places that only the moveable shower head had access to. Madison whimpered softly in return. She wanted to please Damion and reached to do so. She would show him what a tigress she could be, but he shook his head to quiet her and whispered, "relax...."

Obediently, she lay back on the bed, helpless, while Damion worked his magic. He kissed her, explored her, he tried to lick the rich brownness off of her. By the time he slid into her anticipating warmth, she had transcended to a place beyond her fantasies. How unexpectedly fantastic.

CHAPTER 22

**Madison—The Holidays
November 1999**

As quickly as November arrived, the latter part of the month seemed to creep by. Pilar and Mitch made up. After all, it was the holidays, and Pilar could make a mean apple cobbler. Besides, the kids missed their mom, and Mitch couldn't sleep without Pilar by his side. Pilar, relieved, approached the role of happy homemaker, loving mother seriously, her life as she knew it depended on it. Things were tense, at first, but eventually dissolved like liquor in egg nog. You can't see it, but you know it's there, can taste it, but the egg nog is still good. Seasonal.

Madison and Damion were inseparable. They acted like tourists in DC one weekend, and drove down to Luray Caverns the weekend after and stayed in a bed and breakfast securely tucked in the mountains. Their lovemaking grew in fever and intensity. Madison felt on a scale of 1 to 10, their compatibility was off the charts. She was falling for Damion, but didn't want him to know, just yet. Damion convinced her not to go to the A group meetings but to spend her time with him. She'd even missed last Sunday at her parents. Initially her mom balked, but Madison told her she was taking a day trip to Annapolis to get a special fish that couldn't be found in DC. Madison told her mom she wanted to prepare it for Thanksgiving. That did it. Thumbs up. Green light. The bed and breakfast she and Damion stayed in was divine. And, her mom would spend the whole dinner bragging about Madison's excellent taste in choosing good fish, all the way from Annapolis.

Crystal was having a really bad month. She called Damion. Paged him. Drove by his place on several occasions. His black Saab was nowhere to be seen. Occasionally she'd hear him at the station, but not often. The instant void was new and strange to Crystal, as were the sudden, uncontrolled crying jags. The guilt was eating her alive. The guilt affected her appetite. The guilt was beginning to affect her job performance.

Tony was extremely supportive. Crystal began to depend on him more often, for counsel and just, overall friendship. He believed Damion should have been really pleased that Crystal wanted to have a baby for him and would make him a good wife. Tony told Crystal she was stronger than Damion and deserved to be with someone who wouldn't take her for granted and would respect her enough to ask her to be his wife.

Only half-hearing his words, Crystal fretted over an excuse her family would believe during the holidays. Damion would travel with her to Daytona and Atlanta during Thanksgiving and Christmas and everybody loved him. One, he was "easy on the eyes," and two, he didn't have "ashy elbows." That was big in her family. Damion would shamelessly flirt with her grandmother and female cousins. Grandma Rosa, in turn, would chastise Crystal about taking better care of him. "You betta treat that man, right. He's a good one, and you don't need a flashlight to see 'em." Her grandmother was so color conscious, it was funny to Crystal. But nothing was funny now. Crystal began to cry again. Tony hugged her, comforting her the best way he knew how. Through a river of salty, stinging tears, Crystal vowed to get Damion back. The following day she called her doctor's office and asked Nurse Amari to reinstate her birth control pills.

Thanksgiving at the Robinson household was hectic and enjoyable. Paul stayed downstairs with his dad. Cindy, Madison and Mrs. Jahmal controlled the kitchen. Paul and Cindy's kids, Kelly and Scott were going bananas playing with Mrs. Jahmal's twin niece and nephew, Brandye and Darrell. The kids were bound to be asleep by 9:00 p.m., they were playing so hard.

Dinner was delicious, but Madison rushed through it. Damion was working that night, and he'd invited her to the station. She turned on the radio during dinner so her family could hear him. The only comment came from her mom, who said he sounded nice. Nice? Couldn't her mom see he was the sexiest thing on the East Coast? Ah, well. Madison would let her slide. Her mom was from the old school.

Madison prepared a plate for Damion and cut him a slice of sweet potato pie. She cut a slice of pumpkin for herself. After closing the lid on a container full of whipped cream, she hastily said good-bye to her family and kissed the kids, who were so deep into some PlayStation game they barely acknowledged her. Once Madison arrived at the station, Damion programmed an hour medley of Marvin Gaye. He ate, and they joked and laughed together like old friends.

CHAPTER 23

Madison—The Luckiest Girl In The World
December 1999

December rushed in with a vengeance. The city was covered under a blanket of snow for several days. After the snow, came the big freeze. Stacey called Madison at 2:00 am one morning because her pipes burst. Madison called Damion, who didn't answer his phone, then paged him. His cell was probably turned off at this hour. He called back in 20 minutes, alarmed that something might be wrong. Madison told him about Stacey and he said he'd call his boy Eric who would take care of her. He took down Stacey's number and address and told Madison he was at his boy's house, and they were just drinking beer and talking shit. Madison blew him a kiss over the phone and told him he would receive a special reward for his kindness. Damion, who would usually respond with a sexy joke, chuckled a little.

"No problem. Anytime I can help out a friend," and hung up.

Madison thought his behavior a bit odd, but perhaps that was his business side. Or, maybe he was a bit tipsy. He didn't say which friend of his, but Madison didn't know everyone in his life, yet. Just his corny friends Todd and Rod.

She happened to run into them at Montgomery Mall while doing some Christmas shopping. They never called her by her name, just "D's girl."

"I guess that's a good thing," she thought, and headed towards Nordstrom, where she did the bulk of her shopping using Stacey's discount. She left Todd and Rod talking to a couple of girls, of course.

Her days and nights were extremely full. Work was crazy because of Y2K. Freelancing for *The Chocolate City Voice* was stressful. She was under the gun to write stories in advance since her family was going to Seattle for Christmas.

The first three weeks Madison didn't see Damion much at all. He told her he'd picked up a couple of new, demanding clients, and he was filling in more often at the station as the regulars began to take vacation. They went ice-skating on Freedom's Plaza once, but Damion seemed a bit distant. Madison chalked up his moodiness to a busy schedule. She could definitely understand busy.

The schedule was actually Crystal—who was pulling out all the stops for Damion to forgive her. They hadn't slept together yet, but Crystal knew patience, if she didn't know anything else. He would come around.

Before she left for Seattle, Madison met Damion for brunch at Georgia Brown's to exchange gifts and catch up with one another. Damion apologized profusely for being out of pocket lately. He was interviewing contractors for his renovation, if he were to win the housing lottery. He felt pretty confident about it, and proceeded as if he'd already acquired the property. His phone rang constantly.

"That explains his phone ringing off the hook," thought Madison. After checking the display, Damion would make little comments like "Dude can wait, I'm with my baby, now."

They had a pleasant and filling brunch, and Madison was actually pleased with her gift. Damion bought her a beautiful smoke-gray cashmere v-neck sweater. He also surprised her with an exquisite original necklace from his best female friend, Yvette B., a Chicago native who brought her Midwest flair to a slower-paced, but welcoming Atlanta. She was extremely talented, and had an eye for good color and design. According to Damion, jewelry-making was just a hobby for Yvette, but Madison could see her selling her pieces, "Distinct Designs" in Neiman's and Saks, they were that good. As a matter of fact, Yvette was so multi-faceted, she could do anything she wanted. She was a tiny little thing, pretty, with large eyes and a short boy cut that only she and Erykah Badu could get away with. She had two masters and a PhD and was still going to school, and working, and making jewelry. A renaissance woman whose only known fetish were expensive shoes. Madison really liked her and asked for her suggestion of what to get Damion for Christmas. It paid off. Yvette knew Damion backwards and forwards.

Madison gave Damion his gift, a pair of Cole Haan driving moccasins, which he loved and changed into immediately. They just happened to offset his chocolate cable knit sweater and jeans. Stacey warned Madison against giving a man a pair of shoes when she was thinking about buying them in the store.

"Girl, you give a man some shoes and he'll walk right out of your life, mark my words."

Madison just laughed at her superstitions.

After an hour, Damion had to run. He told Madison he wished they could have spent their first Christmas and the millennium together, but that it would be more special next year. 2000. Their year. He hugged her, planted a kiss on her forehead, pecked her lips, and was gone. Their year? He couldn't have been talking about an engagement. Not that soon. Well? Madison felt like the luckiest girl in the metropolitan area. She hugged the sweater close to her and grinned wider than a cat. She was the luckiest girl in the world.

CHAPTER 24

**Damion—Something In The Milk Ain't Clean
January 2000**

Damion was amazed at Crystal's tenacity. No wonder she got through Howard Law with a 3.9 GPA. She had been tender, understanding, womanly, and slightly aggressive, but not too much so, the past few weeks. She was acting more like the woman he was attracted to when they first met. Madison spent the holidays in Seattle, and when she came back, *The Chocolate City Voice* consumed her. Madison explained they were preparing for the Black History Month edition, which had to be huge this year. *The Washington Afro-American* usually dominated sales in February and *The Chocolate City Voice* was vying to compete. Madison was pretty independent. She acted like she didn't need him; well sometimes she acted like that. He still hadn't quite figured her out, yet.

Crystal, on the other hand, really knew how to make him feel like a man. First of all, she didn't go to Florida for the holidays like she usually does. She chose to stay in the District, and hang out with him. They did a lot of first date stuff, like movies, the museums, new restaurants and Damion's favorite adult playground, Dave & Busters. They also went to see Crystal's high school buddy Temika Moore perform at Republic Gardens. Temika was a natural. Petite, cute, with a big 'ol voice reminiscent of Phyllis Hyman. She had the look and she had the presence. She was a star. Damion promised he'd try and get her some run time at the station.

Damion was also beginning to spend a lot more time at Crystal's place again, which was established and cozy. His place was kind of cold, and didn't have any personality. It was a typical bachelor's bad.

Crystal made dinner for him daily. He still hadn't touched her, but it was getting harder not to. She showed him the pills she started again, and wore his t-shirts around her place with no bra on. She knew that turned him on, but never pressed the issue. He would go home around 10:00 p.m., and talk to Madison until he went to bed.

When the Martin Luther King Holiday rolled around, Eric invited Damion and Madison over to Stacey's for dinner. They'd hit it off and Eric was practically living over there.

Madison met him at Stacey's place. She looked absolutely beautiful. Madison was simply... magical. He never questioned her feelings when they were together. He could see the honesty in her eyes. Damion just wanted to get her home and make love to her. Forget a meal. But his boy was pressed, and Madison was always talking about her girl Stacey, so he figured it was time they all meet.

Damion was totally shocked when he met Stacey. She was loud, arrogant, overly confident and had some big ass titties. Not that the titties had anything to do with it, but he figured that's how Eric got hooked. Madison was the total opposite. She was quiet, rather reserved, and slightly self-conscious. But, they were friends for a reason. He needed to study Stacey a bit more before he came to a conclusion.

Despite her brashness, she could cook! She made pork chops, sweet potatoes, home-made macaroni and cheese, collard greens, cornbread and fried catfish. Madison was on some old "cooking light" type program. As if echoing his thoughts, Damion overheard Madison talking to Stacey in the kitchen. She was talking about garnishing the fish with fresh rosemary and sprinkling it with fresh ground ginger. Stacey told Madison to kiss her ass and hand her the hot sauce.

He and Eric got a good laugh off of that one. Dinner was very informal and spirited. No matter how much women and men talked about women and men, the topic never got tiresome. Stacey kept telling Damion he looked familiar, but she couldn't quite put her finger on where she saw him. She was funny, but aloof at the same time. She was definitely a woman who didn't trust easily. He thought she looked familiar as well, but this was DC, so it's possible he may have run into her somewhere.

After rum cake and ice cream, the women went to clean up the kitchen and Eric and Damion chilled in the living room. It was easy to hear them even with the TV on, because Stacey's house was so small. Marion Anderson was singing at the 1963 March on Washington on a PBS special, but the conversation in the kitchen got Damion's attention. It was pretty intense, and the banging dishes got louder and louder. After hearing a succession of muffled sounds, Damion heard Stacey say "Something in the milk ain't clean."

A few minutes later, Madison came storming out of the kitchen, grabbed both their coats and said "Let's go."

Eric looked terribly confused. Damion just stood up and followed Madison's lead. Whatever it was she was upset about didn't need to be aggravated.

Stacey came out of the kitchen with a toothpick in her mouth, drying her hands with a dishtowel and glared at Damion.

"Where ya'll going so soon?" asked Eric, puzzled.

Damion shot a "hell if I know look" at his boy, and looked at Madison.

"We've got to go the MLK library for their evening special on King," said Madison evenly.

"This late?" Eric was the only one pushing the issue.

"Baby you want another beer?" Stacey broke the tension strategically.

"Alright, D," Eric said, giving his boy the "grip" and brother hug.

"Nice meeting you, Stacey" Damion said carefully as she walked back into the kitchen."

It was so quiet, the volume on the TV seemed to raise itself. A little boy of about 12 was reading a poem dedicated to the little girls that were killed in a Birmingham church. His voice was clear and held the promise of power.

"...and we must not forget September 15, 1963
No!
4 little black girls
Bombed
Hatred personified
Crushed broken bones
Burned skin
Bruised souls
Hearts heavier than stone

Grief Sudden Grief
Overtaking the escalating moans
Too much
Way too much pain to bear
Yet
Hope clings desperately in the air

> Someday we will all be free
> But 4 little black girls
> Remain a painful memory"

Stacey stood at the entrance to the kitchen with a dishrag in her hand, gritting on Damion. "Speaking of memories, "I know that's him, Madison, Peace."

She abruptly turned on her heels and disappeared into the kitchen, leaving Eric to see Damion and Madison out.

The sub-zero temperatures at Stacey's seemed colder than the weather outside.

Damion walked Madison to her car. She gave him a peck on the cheek and said she'd call him later.

"I thought we were going to hook up this evening, Madison. I haven't seen much of you, lately." Damion replayed the question in his mind and decided he sounded like a bitch.

"Oh, ummm, okay. Wanna go get coffee at Kramerbooks and Afterwords?"

Madison's brain felt like it would explode. She was hurt, confused and exposed.

"Sure, since parking is so tight, I can drive with you. You mind dropping me back here?"

Madison agreed and Damion hopped in the seat beside her. The car smelled like smoke. Madison admitted she took a puff or two now and again. Damion didn't really like it, but she didn't seem to need to smoke, not around him anyway.

At the coffee shop, Madison told Damion why she was so upset. Apparently, Stacey claimed she had seen Damion with some short, red-headed girl last year and he was buying her perfume. Stacey was so sure it was him, she'd come home and called Madison to tell her about it in one of their "why do bitches always get the man?" conversations. The only thing was, Stacey couldn't remember when the incident happened, but it was Eric calling him "D" that triggered the memory. Madison remembered, though. If Stacey was right, it would have been the same weekend she met Damion.

Damion's first instinct was to lie. His second instinct was to try and make Stacey seem crazy, especially since she sees so many people working retail. But looking at Madison, he sensed that every fiber of her being needed him to tell the truth. So he did, to some extent. He told Madison the weekend he met her, he was so taken by her that he felt guilty because he and his ex-girlfriend were trying to reconcile, so he took her to buy some perfume. But he knew, that after meeting Madison, it wasn't going to work.

He looked at Madison's large eyes and knew she was fighting back tears. He'd never seen her come close to crying, even in sad movies, and it was freaking him out.

"Why?" she asked in a wavering voice.

"Why what?" he answered gently.

"Why did you know it wasn't going to work with you and your girlfriend?" Madison's hands were trembling around her coffee mug.

Under normal circumstances, he wouldn't have even been here, in this place, full of bundled up strangers and hot drinks and pretense. He wouldn't have cared enough to explain himself to anyone, especially a female. But, he did care for Madison, he would just have to stretch the truth, this one time.

"Well, Madison. We'd dated for a few years, and had broken up because I wasn't moving fast enough for her. But after a couple of weeks, she wanted to try and make things work, and told me she would wait for me. But it made me think that she was an impulsive person, and I can't marry a woman like that because I wouldn't be able to fully trust her with our kids, our money, and what if she met someone, decided to screw him because she felt like it, then came home to me and our bed? She was too much of a risk."

"A risk? You call dating someone for years a risk?" Madison was still angry. 'As much as those bastards cheat?' she thought. And he said he was worried about his ex? What brass ones.

"Besides, when I saw you, and talked to you, I felt that I wanted to get to know you and make you my woman, and that wouldn't have been fair to her."

Damion was afraid of what Madison might ask next. She was a nosy ass journalist, and if she started connecting the dots, his ass was in trouble.

"Damion."

"Yes, baby." She was about to drop a bomb. He could feel it.

"When did you officially call it off with her?"

Damion could tell you the scores of all the Super Bowl games, the teams who played and what the weather was like that day, but as for when he and Madison met? He didn't know. And he knew, that she, as a woman, knew exactly the day they met, and would hold the Crystal thing against him. He had to play this smart. He looked at her expecting face, and took the now cold coffee mug out of her hands. She hadn't drank a drop.

"I broke up with her for good before we went to Deep Creek Lake."

Madison's lips quivered. She stood up and put on her coat.

"That was October. We met in September, Damion," she said harshly,

"...find your own way home."

"But Madison, I chose you."

Madison picked up the creamer, looked at it, poured it in his coffee, slammed the container on the table, splattering milk on both their hands and muttered, "Stacey was right. Something in the milk ain't clean."

Madison left the coffee shop without looking back. Damion sat there dazed, wondering where he went wrong. Madison absorbed his thoughts during the cab ride over to Crystal's. He'd have Crystal drop him off in the morning to get his car. She'd do it and wouldn't ask him 100 questions. Good 'ol Crystal. Later that night, with Crystal's warm naked body snuggled in the crook of his arms, Damion wondered what he could do to make Madison forgive him. This was their first fight, and Damion never saw it coming.

CHAPTER 25

**Damion—Mission Madison
January 2000**

"Man, I fucked up."

Damion had made the mistake of trying to share his problems with Todd, the consummate ladies man. He realized his error halfway through the conversation, as Todd ordered his 4th drink of the evening, and checked out all the women with Anita Baker haircuts. They were at Baileys, a local spot in Silver Spring known for its Friday night happy hours, the 'slammin jazz band Spur of the Moment, and hordes of gorgeous women.

"You alright, man." Todd almost broke his neck looking at a couple of honeys. They seemed to travel in twos.

"But, man, I need to win Madison's trust back, and I don't want to do some corny shit, like, send flowers, or something, making a 'nigga look guilty. What 'chu think?"

"Look man," Todd began impatiently. "Just go 'head and bone her like Wesley Snipes boned Cynda Williams in *Mo' Better Blues*. On the balcony. No inhibitions. She got a balcony where she live?" Todd turned to watch a Brazilian girl walk by.

"Man, she ain't the sex make it better type."

"Man, what's wrong with you? Look around. "Todd spanned the room with his eyes. "It's way too many fine honeys around, especially in DC, bruh, shit... homegirl should be calling you... ringing 'yo phone off the hook! I mean, look at that fine honey near the bathroom, the one with the long hair, she is definitely giving you the 'you can have my drawers on a platter, look!"

Damion looked in the direction of the woman, and shook his head.

"Man, she looking at your bama ass—you loud!"

Damion checked the sister out a little more carefully, while sipping his drink.

"Actually, man, she's more your type. Light, bright, damn near white."

"Don't hate, man. Just because I don't want my girl to have to perm her hair, don't hate."

"Whatever, man, all I'm saying is, you have a preference, which narrows your search of all these beautiful black women down to... one."

"I've gotta go water the lawn," Todd said barely audibly, and walked towards the sister—who just happened to dig brown-skinned men—and Todd fit the bill.

Damion gave up on Todd, and went out on the balcony to clear his head. There seemed to be couples everywhere. Women giggling and men macking. Beautiful black folks, all hues, focused on executing the Genesis of man—procreation. He waved to his boy Marcus Johnson, who was trying to make his mark in the music business. The brother was extremely talented, could play several instruments equally well, and unlike many artists, he was able to balance the creative and the business. Long after his music career, he was the type that would continue to make money. Marcus was talking to some trophy chick. That brother was always surrounded by beautiful women. Damion wondered if he was the type of brother that would ever settle down. Probably. Just not right now. Another woman more beautiful than the one he was speaking with approached him. Definitely not right now. Damion pulled out his cell phone and contemplated calling Madison. Women were complicated creatures, and he didn't know how many days to wait until her anger wore off. It had only been a few days since the King incident.

"I have a dream," he thought wryly, and it was Madison. He put his phone back in his pocket and turned to go back inside the club. Todd had his arm around the light-skinned girl. Whenever he got super touchy feely, he was drunk. It looked like Damion would be the designated driver tonight.

After they left Bailey's, Todd insisted on stopping by the 7-11 on Georgia Avenue by the DC line, so he could get some coffee. Damion reluctantly agreed but figured he could get gas while Todd did his thing. Inside the store, Todd met up with one of his old fuck buddies. They came out of the store, arm in arm. Todd unhooked his arm and sidled over to Damion.

"You can go on, man. I'll be alright. Remember Brie?"

Damion looked at her. She smiled and waved victoriously.

"You sure you want to do this, bruh?" Damion asked with a modicum of concern.

"Man, I know what I'm doing, I'm doing this for you."

"Man, I know you drunk, now. Get in the car."

"I may be nice from the drinks, but my vision is fine."

Todd pointed to a woman filling up her tank in a red Acura.

Damion couldn't believe it. "Madison." Though he didn't say her name too loudly, she must have felt his vibe.

Madison looked up, saw him and Todd, and waved.

Damion put the nozzle back in its place, and rushed over to Madison's pump. Todd walked to Brie's car, and opened the passenger-side door for her. Damion couldn't believe this honey was going to let drunk ass Todd drive her car. These women!

Once Damion reached Madison, he gently removed her hand and took over the pumping.

"I'm only putting $10 dollars in, Damion. Don't go over."

"You shouldn't be out at night putting gas in your car, will your tank be full?"

"I know, but I don't want my gas line to freeze, this will give me half a tank. The rest is going towards groceries. I just don't want to get caught in the snow when it's supposed to storm really heavy tonight." Madison was talking to him like nothing had transpired. Maybe she didn't hold grudges like Crystal did.

"Have you been to the store, yet?"

"I'm on my way to Giant by the Blairs."

"I'll go with you."

Madison hesitated. To Damion, it seemed as if Madison was calculating the odds. He shifted impatiently. No need for games. When women knew they had the power, boy, they were a trip!

"I'll carry the heavy stuff for you, water, water, and water. You know. Something Something," he said jovially, figuring she'd buckle with the Maxwell reference. Madison turned into a true groupie when it came to that dude. His music was smooth and all, but Damion couldn't see what the honeys went buck wild for.

Madison smiled, shrugged her shoulders and said,

"Alright then, I guess I can use you."

"I'll pay for your groceries," Damion suggested, hoping they would get snowed in together.

"No need."

Madison was rather stubborn and independent. Crystal would have accepted and gone to two or three stores to get what she claimed she needed. Ah well. Whoever said women were all the same was a freaking liar. It started snowing while they were in the grocery store; fat, heavy, flakes that competed with one another to see who could cover the asphalt first. Damon still felt he should handle Madison with kid gloves. She could be one of those blow-up sisters, smiling in your face and shit, then, BOOM—here comes the anger. But she stayed cool.

They did the grocery thing. Madison even invited Damion up for some hot cocoa. Watching her move about in her tiny kitchen, Damion realized how much he cared for her. Although she was home comfortable, in black velvet sweats and her long hair thrown carelessly in a ponytail, Damion longed for her. It was more than a dick thing, it was ethereal.

"Damion, do you want whipped cream?"

"What was that?" Damion pretended he didn't hear her so he could walk in the kitchen and get next to her. He walked up behind her and squeezed her really tight.

"Sure, I'll take whip," he whispered, and licked her luscious ear lobes, noting the metallic taste of her diamond studs.

She froze up like the icicles starting to form outside her window. Damion berated himself for moving too fast.

"Slow down, bruh," he cautioned himself.

Madison gave him a cup of steaming hot cocoa, grabbed her pink and green mug, and headed towards the living room, where the Quiet Storm was serving up some LTD with "We Both Deserve Each Other's Love." Madison curled up in the big, plaid comfy chair, while Damion sat nearest her end on the sofa. They sipped in silence for a while, watching the snow blanket the universe. Brainstorm's "This Must Be Heaven" flowed softly into Norman Connors "You Are My Starship" before Damion broke the silence.

"They 'jammin tonight, hunh?" Madison looked into his soul and nodded her head. Damion trembled ever so slightly.

"Madison, I have something to tell you."

Again, the unnerving stare sent a slight chill down his spine. He took her silence as an okay to begin.

"I've never told anyone this before, but I feel as if I should share this with you."

Madison slightly tilted her head, paying rapt attention, but remained silent.

"When I was nine, I almost got raped at camp. This big kid tried to pull my sweats off me in a navigation exercise. I bit his hand to keep him off me." Madison had put her mug on the coffee table. Damion continued his story, speeding up like a record, from 33 to 78 rpm.

"From that day and on until my adult years, I felt that if I couldn't protect myself, how could I protect someone else? And Madison, it wasn't until I started hanging out with you, that I began to feel as if I wanted to not only protect myself, but to furiously protect what's mine—my woman. Madison, for the first time in my life, I feel like I could settle down; and not with just any woman, but with you. With you Madison; with you." Damion still had to fight from getting choked up when he thought about the incident, and sensing that, Madison moved next to him on the sofa. He looked at her for a long time, then held her gingerly as he kissed her long, and hard. Madison kissed him back, passionately. When he pulled back to look at her, her eyes were full of tears.

"I'm crying for you," she said.

"Oh, Madison, Madison—you are beautiful," Damion whispered tenderly. Moments later, their syncopated bodies moved in rhythm to each other's heartbeats. After which he held her, as the night faded into the quiet storm.

#Place the numeral 3 by the CD to indicate song #3

CHAPTER 26

Damion—My Funny Valentine
February 2000

Although February was the shortest month of the year, every day was good for Damion. It was his month. Things went so smoothly that he began to wonder when the shoe was going to drop.

First of all, he found out he'd won the lottery for a row house in Columbia Heights, and was able to get it way under market value. Homegirl had come through, though it was a nail biter to the very end. Someone had told her Damion had a girlfriend and was just using her, but she didn't care; she just liked the fact that she was able to use her position to get some from a guy that probably wouldn't have looked twice at her. She was almost right, Damion wouldn't have looked at her at all. The neighborhood was kinda rough, but it couldn't stay like that, not with the Reeves Center down at 16th and U. Rules of economics, whenever the government owned a building in the hood, that hood got 'mo betta.

He and Crystal celebrated at the family-owned soul food joint on Florida Avenue, not far from where his new place would be. He was going to have to do some renovations, but everything should be ready by the spring. And he could make some extra income by renting out the basement. Madison was busy researching a black history piece about historic "U" Street for *The Chocolate City Voice* and was working 12-15 hour days. She was exhausted most evenings and didn't demand much of his time. This worked out well for him, along with Crystal's predictable schedule. With her good government job, she was off at 4:30, no later than 5:00 p.m., and would come home and cook most evenings. They'd eat, talk about the day, and he would roll out in time to touch base with Madison before she went to bed. Damion had Crystal still believing he was mad about the birth control thing, which is why he rarely spent the night anymore.

It was a week before Valentine's day, and Damion was trying to figure out how he was going to juggle Crystal and Madison, when yet another lucky break occurred. Crystal was clearing off the table after they'd eaten. She'd fried some chicken wings and made some macaroni and cheese and mustard greens. He stood up to go in the den and watch TV when she asked him to help dry the dishes.

"Aw come on Crystal, I'm all full and everything, and you want me to dry dishes? Let 'em sit for a minute, and come watch TV with me."

"Damion, you lucky I'm just asking you to dry," Crystal chided. My mom always made us clean up in my household. She was like, 'I cooked! The least y'all can do is clean up,' so that's what I'm accustomed to."

"Well, that was your house."

"You used to help me."

"Yeah, when I first met you, I was trying to impress you."

Crystal ran towards Damion flicking a wet dishtowel at him.

"Go 'head, boy, and get your ass over to the sink. I need to talk to you."

Damion's stomach sank. Anytime a woman said she needed to 'talk,' they usually fucked something up. That phrase translated into the woman wanting to take the relationship to the next level, or wanting to meet your momma, or the ultimatum for marriage or some shit like that.

He dragged over to the sink, and watched her deftly wash the plates. She was so comfortable washing, her rhythm was almost like a song. Pretty hands, nails clicking, dishes clinking against the aluminum sink as she rinsed, hypnotizing Damion, numbing him to whatever was to come.

"Baby, we need to celebrate Valentines day early this year."

Damion jumped to attention. Bracing himself on the edge of the sink, he asked cautiously, "Why is that, baby?"

Sensing he was in an odd mood, Crystal prodded him lightly with her elbow.

"The A group is going to Copper Mountain in Colorado for Black Ski, and I said I'd go. I've always wanted to go to the summit, and we'll get a huge discount. Are you okay with that, baby?"

Damion looked towards the heavens and rejoiced inside.

He hugged Crystal.

"Baby that's fine. I'll be alright here. I'm filling in for Denny at the station, so I would have short-changed you anyway."

Crystal looked relieved.

"Just don't be giving no 'niggas your phone number," Damion said jealously.

"Don't worry, I'm not you," Crystal kidded.

Damion was already thinking of taking Madison to the Poconos for a little ski trip of their own. She definitely couldn't go to black ski with Crystal. That was a no-no.

"Well, baby. I gotta be out. I'll hollar at you tomorrow, and you can figure out what you want to do for V-day. You women are good at the planning thing, better than me."

Damion figured this was the right move. Empower her. Let her plan, feel important.

"Oh. I thought you wanted to watch TV?"

"Naw. I forgot I told Todd I'd scoop him up from Brie's place. Thanks for dinner, baby, it was delicious."

He left Crystal at the door with a dishtowel in her hands and a strange look on her face.

Damion didn't have time to figure it out, he needed to get to Madison, quick. Fortunately, she was just getting in when he called from the car.

"Baby, I need to see you."

Madison sounded glad to hear from him, but she was tired.

"Damion, how about tomorrow, I'm a little tired."

"No, baby. I need to see you tonight, I have a surprise for you."

"Okay, then. But don't trip if I fall asleep on you. A 'sista needs her beauty rest."

Damion sped up Connecticut Avenue, cut through Rock Creek Park, and was at Madison's place inside of 15 minutes. You gotta love the park, he thought, no lights, rarely a DC cop, and depending on the time of day minimal traffic made for a smooth commute. When he got to Madison's, she was in the middle of heating up some leftovers.

"You hungry? I've got some leftover spinach, mashed potatoes and filet mignon from Clyde's."

"Naw, baby, I'm good. I met Cliff at his mom's house and had dinner there."

"Cliff, your friend from Chicago?"

"Damn you've got a good memory. Yeah, that's him."

"Does Cliff live with his mom?"

"Just for a little while baby, I mean, they are in Crestwood."

"So, he's a grown ass man. He shouldn't be living with his mama, that's all I'm saying. Does he have a girlfriend?"

"Yes. Several."

"Several?" Madison huffed.

Wrong move, Damion sensed.

"No I'm just playing baby. He's dating Danielle, you remember the girl we ran into at Carter Baron the day we went to the Angie Stone concert, and I said Cliff was trying to hollar at her?"

"Yeah, I remember. She had on some ridiculous high heels, and I thought how inappropriate they were at an outdoor concert."

"Right, but with regard to his living situation, Cliff's moms is planning to buy a condo near the National Zoo, and leave the house on Mathewson to him."

"Ummm hmmm," Madison said in true black woman fashion as she sifted through her mail.

"Oooh wee," she said excitedly.

"What, baby?"

"Looks like the A group's going to black ski. It's going to be in Colorado again this year."

"Oh yeah, when is that?" Damion asked, trying to play it cool.

"Around Valentines day," Madison said leafing through the brochure.

"Well, baby, that's what I wanted to talk to you about. Your surprise."

"Oh, yeah, what's that?" Now she had a mouth full of mashed potatoes.

"I've planned for us to have our own ski trip for our first Valentine's Day. In the Poconos."

Madison's eyes widened.

"For real?"

"For real," Damion grinned, wondering how he was going to pull this off.

Madison couldn't contain her excitement.

"But it's been so long since I've hung out with the girls, Damion, do you want to go to the Poconos later this month?"

"Naw, baby, it wouldn't be right. It HAS to be on Valentines. This is our first Valentines day, so it needs to be special, right?"

Madison took a sip of spring water, and abstractly picked up another envelope. She opened it, furrowed her brows momentarily, and sighed heavily.

"Baby, what's up?"

"Nothing, Damion. I'm going to have to go to court for all these darn tickets I got."

"Just write them a check that's over the amount of the tickets. They can't cash it because it's not the right dollar amount, that'll bide you some time."

Madison, taken aback, looked at him and chuckled.

"You sure are a little trickster, aren't you?"

"Nah, baby, you just gotta understand how systems work. My boys do it all the time. And if you get a boot, I've got a boot man, too. He doesn't ask for as much as the tow people. Now what about our trip? Don't leave me hanging."

Madison just shook her head and grinned. "Okay, Damion, that'll be great. It will be a nice getaway from the job and the paper, but we'll only be gone for a couple of days, right?"

"Yeah, baby. No more than three."

"Good, because I'll need to be back for the planning meeting for March's paper, it's Women's History Month, you know."

"That's cool. I'll need to finalize the contractors I'm using for the house. So you see how that works out? It's all good, right?"

Madison just nodded her head in the affirmative. By this time, she'd cleaned up her mess, made her tea, and was on her way into the living room to sojourn with her oversized chair and a J. California Cooper book. This signaled to Damion she was ready for him to leave. She never quite said it, but it's the feeling he got; that Madison really didn't need him. Crystal always seemed rather sad to see him go, which gave him a sense of power, but he always felt slightly vulnerable around Madison.

"I know you're not a tea person, but would you like some hot cocoa?" she offered sweetly.

Damion thought briefly about Crystal's place, which would be very warm, she couldn't stand to be cold, and would carry the faint smells of a home-cooked meal. Hell, she may even have a pie or some cookies baking in the oven. But, for some reason he couldn't fathom, Damion wanted to stay right here, at Madison's, inhaling the warmth from her Hershey cocoa brown skin.

"That's cool," he said, not wanting to sound too eager.

Madison flipped on the quiet storm and disappeared into the kitchen. Damion thought about turning on the TV to watch *SportCenter*, but figured he'd surprise Madison. By the time she returned to the living room, Damion had dimmed the lights, lit a few candles and was using the remote as a microphone to sing "My Funny Valentine" along with Will Downing. She giggled as she sat his steaming mug down on the coffee table. Damion grabbed her hand and spun her around, indicating he was ready for a slow dance. She settled in the crook of his arm, wrapped her arms around him, and lay her head on his heart. He held her close, the heat of desire spreading through him as he inhaled her sweet-smelling hair.

"Baby, I can't wait for our trip, he whispered in her ear."

"Me neither, funny valentine. Me neither."

CHAPTER 27

Madison—3 Times Is The Charm
March 2000

Under the hairdryer at Bruce's shop, Madison took some much needed time to relax and reflect. She and Damion had a wonderful, storybook weekend in the Poconos. He seemed to be working hard to regain her trust, and she liked that. Because of her schedule and weekends with Damion, she hadn't taken a lot of time to follow up with her girls, and it had been so long since she'd been to an A group meeting, she felt as if she'd lost touch. Stacey would say this stage was dangerous territory. Madison could hear her now.

"Girl, when you put a man before your girls, you in trouble. Sprung, and on the path to devaluing yourself and your…' good lawd! Ayinde, your fingers feel so damn good you 'bout to give me an orgasm!"

That's not how her speeches usually went. Was she? Could she be? Madison bolted from under the dryer. She peeked around the corner, and sure 'nough, there was Stacey, in the washbowl, apparently getting the scalp massage of a lifetime. She was surrounded by the usual crowd, Tiffany, Erika, Yaema and Keni. They were giggling and cuckooing as usual. Madison checked to see how much time she had under the dryer. 15 minutes. She'd hollar at Stacey and get back under, but she had to keep an eye out for Bruce, as he'd fuss about her wet set if he saw her. "You don't have the kind of hair you can wet and wear," he'd say bluntly if he found her wandering during her dryer time. He could get away with it. He was Bruce.

"So when ya'll getting married, girl?" asked an inquisitive Yeama. She was a beautiful girl, model thin, with perfect features and constantly changed her hairstyle.

Madison jumped out of her chair and walked towards Stacey.

"I don't know, girl," she said. "We plan to live together for a minute, then we'll decide. You know I've been married twice, he's never been married."

"Girl, how do you do it? You must have the magic touch," Erika chimed in.

"You must cook for him," chimed Calvin. "We love women that cook for their men."

"Calvin, a robot could cook for you, and you would love it," quipped Keni.

"Yeah, especially if Roshida the robot had some big robot titties and cooked in a thong," said Ayinde. The entire shop broke out in laughter.

By this time, Madison stood over Stacey, and forced her to open her eyes.

"Stacey!"

"Oh, what's up, trick?"

"You didn't tell me!"

"Tell you, what?"

"Tell me about you and Eric."

"You haven't been around. I'll talk to you after my shampoo." Stacey squinted at Madison with one eye. "Don't you need to be under the dryer, anyway?"

Tiffany and Erika gave each other the look. Madison observed the glance, and feeling slightly embarrassed, walked back to the dryer, where Bruce was guarding it like an overprotective mother hen.

"Madison. Why aren't you in your seat? How many times do -"

"Okay, Bruce. Damn!" Madison exclaimed, cutting him off.

She sat down and thought about her feelings. She was happy for Stacey, but she and Eric had just met. How did they know? It was rather soon, and Stacey herself always said it took a year for the "inner nigga," meaning one's true colors, to reveal themselves. They did look very comfortable when Madison met them, though. It was obvious he loved her. It was in the eyes. You could always tell by the eyes. Occasionally, she saw that look in Damion's eyes, but he hadn't said anything, yet. She thought he would tell her he loved her in the Poconos, they'd had an awesome time, but no confessions of love. Damion treated her well, but in many ways he seemed so 'textbook' to Madison. It's like he did everything right, but something was missing, though Madison couldn't quite put her finger on it. Ah, well. No biggie. She'd have to show Stacey extra love so she wouldn't be mad at her. Her mind was blown about the Eric thing. The whole thing just seemed so out of character for her friend. Madison waited for Stacey to finish up. She spent her time by going next door to the Asians and getting a $10 manicure, and gossiping with the girls at Bruce's shop. You could always get them heated up talking about celebrities and interracial dating.

Stacey and Madison met at Starbucks for coffee afterwards and Stacey was all too happy to tell of her good news. The momentary iciness had vanished. Eric confessed his feelings to Stacey on Valentine's Day. So, in typical Stacey fashion, she asked him, "Alright, so what are you going to do about it?" Stacey said Eric didn't skip a beat.

"He manned up girl. Manned up."

"Wow, Stacey, I am happy for you."

"Yep, and if it wasn't for that sneaky ass boyfriend of yours and my old ass pipes, this wouldn't have happened. So here's to you," Stacey said, touching her cup of java to Madison's.

"I mean, can you imagine me telling the kids, me and your daddy met 'cause he had to fix my pipes!"

Stacey laughed hysterically, checked her watch, jumped up and said she had to go.

"Alright, Stace. I wish you guys the best. Take care of each other," Madison said wistfully.

"Three times is the charm, girl, three times is the charm."

Madison's mobile rang as soon as she stepped out of the coffee shop. It was Pilar, and she had that strange hurriedness in her voice that made Madison suspect.

"Madison, I'm at the office, trying to make some two-sided copies, I need 2,500 of them, and something is wrong with my computer, and I really, really need your help, girl. I will do whatever you need, girl, even talk to Rob about giving you a promotion in place."

Immediately Madison was suspicious. Pilar sounded a bit too pressed. She decided to push back, bait her and see what was up.

"Pilar, it's Saturday, and I'm in the middle of running errands."

"Girl, it won't take you but a minute. Bernard really needs this."

That was it. Bernard. The greatest asshole that ever lived.

"Pilar, I'm sorry, I can't…"

"Madison, wait," Pilar pleaded, "hear me out."

Madison had a feeling this was going to be yet another disaster. She remained silent. First Pilar pulled the house party trick with Bernard. That failed. She then pulled the NY trip with Bernard. That failed. Now she was up to something else with Bernard, and sure as shootin, whatever this is, it will fail, too.

"Yes, Pilar. What is it this time?" Stacey had just said 'three times is the charm,' so maybe Madison was overreacting.

"Well, girl, Bernard is getting ready to go public," Madison heard her frantically shuffling papers in the background.

"And he needs 2,500 copies of his IPO for the company he's presenting to. But for some reason, my computer isn't talking to the printer, and that's where you come in."

Madison could not get over Pilar. Now she was using the company's resources for this asshole! She would never learn.

"Pilar, why don't you call DigiGraph Media, they'll be able to bang that out for you in no time. You have an established relationship with those guys."

"But Madi, this is real quick. I didn't want to bother them for a job this small."

"But yet you would bother me and risk your job," thought Madison. She wished she had never answered her phone. Although she hadn't discussed her disdain with Pilar, she was sure Pilar could feel her pulling back from their friendship.

"Madison, I won't forget this."

Now she's resorted to begging. Bernard is so not good for her. Perhaps Madison could help remedy Pilar's warped situation.

"Pilar, give me a couple of hours. I'm sure you can stay busy until then."

Pilar was silent on the other end of the line. She was probably weighing her odds.

"Okay, Madi. We'll go get something to eat, then we'll be back here shortly."

"Yep."

Madison immediately dialed Pilar's home number. As expected, Mitch picked up.

"Hi, Mitch, it's Madison." She listened intently.

"Ah, no, I know Pilar's not there. Umm hmmm."

She shifted on nervous feet.

"Is your cousin Roughhouse still in Philly?"

Madison smirked.

"Good. How long does he plan to be here?"

"No, I'm not in trouble, but I have some information you may be interested in."

Madison met Pilar at the office exactly two hours later. Bernard's punk ass was nowhere to be found. Madison could not fathom how a beautiful, talented, lucky woman like Pilar could continue to jeopardize her marriage for this clown. He was selfish, and motivated by what was best for him, and Pilar just melted into the mold he carved for her; but whose role could easily be played by someone else. When Madison left the building, she had yet another freaking ticket. This was getting ridiculous. She'd have to go to court to try and talk some judge down.

Pilar called Madison several times that night, but thank God for Caller ID, because Madison didn't answer. If asked, she'd tell Pilar she spent the weekend with Damion.

On Monday, Demetrius was outside smoking a cigarette when Madison walked in. He was so excited, he put a fresh cigarette out to talk to her.

"What's up, Madi, man, you won't belieeeeeve what happened Saturday, damn!"

Madison, genuinely interested in something he had to say for once, looked appropriately inquisitive, and asked softly, "What wouldn't I believe, Demetrius?"

"Madison, it was crazy here, yo. Mad crazy. Shoot, you be looking for stuff to write about, this it right here. This is it!"

"Demetrius, I don't have much time, so—"

He cut Madison off quickly and began to make wild gestures with his hands.

"Well, Pilar asked me to come in and help her out with a pet project, so—"

"Wait, Pilar called you?"

"Yeah, man. She said she'd pay me $100 bucks. I wasn't doing shit, and I could use the duckets, so I said aight."

"Mmmm. Okaaay," Madison said, rubbing three fingers against her chin. "Continue, and tell me like I'm interviewing you. Don't leave anything out."

This was Madison's manipulation at its best.

Demetrius, who'd never captured Madison's attention like this, was amped to tell the story, even if he had to embellish a little bit.

"Well, I was collating all these copies for Pilar downstairs, some IPO shit, and I run up to the lobby to smoke a ciggy and I see Pilar's husband walking up to the building with some huge ass dude. So I let 'em in. Mitch said something about the dude's name being 'Roughhouse' or some shit like that. But I ain't think nothing about it, you know? Then Mitch asked where Pilar was. Just like that, like, he had to know his wife was there, so I didn't get why he was asking me where she was. Antyway, I told him she was upstairs, but she was supposed to come down to the mailroom to pick up the extra copies for me in 15 minutes. Mitch asked if he could see what I was working on for her, and I didn't think to say no, I mean, that's his wife and all, right? So anyway, Mitch and this dude come downstairs with me and he's looking at the papers, checking his watch, and whispering to his boy. I figured since he'd be in there, I'd go and holla at one of my girls. So I went into an office to use the phone in private, and a few minutes later, things got real quiet. The copier machine had stopped, and when I tried to get back in the mailroom, the door was locked. I was getting ready to knock on the door when I heard some man saying,

'Mitch, this is not what it looks like. Pilar is doing me a favor as a good friend. No need to be suspicious, I'm engaged, and Pilar is just…' Madison, I ain't hear the rest, 'cause somebody stole homeboy right in the face. I know it. I heard it. I swear I didn't see anything, Madison, but I can tell you right now, someone administered a ass whoopin on dude like he stole something. The whole thing was just 'ill! I was trying to peep through the old lock hole, but that ain't work, so I just put my ear to the glass part. So when they finally opened the door, I didn't want to disturb them 'cause I ain't want my ass beat, but they had homeboy in between them like a wet blanket, and told me to call 911 for slim. I didn't ask no questions, but in a few minutes, the ambulamps picked up shorty from outside the office building where Mitch and that dude just left him. It was 'ill, Madison, the whole thing was just 'ill! I ain't seen no shit like that go down since *Shaft*, and that's a movie. Demetrius was speaking so fast he was almost out of breath.

"Wow, Demetrius, that's deep. So what else happened, I mean is that it?"

Demetrius shifted his feet and looked around nervously. Madison was really into this story. He wouldn't disappoint her.

"Well, Madison, when they dropped this dude in front of the building, Mitch told me when Pilar wondered what happened, to tell her this, which seemed weird to me, "Three times is the charm.""

"Yeah, Demetrius, I'm with you, sounds strange. You didn't tell anyone, did you?"

"Nah, man. But that was some wack shit, and I figured since that's 'ya girl, you may be able to find out."

"You're right, Demetrius, I may be able to find out something. But let's keep this between us."

Not only was Madison giving him more attention than usual, she was trying to bond with him by keeping secrets. Okay. He'd play.

"Oh, I see, yeah right, it'll be our thing. Three times the charm, baby, three times the charm."

Madison mustered a slight smile as she walked to her desk. Hopefully, three times would be the charm, and teach Ms. Pilar to appreciate what she had at home.

CHAPTER 28

Crystal—Cherry Blossoms
Last April

"Girl, it's time."

"Ciara, I don't know. He's just begun to trust me again."

"And how many times have you caught him out there, Crystal? It's not like you were with another man...."

Crystal was speaking with her best girlfriend, whom often pushed her to make hard decisions. It came naturally to Ciara, who worked for one of the Congressional Black Caucus Congressmembers, and had to make critical decisions daily. She was a good person to talk to. Crystal didn't trust easily, especially women, but Ciara had been her friend since jr. high school.

"I know Ci Ci, but, if I give Damion the ultimatum, he might walk."

"Umm hmm. Kennedye! Leave your sister alone. Khalie, listen to Sarah or else I'm coming in there!'"

Ciara had two girls, and if Crystal didn't get her point across soon, she'd lose Ciara to the girls.

"Look, Crystal. It's your birthday, and you guys have been together, how many years?"

"5", Crystal murmured weakly.

"Alright. So if it's been. Wait...'Kennedye! I'm warning you, little girl. Barney will be a distant memory in 3 seconds if you don't stop messing with Khailie!!!' So if it's been five years, what's his excuse, Crystal?"

"Well, he says he wants to get himself together financially, first, before he gets married."

"He or we, Crystal? Have you discussed marriage with Damion, before?"

"Not specifically."

"Well, it's time for specifics. Take the plunge. It's been 5 years. Trust me. He knows what he wants. I've got to go turn off Barney. Call me and tell me what happens, and happy birthday, girl." Ciara hung up before Crystal could say anything.

Secretly she hoped Damion would give her a ring for her birthday, but her gut told her it was wishful thinking. However, she was really starting to be embarrassed in front of her peers, whom she knew talked about her and Damion and their marathon relationship. Now would be a good time. She was settled in her career, she could help Damion escalate his, and they would be a good power couple, envied my many. Since she didn't have the lineage, Crystal needed to climb her way up the bloodline ladder the old fashioned way, starting with Jack and Jill, Cotillion participation, and associating with DC politicos and the Old Money Socialites. It was all about being in the right circles.

Crystal's birthday turned out to be a glorious day. She and Damion planned to have brunch at the Corcoran Gallery of Art, and walk along the tidal basin and admire the cherry blossoms. It had become their tradition. But this year, if Damion hadn't given Crystal the gift she wanted by the time they reached Potomac Park, that's when she would give him the ultimatum.

Brunch was spectacular. Damion looked good, smelled good and still made her heart pitter patter, even after 5 years. He had to see how good they were together. Their status as a super couple of the DC Elite wouldn't be complete until Damion blew up and/or they got married.

Damion paused and looked at the Jefferson memorial. He cocked his head as if pondering something really deep. He put his arm around Crystal, and said thoughtfully, "Baby, I think Jefferson was obsessed with the circle. I mean look at his memorial, look at the Rotunda at UVA, and I bet ten to one Sally Hemmings had a big, round, ass. I mean, he kept her around when all hell broke loose, took her to Paris, everything. Round."

"Maybe he liked circles because they represent infinity."

Damion looked at her and smiled.

"Okay, I give it to you, You might be right, rabbit. You might be right."

"I can get deep, too, Negro, you ain't the only one."

Damion laughed and took out envelope out of his jacket pocket.

"Okay, baby, ready for your birthday present?"

Crystal pretended like she was trying to see through the envelope.

"Sure, but that envelope doesn't look like a small jewelry box to me."

"Girl, you've got jokes!"

"I'm serious, Damion."

"Anyway, baby, for your birthdayyyyyy, we are going to spend the weekend at the Four Seasons in Georgetown, and catch a show at Constitution Hall, featuring…"

Damion pretended like he was doing a drum roll, dramatically slicing his fingers through the chilly air.

"Our very own homegrown Michelle N'dege Ocello and Maysa! You KNOW they 'gone jam, baby… I can't wait!"

Damion ended with a huge smile and raised his arms Rocky victory style and waited for a reaction from Crystal. He'd gotten the tickets from the station, but springing for the Four Seasons would cost him a grip. But Crystal was cool. She'd been very understanding about his schedule, lately. Working with the contractors for his rowhouse was tedious. He had to constantly stay on them.

"That's great," Crystal said less than enthusiastically, as a tear betrayed her and fell from her face.

Damion looked confused and led Crystal to a nearby bench.

"What's the matter, baby? Why are you crying? Are you not happy with your gift? I know how you feel about Constitution Hall, but we have REALLY good seats."

"Damion," Crystal began slowly. "You see these cherry blossoms?"

"Baby, what do cherry blossoms have to do with you crying?"

Crystal ignored Damion and continued her story.

"The Japanese gave these to us as a goodwill gift. They are a symbol of beauty and we expect them to bloom every year. We know they are going to be there, and people come to DC from around the world to admire them year after year."

Damion shifted uncomfortably.

"What I'm saying is, we've been dating 5 years. You expect me to be there, day after day, year after year. Same 'ol Crystal, faithful 'ol Crystal. Guys try to hollar at me all the time. They admire me. But the one person I want to be a gift for, lay down roots with, seems to take me for granted. Like I'll always be here, blooming for you, on the daily. I don't know how much longer I can do this, Damion. I want a family, a husband, children. You know this, but you keep messing around, giving me excuses. I just…" Crystal was so caught up in emotion, she couldn't continue with her thoughts, and began to sob uncontrollably.

Damion was more than uncomfortable, and thought only of escape.

"Baby, baby, please don't cry." Damion held her close and tried to fight the feeling of suffocation creeping through his veins, racing for his heart. He didn't know why Crystal couldn't just talk to him, making some shit up about some cherry blossoms was just unnecessary. But he didn't want a scene, not here, not now. He'd do his best to placate her and then figure out what he would do, later.

Crystal felt awful. She was caught between trying to do what seemed logical, and struggling with matters of the heart. If he walked, she would lose him to someone else, she was sure of it. On the other hand, if she didn't force the issue, the relationship might continue like this for another five years. Then she'd be past 35, with no guarantees, and that wouldn't be good, that wouldn't be good at all.

"So what are you saying, Crystal?" Damion said softly, knowing he had to tread carefully at this point.

Crystal swallowed deeply, and tried her best to control her queasy stomach. She continued a few minutes later, after the tumultuous waves of fear subsided.

"I think you need to think about what you want. What you want from me," she mumbled, and absent mindedly plucked a cherry blossom from one of the trees. "I am here for you Damion, and I love you deeply, but I love myself more."

Damion released his vise-like grip and positioned himself so they were face to face. His shallow breathing engulfed her. He was so close he could have kissed her full, luscious lips. Crystal didn't like having him this close. He clouded her thoughts and jumpstarted her emotions. She loved him so much, she thought she would faint. But she called on the ancestors of all the strong women in her family, took a deep breath and let the ultimatum fly.

"What I want, Damion, is for you to call me when you've had some time to think about whether you want to marry me or not."

Damion stood rooted to the spot. Was she giving him an ultimatum? Not Crystal? She must have been talking to one of her girlfriends. Damn! And she had been so cool, lately. Ah, well. He would get through dinner, and then see what happened. Crystal never stuck to her guns. When she caught him cheating the first time, she swore if it ever happened again, she'd leave him. He straightened up for a little while, but the ass kept calling, just like the crack called Pookie in *New Jack City*. Crystal fumed for about 6 weeks, but eventually she came back around. He'd probably just wait her out, see what happened. He needed to concentrate on getting into his place, anyway.

Crystal was so scared she was trembling. She knew Damion well, but not well enough to know how he would respond to an ultimatum. He hadn't said a word.

Just looked at her with his big pretty doe eyes and took in every word she said, spoken and unspoken. Should she walk away now, or let him take her to dinner? She deserved that much, but it would be more dramatic if she walked away. Crystal looked at the blossom in her hand for a long time, and said to Damion, who hadn't moved an inch, "It will die, now," and threw it in the Potomac. Both Crystal and Damion watched it float for a minute, and then sink into oblivion. That's when Crystal decided to make her exit. Hooray for the damn cherry blossom. Who would think nature would have helped her make her case so eloquently?

Damion watched helplessly as she walked away, but didn't try to stop her. He knew Crystal well enough to know now was not the time. He turned back towards the water where the delicate flower submerged and shook his head.

"Fucking cherry blossom," he muttered, and walked towards his car.

CHAPTER 29

Damion—A House Becomes a Home
May 2000

Madison had an eye. She could take a color from some abstract thing, like a towel, and use the scheme in acquiring just the right pieces, the combination of which made a cold room warm. Damion gave her the green light for decorating when he moved into his place. She responded to the challenge, too. Madison lit up when she spoke of a throw rug she saw that would go great in front of the fireplace, or a specially carved paper towel holder that would offset the kitchen cabinets, and so on and so on. She was a natural, and Damion could see how this was bringing them closer together. He realized that Madison was really loving, she just needed some time to warm up.

One Sunday she came over especially buoyed.

"Baby, I saw a great entertainment center at Best Buy that would be perfect for the family room."

"How much, Madison?"

"Only $850."

"ONLY $850!" Damion pretended to leaf through his wallet checking for cash.

"JUST $850!" Madison snatched one of his credit cards.

"Next you'll be wanting a washing machine."

"I saw one at Sears, but it will be less during the Memorial Day holiday. So let's go get that entertainment center, Daddy."

Damion loved when Madison played like that, she was usually so reserved and serious.

"How do I know the entertainment center won't be on sale Memorial day?"

"I spoke with the manager, who told me they were going to mark it up to mark it down during the holiday."

"So how can you trust him, baby?"

"He's dating my girl Heather. And if Heather's not happy, he's not happy. He knows the rules. Plus he's going to give us a 20% discount. So let's go!"

"Okay, baby, you should have been a litigator."

"Come on Damion," Madison chided, pushing him towards the door. "You have no sense of urgency, so let's go, and I'll drive."

"Baby?"

"What!?"

"Can I get some pussy first?"

"Damion let's go!"

Damion happily followed Madison out the door and thought about how easy most things were with her. She seemed complicated, yet didn't complicate things with them. She kept things, simple, clean, predictable. In bed she was willing, eager, experimental. Madison was turning out to be a real keeper.

When he got in the car, Madison told him to make a list of the groceries he thought he needed so they could go by Costco since they'd be on the Maryland side. He didn't have a pen, so she told him to get one from the glove compartment, which was stuffed with DC parking tickets. Madison was so funny sometimes, most of the time, she was Ms. Goody Two Shoes, but she hated bureaucracy, and to her, there was something wrong with an inefficient government that had somehow mastered the art of ticketing, so she wasn't diligent about paying her infractions. Seeing the crumpled up pink menaces, Damion turned his thoughts to Crystal.

True to her word, she hadn't called in the past month. He'd give her another two weeks to break down, but he'd give her a courtesy call next week, to show he missed her. That was expected behavior, so he'd go along with it.

They had to go to a Best Buy in Maryland to get the discount. Surprisingly, they ran into Rod with his new girlfriend Tyra. They gave each other a hug and the grip, and started talking about his new place. The girls bonded after they caught each other rolling eyes at their men. Before long, Madison and Tyra were acting like old friends, and were making plans to have a small set at Damion's place in the next few weeks. They even talked about double dating for the upcoming Frankie Beverly and Maze concert. Rod called Damion over to look at car speakers.

"Baby you don't need car speakers," Madison chided.

"Rod. I don't need to remind you that YOU really don't need car speakers," Tyra teased.

"Woman, be quiet!" Rod joked. "This is man stuff, you wouldn't understand."

"Whateva, nigga!" Tyra whispered loudly as she and Madison walked towards the movie section.

"Damion. Man WHAT the fuck is going on?" Rod asked once he figured he was a safe distance from the girls.

"Nothing, man. Chillin."

"Man, I'm talking about Crystal, man." He looked over at Madison. "I thought homegirl was just temporary."

"Man, Crystal gave me an ultimatum, and I'm giving her her space."

"But man, you need to make up your mind. You 'gone mess me up with Tyra, because now she knows Madison, so what happens when she meets Crystal?"

Damion shrugged his shoulders.

"Man, she's 'gone to think I'm a 'playa too. You know, that birds of a feather flock together bullshit?"

"Rod, man, you reading too much into it." He thumbed his finger towards the last direction where he saw Tyra. "How you know this babe is gonna be around for awhile?"

Rod looked at Damion.

"Man, you really don't know do you?"

Damion looked at him quizzically.

"Naw, man. Apparently I don't know."

Rod lowered his voice confidentially, checked to see if the girls were in sight, but far enough where they could speak with no inhibitions.

"It hasn't been that long, but it feels like—well, when I'm with Tyra, no matter if she's dressed up with some nice heels, or we're just hanging out and she's in sweats, it just feels like home."

Funny how you know truth when you hear it. Damion knew exactly what he meant because that's how he felt about Madison, and Rod was able to put it into words.

By this time, Madison had used Damion's card to pay for the furniture, arranged for the free delivery (courtesy of Heather's man) and was whisking them out the door. When they got in the car, Madison stressed the importance of going to Costco while they were on the Maryland side. She gave him the Best Buy receipt and Damion noticed she'd written Tyra's number on the back. Shit, there might be some merit in what Rod said after all. Ah well.

The trip to Costco was relatively painless. The parking lot was a labyrinth, and the shoppers hovered over the merchandise like Atlantic City gamblers hungry for winnings. But those things were expected. What was unexpected, however, was a

Crystal friend spotting. Damion heard insistent honking as he and Madison loaded the car. He turned around and saw Beverlyn, one of Crystal's golf buddies. After she saw that he saw her, she left Damion with the searing image of her middle finger and spun off. She would most certainly take the report back to Crystal. Maybe this would make Crystal call, but no worries, he would tell her he was helping his boy Rubin's cousin acclimate to the area, as she had just relocated, something like that. Mentioning names was always better than just saying, "a buddy of mine, or a friend," women always got suspicious when they think you're evading them, not trying to tell the whole truth. Damion was good. As smart as Crystal was, she didn't realize that every time she caught him in a lie, or some ill-intentioned thing, she would tell him. So he'd figure out another way. It's the same concept behind first time law offenders going to jail—they just become better criminals.

When they got back to Damion's, Madison went straight to work, putting away food, and preparing a quick and healthy snack for them. She did all of this while Damion plopped on the sofa and idly flipped through the channels, settling lazily on a basketball game.

His phone rang. The Caller ID told him it was who he thought it would be. Crystal. He didn't answer.

Madison came out of his kitchen with a tray of food for him; she'd insisted he purchase a couple of TV trays from Pier One, and laid it on his lap. He was glad he listened to her. She had a smidgen of flour on her cheek, and her hair was slightly askew. Madison would have probably died if she knew her hair was out of place; but this made her so, so, vulnerable. He wanted to tell her then and there how much he loved her, but made a joke instead.

"Baby, you doing lines in there or something? You made this wonderfully-smelling meal lightening quick, and you've got white powder on your face. What's up with that?"

Madison looked confused, then broke into a hearty laugh, when she understood the joke.

"And that's why I'm 'gone take my peach cobbler home with me, because of your wild imagination," she threatened.

"Who's cobbler? Yours or your mama's?"

"Mama's, asshole. I just got the recipe from her last week."

Damion put his tray on the coffee table and grabbed Madison and squeezed her until she complained of not being able to breathe.

"Madison, you know I can't wait for that cobbler, girl." He was interrupted by the incessant ringing of the telephone.

"Answer that, I gotta check on my cobbler," Madison said gaily and wrestled out of his arms, then high stepped into the kitchen like she was a majorette.

Damion watched her until he was out of sight, and against his better judgement, answered the phone. He couldn't risk Crystal doing a drive-by, and coming over. Because she would.

"Hello?"

"Who is that bitch, Damion?"

"Well, it's nice to hear from you, been a long time," Damion said sarcastically.

"I know she's there, Damion! So is that why you don't want to marry me?"

"I don't know what you're talking about." Damion refused to call her name, just in case Madison could hear.

"For some tall bitch in a red Acura?"

"Oh, that, Damion said. Why don't we meet later, and I'll explain the mix up to you, say around 8:30 or so? At the Diner? See you there."

Madison came out of the kitchen drying her hand on a dishtowel as Damion hung up the phone.

"Who was that, baby?"

"Oh, some contractor I kicked to the curb last month because they were taking shortcuts. We're getting together tonight so we can finish talking about how much he's going to discount me, you know?"

"Alright, the cobbler will be done in about 20 minutes, then I gotta run. I didn't see any ice cream in the freezer, you sure do go through that stuff fast, we could have gotten some from Costco."

"That's alright, baby, I can just run to the corner store and get some vanilla bean."

"Right, and it will be overpriced, too, Damion. You've got to watch your spending, baby, you're a homeowner, now."

"You're right, baby," Damion said, and kissed her passionately on her unsuspecting lips. She returned the kiss and looked deeply into his eyes. "I want to thank you for making my house a home. I love you." He couldn't believe he'd said it. But, he did, and he meant it.

CHAPTER 30

Madison—More Hot Water?
The Present, June 2000

"Where is she? I know that bitch is here?!"

The screaming jolted me out of my reverie. I was pruning in a tub full of tepid, sudless water. Yuck! I'd told Damion to get a jet tub, he could be rather hard-headed at times.

The neighbors next door must have been going at it! One thing about these DC rowhouses, when your windows were raised you could hear everything in the neighborhood.

I got up and dried off. I don't know how much time had passed, but Damion should have been upstairs by now. Maybe his boy, Rashaud, was coming by to clean Damion's throw rugs. Several of them received paint spots from the "professional" painters. But Rashaud was good. He could get a spot out of a leopard. I moisturized, slipped on something comfortable, walked from the bathroom and flipped on the TV. It was 9:00! What the heck?! Thirsty, I opened the door to head downstairs to get some water and Damion nearly ran me down from the opposite side.

"Baby, what's wrong with you? You look like you've seen a ghost. Have you? Maybe they don't want you here," I said jokingly.

Damion gently took me by the shoulders and led me towards the bed. He hadn't looked this distraught since the first time we made love last November.

"Baby, I need you to do me a favor," Damion looked mega nervous.

"You trust me, right?"

"Of course baby, what's wrong? You have me really scared, now. Is Nana okay?"

"Nana is fine. But an old friend of mine just found out her mother has terminal cancer. She is a wreck, and I'm just trying to make her feel better. So if you don't mind, I'm going to ask you to give me a minute with her. We'll go to dinner this evening, ok?"

"Wow," I said, immediately feeling horrible for the girl downstairs. "What would you like me to do? You want me to cook something?"

"No, baby. I'm sure she doesn't feel like eating."

"Well, okay," I said hesitantly. "Let me get dressed and I'll see you in a few minutes." Geez. I can't imagine how I would feel if I found out my mom was terminally ill. I'd just leave most of my stuff here and see Damion later. He had one more nugget for me, though.

"Uh, baby?"

"Yes, Damion?"

"Can you just let yourself out the back door? I don't want my friend to get all nervous, or feel bad because she disturbed me, which she did," he managed to joke while tapping my behind, squeezed in my favorite pair of Levi's.

I'd have to watch it. Since Damion and I have been dating, I've picked up a few pounds.

But now wasn't the time to worry about extra pounds, I had to fight the red flag that jumped in my soul from nowhere. It would be okay. I trusted Damion. He wasn't like some of these other brothers, who were assholes and proud of it.

Damion watched me expectantly, as I wrestled with my gut and breeding, which taught me to be a lady in all cases, and to never, ever, show anyone what I'm really feeling.

"Not a problem baby," I managed to eke out between gritted teeth. "Take care of your friend. I'll just speak with you later?"

Damion looked relieved.

"Thank you so much baby! You are simply righteous!" Damion's face lit up like a little boy, which made me feel good inside. "I'll hit you up."

Damion turned and left the room just as hurriedly as he'd entered.

Still not quite sure what just transpired, I put on one of Damion's long-sleeved tees, since my jacket was in the downstairs closet, and dug my car keys out of my handbag. I'm glad it was June. When I went downstairs, I had an uneasy feeling about leaving through the back door. I mean, I felt like I was the other chick who had just gotten busted with the man she knew she was sharing, and had to sneak away.

"Shit!" I murmured when I realized my car was blocked in by a white convertible BMW with personalized tags that read, "DCJUDGE." I called Damion, but of course he didn't answer. I thought about knocking, but didn't want to disturb his friend, or make her feel uncomfortable. Against my better judgement, I walked to the bus stop, and took the S4 home. Damion called around 7:30 that evening, and begged off dinner, saying he was called into work. He stopped by and took me to get my car, but then he needed to go. He offered no further explanation of what transpired earlier. I was ok with that. I was still feeling weird about the back door thing, and wasn't quite sure how to deal with it. I got carry-out from Chipotle, and went to bed early. I had a long day tomorrow, plus I had to go to court after getting so many freaking tickets.

The next morning it seemed as if God just opened up the heavens and gathered up all the emotions of the sad women in the world, and just let 'er rip. It rained buckets non-stop, which did nothing for my mood. When I got to parking adjudication on K Street around noon, it seemed like everyone and their mother showed up to fight tickets, and they all parked close to the building. It was hard to see through such a downpour, but I decided to take one more turn in front of the building before I parked in the last available spot in the hinterlands. As I slow-rode close to the front, a car was pulling out of a space less than 10 feet from the building. That's what I'm talking about! My luck was beginning to change. I squeezed in the space and jumped out of the car, dodging soggy potholes full of pebbles and dirt.

I successfully stayed on solid ground until I was one step away from entering the building. I'd celebrated too soon. My left shoe stepped into a puddle the size of a large ice bucket. Hopefully the leather Via Spiga's would not stretch. My pantyhose would dry. I got in and checked the docket. No Madison Robinson. Undaunted, I went to see if the girl behind the information desk would be able to point me in the right direction. I waited 10 minutes while she spoke with Pee Wee the security guard, who weighed about 300 pounds. Their conversation was uninteresting and mundane to me, as they compared the best go-go band of all time. It seemed that Trouble Funk and Rare Essence were running neck and neck, and Experience Unlimited had just been eliminated. I had a legitimate issue, and they just didn't give a damn. Typical. I cleared my throat.

"Excuse, me?"

Little Ms. Go Go peeked around big man, and curled her lips while glaring at me, daring me to disturb her petty ass conversation. I had lost my patience. Sometimes you had to fight ignorance with ignorance, and I was in no mood.

The thing with Damion was not sitting well with me. Part of me wanted to talk about it with my girls, especially Stacey, but I didn't, because I knew she would have something to say. Something I didn't want to hear.

"I'm a reporter working on a story for *The Chocolate City Voice*," I said firmly. Their necks jerked around like swizzle sticks. I had their attention. "My name, Madison Robinson is not on the docket, and I want a judge, now, or else the article will not shed DC Government in a good light, and trust me, I'm sure your supervisor won't be happy when you make the front page, Ms. India," I emphasized, reading her name badge. All of a sudden, Pee Wee moved like he was sliding on grease. He could move for a big man. And Ms. India started stuttering and apologizing while picking up the phone and calling into chamber neverland. She called until she got someone. I arched my neck to let her know I was paying close attention to what she said. I even took my reporter's notebook out of my bag for emphasis. I watched her intently as she tried to turn her back and cup the phone so I wouldn't hear. Poor Pee Wee, he was standing at the door greeting people as they walked in and saying 'good bye, and have a nice day,' when people left.

"Yes, maam," she whispered. "Yes, maam, your last case of the day... yes, maam. Uh, and she's a reporter."

I shifted my feet and looked at my watch.

"Yes, maam, I'll send her right down, Ms. Leonard."

She hung up the receiver and looked at me with big scared, eyes, like I had her trapped in a cage she couldn't escape from.

"Maam, if you could just go down the hall and turn left, you'll be in the judge's hearing room, room A 101." I looked really hard at her, peering at her name badge for effect, making it appear as if I was going to report her trifling behind. She shirked from my steely gaze, and I rolled my eyes, DC-style, and walked down the hall, with one wet foot and saggy pantyhose, laughing inside. Leverage.

The hearing room was empty when I walked in, with the exception of a bored rent-a-cop and a tired-looking dried, slow-moving cleaning woman dusting the benches. A petite red-head sister was behind the dais and kept looking at her watch. She looked familiar, but then again, DC was like that. Everyone looked like you'd seen them at one time or another. She looked at me, sighed heavily and picked up my file. It was pretty thick. "Ms. Robinson?"

"Yes."

"You can take the first seat on the right. You're my last case for the day."

"Thank you," I leaned over to straighten my wet, wrinkled panyhose.

"Ms. Robinson, you've got over $500.00 in parking infractions. Do you deliver pizzas?"

I chuckled.

"No, no. I'm just on the go a lot."

"Well, you need to slow down."

"You're right," I said matter of factly. "I don't have any excuse, just need to take more time trying to find legitimate parking."

The woman seemed relieved that I didn't make up some elaborate story. Who knows the type of lies she was told on a daily basis?

"Well, since you're not full of excuses, I'll reduce your fee. Just pay half, and slow down!"

I wondered if the little woman behind the big dais wanted to seem amenable because she knew I was a reporter.

"Thank you... uh, what's your name."

"Crystal Leonard." I did know her.

"Oh, Crystal. I thought I recognized you. You know Six, right?"

Crystal stood up, grabbed her handbag and stepped from behind the desk. She was a little thing, but you could tell she had a lot of fire in her belly.

"Of course I know Six. Doesn't she know everyone?"

"Yep. Just like the theory, six degrees of separation."

We both laughed in unison, thinking about Six.

"Where'd you meet Six?" Crystal asked.

"We met at an A group meeting, and—"

"What?!" Crystal interrupted excitedly. "She brought me in the A group, but I haven't seen you."

"Well, my boyfriend takes me out of town most weekends."

"I hear you. I hardly see my boyfriend on the weekends," she said somewhat melancholy. "I'll walk out with you, Ms. Robinson."

"You can call me Madison," I said amiably. "I really like your bag."

"Thanks, Madison. It's a Jackie Ashton bag."

"Nice. I haven't heard of her though, can I get one at a major retail store, or a Trade Secrets or something like that?"

"You can get one by calling her. I have her card in my car."

"Really? She's that talented and that accessible?"

"Yep. She's that cool, too. I'm right out front, so it won't take long."

"Okay, let me stop at the window and pay these tickets real quick—"

"Don't worry about it," Crystal said, "I'll take care of them. No worries."

"But, the least—"

"Don't worry about it," Crystal said. "You're going to need that money to buy a Jackie Ashton bag."

"You know it!" I said, laughing. Funny how men could bond over sports, and women could bond over shoes and handbags.

I waited while Crystal went to speak to one of the clerks. The girl peered around Crystal and rolled her eyes at me before printing out a zero receipt for my infractions. My slate was clean. What a cool gesture by Crystal. We just met and she's already demonstrating value add. It pays to know the right people.

"As we passed the information desk, India found her voice. "Have a good day, Ms. Leonard. Good-bye, maam," she said apologetically, and lowered her eyelashes in perfect submission. Pee Wee was right there, too, as if he'd never left. "It's stopped raining, out, but be careful of the mud holes, Ms. Leonard," he wheezed. Big negro like that, he looked like he had respiratory problems. "Big man ain't lying," I laughed, looking at Crystal. "I stepped in one on my way in," I ventured, holding up my foot with my slightly wrinkled hose.

"Oh, I wondered why you kept picking at your legs." She had a hearty laugh.

Before we hit the sliding glass doors, I looked back at the Keystone cop and Ms. Thing and said "By the way, Chuck Brown is Go-Go," leaving them with their mouths open. We walked out front, and the sun was shining like it was auditioning to be the sole natural heat source for the world. It didn't take long to get to Crystal's car, a convertible white BMW, parked right next to my car.

"Oh, I'm right next to you. The red car. How ironic is that?"

"Yep, it was meant for us to meet today." Crystal used her remote to unlock her car, which looked frighteningly familiar. When I parked, I hadn't notice it with all the rain. I slowed down to a mere crawl while she searched a bag in the back seat. When she couldn't find what she was looking for, she went to the back and opened the trunk. I asked myself, how many white convertible BMWs could there be in the District of Columbia? There had to be several. "I know I have her card in here somewhere," she said, sounding muffled since her head was buried behind the lid of the trunk.

"I keep her cards on me, because women are always complimenting me. I have four Jackie bags, already. I'm just waiting for her to blow up," Crystal mused.

I found myself drawn like a magnet to the front of the car. I couldn't take my eyes off of her personalized tags. The words "DC JUDGE" went in and out of focus as I fought the urge to cry and regurgitate simultaneously. Her voice startled me out of my trance.

"Here you go, Madison," she said cheerfully. "I knew I had some."

I couldn't move. Crystal forced the card in my hand. "Don't worry, girl. Ms.

Jackie's prices won't make you cry too bad, are you okay?"

"I should be asking you, that, Crystal. I am sooo sorry to hear about your mom."

"Excuse me?"

"Your mom. Damion told me yesterday when you came over that she had cancer, and..." I trailed off, feeling totally stupid.

Crystal's expression changed in an instant. Her squinted eyes made her look Asian all of a sudden. After looking me up and down, she stared really closely at my car. The same car she'd blocked in yesterday.

"You? My mother? You??" Crystal twisted her mouth to the side while she contemplated what to do next. I stood there feeling like this was some serious twilight zone shit. Maybe, just maybe, the mother story wasn't true after all. "You are the woman that was upstairs! Damion told me you had plumbing problems in your house, and you needed to use his shower, and that you were just someone he met in his neighborhood who organized the block parties."

"I live in Brightwood," I said, wondering why I offered so much information to this woman, who now seemed like the not-so-nice stranger you meet freshman year in college, and you're forced to share the same dorm room. She got it out first.

"How do you know Damion?"

"He's my boyfriend."

My voice sounded hollow.

'He's my boyfriend," she said confidently. "Of five years, and there ain't nothing wrong with my momma." This was about to get ugly. Why is it when something traumatic happens you never feel like you're existing in that movement and time, like you're on another planet or something, on the outside looking in? Go figure.

"We ARE dating," I looked down on her. My heart was pounding so fast it felt like a newborn's heartbeat. "...and there ain't nothing wrong with my pipes!"

She stood her ground. I stood my ground, although I was trembling inside. I couldn't believe this. I couldn't believe I was in this situation. I needed Stacey. Although tiny, this woman had spunk. I was so confused, I was immobilized. Crystal's phone rang. She ignored it. It rang again. She looked at the display, glared at it, and answered with pure ire in her voice. "You're in hot water, mothafucker!" She walked towards the back of her car and turned her back to me while she rivaled the vocabulary of any seasoned marine. I used the moment to jump in my car and roll out; I would deal with Damion later. Maybe. But Crystal was right. He WAS in hot water.

From Madison's Journal

June, 2000

Dear Journal, I know I haven't written in a while. I've been caught up with work and Damion, whom I just found out has another woman. I'm sick. I hurt to my bones. I can't believe it. All this time, and he was hiding this... secret? This fucking sucks.

A Secret's Not a Secret
He trespassed on my heart
Trampolined on my soul
Torn asunder, now we must part
As I fight to restore my half to whole

How could this have occurred
I thought I did everything right
Believed in him, renewed dreams deferred
And Loved heartily, with all my might

What makes a man stray
What makes a man cheat
What makes a man lie
What makes a man play
What makes a man try
What makes a man attempt to beat—
The odds?

My whole world has turned upside down
My stomach has turned right side up
My insides are pinched in an infinite frown
My outside, emotional dishonesty abounds

I should have seen the signs
They've been there a long time
Sometimes crooked, sometimes a straight and obvious line
Unraveling the ties that bind
Leaving me to find…and rediscover…myself

A secret is not a secret—just a shadow of doubt
Then your gut comes to life
Whispering so loud it shouts
Slicing your hopes and dreams with a knife
Turning a blue sky gray, hiding the sun, bringing the clouds out

But after the rain
Comes a new day
And after the pain
That 'ol road paves a new way

To survive
To live
To love…
Again

CHAPTER 31

Madison—The Hottest Summer Ever
July 2000

It was July 15. It was hot, funky, humid and 97 degrees. My air conditioning unit was fighting a losing battle with the savage heat. And Damion had called me approximately 147 times since I ran into his...his.... I still can't say it... special friend. They can have each other. I have lost 10 pounds, two girlfriends, and the respect of my father. Okay, I'm exaggerating there. I can't tell my father. He will kill Damion and who needs that? My work has suffered, for real, and I had to take a small sabbatical from the *Chocolate City Voice*. I am not handling this well. I don't know if it's the betrayal, the big fat Lie that we were, or the fact that I am single. Again. I'd allowed myself to be happy, to believe I was on my way to what my parents have. I was a fish on a hook with my nose wide open. Now I'm flapping on dry land, balled up in a fetal position on my unmade bed and I can't stop crying. I failed. And the hurt is deep. Soul deep. Gut wrenching deep.

The past few weeks have been hell. After I left parking adjudication, I drove straight home, put on my flannel pajamas to try and warm my cold soul, and started playing records and tapes, yeah, I said records, from the 80's and 90's. Sad records. Artists like Marlena Shaw, Phyllis Hyman, Nina Simone and Cassandra Wilson. I lay there and unraveled the past several months searching for what I should have seen, clues, innuendos, red flags. The pieces came together like an advanced jigsaw puzzle slowly, surely. I would begin a sequence, reviewing a fact, an incident, an expression. It wouldn't add up, I would start over. I was obsessed with figuring it all out before I could move on. Meanwhile, I could only really drink tea. My stomach was a bundle of nerves that never stopped churning. It felt like my stomach lining was on the edge of a precipice and leaned, but never quite fell over, like I was on my tippy toes, tempting the edge to crumble so I could fall into the blank, dark world of nothingness and oblivion. And believe me, that was enough to keep me from solid food, for if I forced myself to eat, I paid homage to the porcelain god, until I excreted my insides, beckoning dehydration to invade my body and reign supreme.

My mom came over and left chicken soup and groceries and Gatorade in front of the door I wouldn't answer. The last time she'd seen me like this I was 7, and had grown too tall for gymnastics. I just knew I would be the next Nadia Comaneci. Then I got cut from the traveling team. Reality is a bitch. But now I needed to finish the puzzle to put some of me back together again.

It wasn't until I listened to Phyllis Hyman's "Living in Confusion" did I get some clarity. Her pain was palpable, her voice so pure and genuine. I remember when I first met Crystal at the Black Family Reunion. Six said her boyfriend "D" was DJ at the WJAZ tent. Now it makes sense. Puzzle piece 1. Then Stacey put the answer in my hand when she called last year to ask me, "Why do bitches always get the man?" She'd actually seen Crystal and Damion, handed me the bastard on a platter, and I didn't make the connection, didn't want to see it. I chose instead to believe his sorry ass rape story, and didn't listen to my gut. Momma was right. The gut always knows. Then what about that night I called Damion to tell him about Stacey's pipes, he seemed so standoffish. Was he with her, then? Puzzle piece. Damion gave me lots of advice on how to handle all the parking tickets I received. The key was, how did he know? Now I knew. Then, let's see, I knew there was more, I just needed to concentrate on the pattern. The ski trip, the A group, the countless weekends out of town. The strategy locked more puzzle pieces into shape; click. He didn't want to get caught. Click. He didn't want me to meet Crystal at any of the A group meetings; click click click. Tap tap tap. Someone was at my door, knocking timidly but incessantly. Tap tap tap tap tap. Geez Louise. Whoever it was, I wished they'd go away. Tap tap. I went to my room and plopped on the bed and turned on Oprah. Tap tap. Pause. Tap tap tap.

Maybe it was Damion. I could actually cuss him out. I'd experienced a slew of emotions. I was past the shock, the hurt still hurt like hell, but now I was angry. How dare he? I jumped off my bed from the strength of anger and propelled myself towards the front door. I was so sure it was him, I didn't think to look through the peephole. When I swung open the door, I saw my neighbor Penelope, who looked both resolute and apologetic at the same time. She took in my raggedy appearance, matted hair and bloodshot eyes and permanent frown (for the moment) and shifted her feet nervously or impatiently, I couldn't tell. I really could care less, she wasn't Damion. It was then I realized how much I wanted to, make that needed to see him. This couldn't be real. Did I really feel a twang of desire? I shook it off. No, it couldn't be.

"What do you want, Penelope?"

"I need some of your Braggs amino acid to season some string beans I'm 'cookin,'" she explained. "You 'bout the only person I know in the building that would have it."

"When are you going to return it, Penelope?"

"Girl you know I'm 'gone give it right back to you!"

Penelope shifted and grinned, evidence of not so good intent.

"You still haven't returned my Zane collection, and I'm waiting for it," I teased walking towards the kitchen.

"Girl, you know I'll get those back to you, soon. I like to read them over and over again." Penelope was funny and chock full of contradictions.

"Well, maybe you need to buy your own," I half-shouted while I shuffled through my cabinets.

"Girl, you know I need the bang bang!"

I genuinely laughed. Penelope was a little older, probably in her mid-forties, but she had a libido to match any teenager.

It took some time, but I finally found the dark liquid, and as I turned to go back in the living room, I heard the door slam. I don't know why, but the hairs on the back of my neck rose. I stopped like a deer in headlights, hands in mid-air. I heard a slight scuffle, then a suppressed, high-pitched squeal. I peeked my head out to see if I'd need my great-grandmother's black skillet, which she affectionately called, "the spider." You can say what you want to, but that spider pan could and would knock the living daylights out of an intruder, if need be. I must have been hallucinating; no way Paul and Stacey were sitting on my sofa. It had to be my imagination because they weren't at each other's throats. I tiptoed to the living room, vying to get out and get some fresh air. They both spoke simultaneously.

"What's wrong with you, little sis?"

"What the hell is wrong with your dramatic ass, Madison?"

I snapped from my brief reverie.

"Paul? Stacey? What? Why? Penelope?"

Stacey looked at Paul.

"She really must be sick. Since when have you known Madison to state the obvious in such a fascinating manner?"

Paul nodded his head in agreement.

"Baby sis. Mom told me she left groceries at your door. You're not a little girl anymore, so I know it's not the fact that you didn't make the gymnastics team."

"And Maisie hasn't seen your little crusty fingernails for a month, and Bruce hasn't washed your nappy head in three weeks. That says T-R-O-U-B-L-E," piped Stacey. She always accentuated the negative when she was nervous.

I was stunned.

"I can't believe I'm getting ambushed by my brother and best friend. It's not that serious!" I shouted, my voice trembling uncontrollably. "And where the fuck is Penelope! I need to give her this Braggs Amino before...before..." I couldn't finish my sentence. I crumpled and dropped the little bottle on the floor.

Paul jumped up and grabbed me before I followed the bottle. Of course my tears betrayed me. I cried until I began to dry-heave. Stacey stayed rooted to the sofa, speechless for once, big, fat, teardrops wearing a path down her soft cheeks.

Paul took over. He led me to my favorite big chair, sat me down with such tenderness and gentleness, it seemed to accentuate my helplessness. I broke down again. Freaking A! I wish I wasn't so weak. Paul went to the kitchen and I heard him opening cabinets, probably trying to find some tea or a snack. Good luck, Paul, I hadn't been to the grocery store, either. Stacey handed me some rumpled up tissue she found in her handbag, and rediscovered her voice.

"It's that nigga isn't it?"

I waited a long time before I answered. Stacey's determined silence dared me to not to speak.

"I, I met his ex-girlfriend," I stammered. Leave it to Stacey to get right to the point.

"If that is his ex, then why are you tripping?"

"I—" It registered on Stacey's face that she got it.

"You what, Madison? I told you that nigga was shady from jump. Didn't your gut tell you something?"

"Is that a rhetorical question?"

"Madison, baby. This is no time for 'trippin and using big ass words, this is a time for you to get up. Look at yourself. Check your insides. Get up. Get over it. Survive him. Women share their men everyday, all over the world, and in some places it's legal, but how do you feel about that?"

"Feel about what?" Paul asked, coming from the kitchen with a bag of pretzels and three bottles of green tea.

"Madison met her man's other woman," Stacey volunteered.

Paul looked as if the wind had been knocked out of him.

"Madi, this isn't the same dude I told you to take it slow with, is it?"

I nodded like a little girl who'd just been caught with a clenched fist full of forbidden but sweet, sweet, candy.

"Damn, Madi, I'm not here to beat you up, but I've been talking to you since you were a little girl so this very thing wouldn't happen. I know my species."

"I know, Paul, I was kind of icy for months, but he just got this house, and let me decorate, and I forgot to be aloof, and—"

"He let you decorate?!" Stacey piped up. "And while you're doing all this for him, and he's busy screwing some other chick, what is he doing for you?"

I just looked at Stacey, her words pimp slapping me into submission. I hung my head low.

"Madi," Paul took a simpler approach.

"What's so special about this guy that you've allowed him to rock you off of your axis, your center?"

I took a sip of my tea, and seriously contemplated his question. This one was easier than Stacey's.

"He makes me feel like I'm the only woman he ever loved. He makes me feel like its okay to be vulnerable. He seems to accept me unconditionally. He makes me feel, safe."

Now it was Stacey and Paul's turn to be speechless. They really didn't know what they'd walked into.

Stacey's t-shirt was beginning to gather moisture under her boobs, and small wet spots appeared under her arms.

"Shit, I'm hot. Madison what's up with your air?" she pronounced it "er."

"I don't know," I said sheepishly.

"Well, I want some ice cream," she demanded.

Ice cream sounded like a really good idea.

"I know you don't have anything in that freezer, chickie, so let's go out."

"Good idea!" chimed Paul. "But Madi, you've got to do us both a favor," he said wrinkling his nose. I looked up at him with tear-stained eyes begging to be saved.

"Take a shower, first!"

I thought about it, and it would probably make me feel a little better. Perhaps I'd call Foluke and see if she could come by my place later for a massage. She was the absolute best. She worked on you well past the usual salon hour, until you felt healed, renewed.

I positioned myself between Paul and Stacey, and squeezed them heartily.

"I love you guys!" I whimpered. Although I was slightly relieved, I realized I hadn't stopped loving Damion. I wasn't going to tell them that, though. I mean my brother came all the way from Seattle because he cares. Now that is special.

"We love you, too, when you're clean. Now go bathe!"

"Okay, Paul. But don't tell ma and dad about this okay?"

Paul did something we used to do when we were little and joined forces against our parents. He touched two fingers to his heart, and to his lips. That was our way of protecting each other. We'd bury each others secrets in our hearts and seal our lips, promising never to tell.

Stacey rolled her eyes.

"Oh God, let's keep it moving, please, I'm hot and I'm hungry!"

Vintage Stacey was back. As I walked out of the living room I heard Stacey say to Paul.

"What's the weather like in Seattle this time of year?"

I couldn't hear how Paul responded, but I could hear Stacey's response when she said matter of factly,

"This is the hottest summer ever, and we've got the drama to prove it!"

Amen, Sister Stacey, Amen! I agreed, as I stepped into the shower and adjusted the temperature, the cool water tried to heal my aching soul. It was the hottest summer ever.

CHAPTER 32

Madison—Pride Goeth Before a Fall
August 2000

"Pass the greens, please mommy." It was Soul Food Sunday, and my mother was beside herself. She hadn't seen me in ages and her baby Paul was home. Daddy had even unglued himself from *ESPN* long enough to spend some one on one time with Paul on the front porch. I hoped Paul didn't get the urge to tell daddy what happened. If he did, I'd have to swallow my pride and lie to my daddy. Stacey had decided she wasn't going to take any chances with me backsliding and trying to contact Damion, this weekend, anyway. She figured I might once I broke out of my funk. She was right. At times, I felt she knew me better than I knew myself. We spent all day Saturday hanging out at Eastern Market and Adams Morgan. I was doing a lot of talking to keep the focus off of my personal life, but daddy slid right in when my mouth was full of cornbread.

"So baby girl, what's got you so upset you don't even open the door for your momma?" I stopped chewing and looked at Paul. Stacey reached for the macaroni and cheese, anything to stay busy. The awkward silence opened the door for my mother, who would have thought it impolite to pry, but gained strength from my father's boldness. "Answer your daddy, baby. I haven't seen you this upset since you didn't make the gymnastics team, though it wasn't your fault, you were just too tall."

"Mama!" Paul stopped her before she could reach full throttle. "Madison's upset because she's been working very hard at work, and they passed her over for a promotion." Stacey choked on a rib, and looked hard at me. For once she was quiet. Thank God. Both parents looked at me as if I'd just sprouted a new head.

Mom broke the ice. "Oh, is that it? I thought you were upset over some boy. You've never really had a real relationship, Madi, so you're a little immature in that area." My mother paused for effect.

Daddy began to speak before mom could catch her breath. Again. Thank God. "Baby, don't you worry," daddy's words soothed. "You have so much life and talent inside of you, and God knows it. You're better than that company, and the top brass know it. They just want to keep you in your place. Getting passed over for the promotion sends a message. But unfortunately, baby girl, you probably didn't get passed over, they probably didn't consider you." The weight of my father's words hung over me like a slab of fresh cut beef. Did Damion consider me, my thoughts my feelings when he was sleeping with me and another woman? He couldn't have, the selfish bastard. I put on my best game face.

"You're right, daddy. Thank you so much." I sighed, hoping this was over.

"I can go talk to them, pumpkin. Nobody treats my baby girl like this!" I saw his anger mount.

"No, daddy. I know what I'm dealing with, now. I'll be okay."

The only thing that saved me was Paul's announcement that he had to get to the airport. God was definitely in the house.

Stacey jumped up and volunteered to take me home.

Mom barely paid me any attention, as she was scrambling to get to Paul before he left. Women and their male children. She kissed me and Stacey lightly on the cheek and told me I needed to go to church. That was her solution to everything. I'm not mad at her, though her life was great.

I hugged my brother with all my might. The harder he squeezed me, the harder I cried, inside of course, I didn't want to press my luck with my mother's keen intuition.

Stacey dropped me off. She was scheduled to meet up with Eric. Thank God, I needed some alone time. I was getting tired of pretending. I ran into Sabreena and Terry, who lived across the hall from me, getting off the elevator. They grinned mischievously and Terry said, "Girl, I wish my man loved me as much as yours loves you." Sabreena laughed heartily, and said "What man?" They giggled like schoolgirls who share special secrets and walked into the sunshine, as the elevator door closed and left me wondering what the hell they were talking about. When I got to my floor, I had three items in front of my door. A ficas tree, a dozen long-stemmed roses, and a dozen of fresh cut tulips. I cautiously approached my door to read the note attached to it. When I peered to see if the note told me who I knew it was from, Damion came around the corner. I didn't know whether to punch him or kiss him. My mouth flew open. I didn't have to decide. He grabbed me and kissed me hard as my body slid away from his. I guess I wasn't ready after all.

"Damion, please."

"Shhh..." he put his hand over my mouth, and gently slid my keys from my hand to open the door. I didn't realize how exhausted I was until this very moment. I succumbed. Damion quickly moved the flowers and plant into the house. I'd always wanted a ficas for the corner by the window, and this asshole remembers. He remembers tulips are my favorites but that I believe roses make a statement. The asshole is showing such thoughtfulness, it's increasingly difficult to be mad at him for something I don't have all the facts about. I decided I would hear him out. Damion led me to my favorite overstuffed chair, asked if I wanted some tea, and sat on the floor in front of me and took my hand. Okay, this was a bit much.

"Madison, I'm at your feet, and at your mercy. Please hear me out."

"I looked down at him, with conflicting emotions. Kick him in the face, or wrap my legs around his face so he could take care of business. I refrained from doing either. Damion looked as if he'd aged since I saw him last.

"I've spent the past few weeks figuring out how to prove to you that I love you," he began earnestly. "I'm not sure what Crystal told you, but we aren't together." I stared at him.

"Go on."

"She's someone I dated for a while, and whom I care about as a friend, but it's you I want, Madison. You."

"How long did you just "date" her, Damion?"

He shrugged his shoulders.

"I don't know, three, four years?"

"I'm asking you the question, Damion."

"I don't really know, Madison, she's been around a while."

"Damion, why would she act like that if you didn't make her think it was something?"

"You don't know her, Madison."

"I know something. We obviously have the same taste in men."

"Madison, baby, please hear me out."

My silence prodded him on.

"Crystal is very focused. Very driven. When she wants something, she goes for it, and nothing much stops her. She's on some trip about how we would make a good power couple or something, and I'm the one she chose."

"Maybe she just loves you, Damion." I wondered how she could think they'd be a power couple and Damion was just a DJ, and a back-up one at that. No, it was love. She must have told him that to inflate his ego or something. She seemed like a smart one. Crafty.

"Well, we had broken up before you ran into her, and she's just having problems letting me go, baby. That's all."

Damion stood up.

"Well, she seemed pretty convinced that you are a present and not a past item."

He pulled out his cell phone and looked me straight in the eye.

"Madison, I will call Crystal right now and reiterate that we are through. Will that make you believe me?" Damion began to dial her number. I thought how humiliating that would make me feel, let alone another woman who still really loved Damion. I stopped him.

"You don't have to do that, Damion."

"So do you believe me?"

He looked like he was going to cry. Either he missed his calling as an actor, or he was actually being genuine, I couldn't tell, but what I could tell was that some of my innocence was gone, because now I was starting to question everything. There was no doubt I still loved him. I couldn't trust him as much, but was willing to give him another chance, but this time I'd take it even slower.

"So do you believe me, Madison?"

I stood up and tilted my head up so we were close to being face to face. He watched me expectantly. I picked the roses up from the table and inhaled their sweet, yet musty fragrance. Was it time for me to wake up and smell the roses? Or was my nose still wide open like the tulips, which by now had spread to full glory in their packaging. With such conflicting, hazy and gut-wrenching emotions, I was neutralized.

"I'll make it up to you this week, Madison. I know you're not working this week, I heard it on your voicemail."

I sat down, and Damion took his thumb and begin to massage the nape of my neck while I absorbed his words.

"I have something planned for every day of this week, and Sunday we'll end it by celebrating Nana's church's 100 year anniversary, followed by brunch on the Spirit of Washington. Nana really wants you to come, she's been a member of that church for over 50 years. It's one of the oldest black churches in DC. Come on, Madi Madi, we'll have a good time, baby, you'll see."

Damn! Damion had done his homework stalking me, though it couldn't have been too hard, I was so freaking predictable.

Damion kissed me lightly on the cheek and told me he'd pick me up first thing in the morning.

"Damion. I have to stop by the office real quick, but shouldn't be more than an hour, so why don't you come by around noon? What do you have planned, anyway?"

"Nunya", he smiled seductively and let himself out. My emotions were swirling like milk in black coffee. My heart and mind were at opposite ends of the spectrum, and I stood in middle ground limbo. I'd see how tomorrow transpired, and one wrong move, Damion is kicked to the curb. I went to bed early, and woke up around 6:30 am. I got to work around 8:30 and stopped by the pantry to get a cup of coffee. I'd tossed and turned all night long wondering if I were doing the right thing with Damion.

The first thing I saw were the split seams in the back of Mrs. Portals' patent leather kitten heels while she stood in front of the vending machine. She was wearing a purple knit skirt set. Geez Louise! I felt sorry for the knit, which seemed like it was struggling to conform around Mrs. Portal's rolls. She looked very Pillsbury pop 'n fresh doughy. Someone needed to tell her, but it wouldn't be me. Not today. But you couldn't tell Mrs. Portal she didn't look good. She'd been married 35 years, and I wasn't mad at her; just her lack of discipline when it came to food. She must have sensed me staring at her, or caught my reflection in the glass, because she whipped around as fast as a heavy person could, and tried to balance on those kitten heels. She lit up like the national Christmas tree.

"Hey, baby! It's been a while since I've seen 'ya. You looking right 'po. You need something to eat. You want to split some Oreos?"

"No thank you, Ms. Portal. I won't be here long, and it's too early in the morning for me to eat Oreos, don't you think?"

"Naw, baby. Never too early for Oreo ee ohs!" she sang with only a pitch a dog would understand, and pushed E4 on the vending machine.

"Whatever makes you happy, Ms. Portal," I said as I poured a cup of coffee.

"No, apparently it's whatever makes YOU happy," she said slyly as she sidled by me, cutting her eyes like she was sharing a secret or fishing for one. I decided to take the bait.

"What do you mean, Mrs. Portal?"

"I mean all them flowers at your desk," she informed while opening the package of Oreos.

"It's obvious the boy is sorry."

I was floored. No Damion didn't invade my job as well.

"I'm not sure I follow you, Mrs. Portal."

"Baby, no matter what he did, you've got to forgive him. You know the good Word says that pride goeth before a fall. Read about Nebuchadnezzar."

I looked at Mrs. Portal like she was crazy, but she stayed right on course.

"Remember, men are going to mess up," she said stuffing an Oreo in her mouth, that's how they are built. But you have to decide what you can live with." Mrs. Portal wobbled out of the pantry, her thighs swishing like rubbing sandpaper. Go figure; Mrs. Portal, offering unsolicited advice that had a smidgen of truth. Geez Louise.

I was just logging off when Pilar popped by. I groaned inwardly. I was not in the mood for Pilar or any of her drama. She's the type who had everything going for her and brought shit on herself. I used to admire her; now I didn't want to see her coming. How does that happen in less than a year?

"Hey, girl, how's it going?"

"Pretty good, Pilar, on my way out."

"When will you be back? I've got lots to tell you."

"A week, Pilar." I looked at my watch and jumped up.

"I'm sorry, Pilar, I've really gotta go. Give Mitch and the kids my love," I said briskly, thinking how lucky she was that two men, at least two that I knew of, totally loved her, worshipped the ground she walked on, and she just didn't get it. She just didn't get it. I left her staring at me, her lips were forming a 'B', probably for that bastard Bernard.

I realized at that very moment how vulnerable I felt. How insecure. And lonely. And worst of all, betrayed. Could I ever fully trust Damion again? I didn't know. Most dangerously, I viewed our relationship for what it could be, as opposed to what it was. My heart and mind were at war, but I would give him this week, and then I'd decide. For sure.

True to his word, Damion picked me up at noon, and whisked me off to a whirlwind week, in which he was a perfect gentleman, the perfect companion, just… perfect, and we did everything in town. On Monday we started off on a historical note with golf lessons where the first black golf clubs were formed, the Langston Legacy Golf Course. I sucked, but we had fun. That evening we went to Blues Alley to see Kenny Rittenhouse. Whoo, that man knows he can play the horn! On Tuesday we started the day with breakfast at Annies, one of my favorite breakfast spots, then we rented paddle boats on the Potomac. Later that evening we dined

Moroccan at Marrakesh and I grooved with an exotic belly dancer. On Wednesday we went to the National Arboretum and marveled at nature's glory. Thursday evening we went to the Lincoln Theatre to see Damion's friend T-Rexx perform in a comedy show. He was very funny, and spared no one. Damion loved when he talked about the homeless, the handicapped and rednecks. He was so into T-Rexx's routine, it seemed as if he forgot about me momentarily. He kept slapping his thigh and saying,

"That nigga's funny as shit! He is ignorant! He is funny as shit!"

On Friday we went to hear spoken word, where this time I got caught up. This brother named Kwame Alexander did a Minnie Riperton and killed me softly with his words. His poetry was so poignant, and so relevant, I just melted into his words, slid in between his consonants and tripped over his vowels. The brother was bad! Bad meaning good, for some of my friends of another culture out there reading my story. Damion and I ended up at a small bar on U Street where we both disappeared into oblivion with the best Marvin Gaye had to offer. We made love with our eyes on "I Want You" and then with our tongues on "Come Get to This," and by the time they played "Sexual Healing," we were headed back to my place, where we spent Saturday. We stayed in my house all morning long, making up for lost time. Yeah, ladies, I gave him some. Actually, I gave him a lot of some. Don't judge, I needed it; him.

On Saturday night, we had a nice dinner at Georgia Brown's, then went to a Marc Barnes party. Sunday morning I got up, made breakfast, and he went home to take a quick shower and dress, and picked me up at 10:30 am sharp so we could go to Nana's church.

The church was jumping. I had to keep reminding myself I was in church, and not the club, the choir was grooving so hard. Nana was glad to see me as always, and she sat in between me and Damion. Pastor Benny Corey preached on being at a crossroads, and how important it was to ask Jesus for guidance in making the right decisions. The choir began to sing "Order My Steps" when Pastor called all members who'd been with the church 30 years or more to come to the front of the church. Nana hopped up and made her way down the aisle with pride. Damion moved next to me, leaving an empty space in the pew, which a lady with her big 'ol Sunday go-to-meeting hat filled almost immediately. I couldn't see who it was, but her fragrance was nice. Damion visibly tensed. The hat looked around Damion and cut her eyes at me. My stomach turned into licorice. It was Crystal. No way, Lord. How could this be?

"And God is not a God of confusion," Pastor Benny was shouting. "But you need to pray for discernment, that you'll recognize him when he shows you the right path. Now some of you need a place to do God's work. You've been coming here for years, let God order your steps and lead you to a warm, waiting and loving family."

Damion whispered something in Crystal's ear. She snatched away from him and looked at me and mouthed, "bitch" before getting up and walking out of the church. I can't believe she called me a bitch in church, then had enough gumption to walk out during alter call. What a piece of work! No wonder Damion dumped her. I put my arm through his as Pastor welcomed the hopeful into their new church home.

Afterwards, there was a lot of grinning and shaking hands, and "Don't you remember me, boy?" questions for Damion. I stood by his side, proud to be there, but looking out for little psycho queen. The nerve of that girl. She must really be desperate. I felt sorry for her. Nana came up to us glowing. She was definitely in her element. "Ya'll coming to the brunch, right?"

"Yeah, Nana, we'll be there."

"Good. Baby, you look really pretty in that yellow dress, see ya'll on the boat."

The Spirit of Washington was Washington's crown jewel; a huge yacht that sailed around the Potomac, while food and music was served on the inside, and breathtaking views of the nation's capitol were naturally served on the outside. After stuffing ourselves like hungry puppies, we decided to walk to the upper deck, and leave the food, the singing and the testifying behind us. Plus we couldn't stop laughing at this man that would give a periodic "yeah!" and "that's right!" whenever someone said something that sounded deep.

The day was simply gorgeous, and the sun was puffed up with pride, showing off her son clouds and daughter rays. Damion and I stood hand in hand, silent, enjoying nature and love, and for me, forgiveness.

I broke the silence after a while.

"Baby, I'm thirsty."

"Okay, I'll go get you something to drink."

"Nah, that's okay, I can get my own drink. Thanks, though."

"Alright, baby. I'll be right here."

"Yep. I'll check on Nana while I'm in there."

"Madison. You don't have to worry about Nana. She can hang longer than all of us. Remember, she is from the Chi."

I smiled, and took my time walking inside, lost deep inside my own head. It was

#Place the numeral 4 by the CD to indicate song #4.

as if Damion and I were in our own world, and everyone else was like a silhouette. It was only when I accidentally bumped into an old friend of mine and her husband did I come back down to earth.

"Ms. Madison. Still clumsy!"

I was prepared to apologize profusely until I recognized who it was.

"Tamara, Alex, how are you!" "How long has it been?"

"Too long. I didn't know you belonged to this church."

"Well, I don't but my boyfriend and his grandmother are members."

"Oh, cool. What's his and her name?"

"Damion Cross and Nana is Lea Jeffries."

"Yeah, we know Ms. Jeffries, she's on a lot of committees, that's a funny lady." Tamara and Alex had been together since high school. And when they spoke, they usually spoke in unison, as if their lines were rehearsed.

"Let me pour you some punch, Ms. Madison, that's the least I can do."

"Girl, no wonder you still got him. He's a gem." I said playfully punching Alex's shoulder. While he poured the punch, a commotion ensued outside. I couldn't see what was going on because a crowd had gathered and formed a circle around whomever the drama was about. Now I know church folk weren't going to fight. At least I thought I knew. A set of teen-aged twins came flying in the dining area and grabbed the guy behind me.

"Derwin, come quick! You've gotta come see this lady. She is straight up trippin! Hurry up, before you miss it!"

The guy looked around like he was embarrassed. He apologized. "Sorry, these are my sisters." "Ada and Rachel Petties…stop being so loud!"

We followed the little band of curiosity seekers to see what was going on. I excused myself through the crowd until I was close enough to see none other than Crystal propped on a chair looking down at Damion. He was asking her to come down, but his voice was lost in her tirade. "…And I've given you all my good years! My prime child-bearing years! I would have died for you, and this is the thanks I get? You selfish motherf—"

Someone made a move to grab her.

"Get off me!" Crystal yelled and jerked away from the member's grasp. The sudden movement threw her off balance and she slipped somehow, and the next thing I knew, I heard a splash. Crystal was in the Potomac. What a nightmare! The church members let out a collective gasp, and were frozen for a moment in time. Someone sprang into motion and called for help, while a small group started praying for Crystal. By this time I was face to face with Damion, who looked concerned, but drained, empty. He brought me close and shook his head apologetically. "Baby I'm sorry you had to see that. I would have never exposed you to something like this, some 'ol ghetto drama. I am sorry." He rubbed the back of my neck but kept looking overboard. Crystal had grabbed onto a large orange life support and was still scowling. Some of the members began to snicker.

"Hmmph," said one sister. "She ain't got no pride about herself. Tsk Tsk…"

"I know. Carrying on that way over some man. Poor thing," chimed another.

I was too distraught to ask Damion how Crystal knew to show up in the first place, at the church or the cruise. I really didn't think about it, but I did think about Mrs. Portal. I guess she was right. Pride does goeth before a fall.

CHAPTER 33

**Crystal—Flight 733
September 2000**

"I am sick of Damion Cross." Crystal was lamenting to Tony during lunch. They'd been going to lunch more often these days, as Crystal needed to vet with someone who would listen.

"Crystal, I've been telling you for years you were better than him, and deserved better and more. We'll talk about it more during our conference."

Crystal felt like a hypocrite. She was telling Tony one side of the Damion story, but she didn't dare tell him they'd slept together recently; but he'd just gotten some gig in Chicago, and they got caught up in a moment. The sex was good, but mentally, Crystal felt different. Well, maybe different was the wrong word, she felt... tired. Tired of the fact that Damion seemed to be stringing her along. Tired of the fact that she gave constantly and he took constantly. Tired of the women she found out about that kept popping up every so often; tired of him just talking about himself, his goals and dreams. Plus there was the Potomac incident. It was embarrassing, and served as a kind of wake-up call, really. It made Crystal think about what was really going on with her and Damion. When she spoke of her dreams to him, it was always about them, and what they could do together. He always received carte blanche in her future fantasies. She couldn't say the same thing about him, though. His dreams were always "I, I, and more I." Their relationship as of late just seemed one-sided and empty, and for that, Crystal was tired. She was glad to be getting out of town, and it would be fun to spend some quality time with Tony. He and his girlfriend had broken up, so they'd been talking on the phone every night, sharing all types of fun stories.

True to his word, Tony and Crystal talked about Damion and their relationship in Lake Tahoe. They took long walks, and even blew off a couple of workshops, to talk. On the third day, Crystal realized she was fretting over what to wear. That behavior struck her as peculiar. She couldn't have feelings for Tony, could she? Nah, it must be the beauty of the resort, or the crisp lake air, which would cause anyone to be giddy. Tonight they were going to try their luck at the Casino, and afterwards had a hot air balloon ride scheduled. That should be a nice adventure. It was more than nice, it was breathtaking. Although the days were warm, the nights were a bit chilly. Tony pulled Crystal close in the balloon to share some of his body heat. It felt nice, and Crystal realized, natural. The next day, Tony and Crystal scheduled spa time, and agreed to meet at the pool to get in a workout first.

"What's the purpose of doing a spa, if you're doing all this work before?" she teased.

"Crystal, you want to work out, get sore, and have the masseuse get the kinks out."

"Well, I can't swim that well, but I dog paddle like a champ."

The Olympic-sized pool dwarfed Crystal. She piddled around in one place while Tony swam several laps. He did the breaststroke, the butterfly and freestyle. He looked like an Adonis with dolphin blood. And he was in really good shape.

Later in the hot tub, Tony really put a nail in the Damion coffin.

"So Crystal, have you thought about what you really want from Damion?" he asked.

"I'm not sure anymore, Tony," she said thoughtfully. "Sometimes I feel like I'm more caught up in the memory of what we were as opposed to what we are. I mean, I feel like a crack addict. I keep looking for that euphoria I felt when we first started dating, and have yet to find it."

Tony took his toe and playfully touched Crystal's leg. Although they were in hot water, Crystal felt a chill travel down her spine. She didn't want him to stop.

"Crystal. You are so much better than your history with Damion. It's time for you to concentrate on your future. You have done so much to help him, lift him up, make him a better person, what has he done for you? Or more importantly, what have you done for you?"

"I hear you, Tony, but I don't want to feel like I wasted all this time shaping and molding him and he gives his best self to some other woman. I made him, Tony.

#Place the numeral 5 by the CD to indicate song #5.

How dare he?"

Crystal began to cry, breaking her vow to stay strong. Tony immediately moved closer to her and wrapped her in his arms. Despite her tears, Crystal got goosebumps when Tony's flesh touched hers, which didn't go unnoticed by Tony.

"Crystal. I'm going to say this, and I'm not going to repeat it ever again." Crystal positioned herself so she could look into his eyes.

"Damion is not going to marry you. You can play all the games you want, give him deadlines, and ultimatums. You are not the one. For him. He will date you forever. He will continue to cheat on you. Take you for granted. You allow it, Crystal. And he will forever see you as the woman that continues to give him one more chance. As soon as a woman comes along who checks him, whom he really wants to be with, he will marry her, and there won't be any question about it. It's just a matter of time. And you have to ask yourself, 'do you want to hang around until that happens, or do you want to do yourself a favor and get out, now?' Crystal, you have to love yourself more than you love Damion."

Crystal let a few minutes pass while she absorbed the true meaning of his words. Tony was extremely astute, and Crystal felt the weight of his words tear through her logic, her stubbornness and her delusion. Tony was right.

"Well, look at me. I'm all pruny. I'm getting out."

"Okay, I'm going to stay in a few more minutes and then go up to the suite and shower. I'll see you in the morning for our mountain biking?"

They had totally blown the conference activities off.

"Let's go in the afternoon, I need to show my face at the first session." Crystal got up and wrapped her towel around her emotional nakedness. She had allowed Tony to see through to her soul, and didn't know how she felt about that.

An hour later, Tony knocked on her door. She was sitting on her king-sized bed staring at the TV, lost in thought. She opened the door and Tony stood there, in a t-shirt and some sweats, and Crystal couldn't help but look down at his groin to see if she could see something. She did, and it looked juicy.

"You forgot your rings at the hot tub, and I didn't want you to freak out when you noticed they were missing."

"That's cool, Tony. I appreciate your thinking of me. Actually, I appreciate you."

Tony shifted uncomfortably.

"Okay, Crystal, have a good night."

"Tony?"

"Yes, Crystal?"

They didn't speak another word. Tony lifted Crystal like she was a rare piece of

Lladro. She wrapped her legs around him like he was a trapeze. They locked lips like magnets, and it was on like popcorn. They tore that room up! Tony was a strong, sensitive, attentive and passionate lover, and he explored every inch of Crystal's body with his tongue and lips. He unleashed several years of pent-up passion and love for Crystal on Crystal from that moment, and throughout the next day.

They were supposed to leave on Saturday, but Crystal wanted to fly back to DC early and meet Damion at the airport to tell him good-bye forever. If she planned it right, she could catch a red-eye and meet him before he took off. When she shared her plan with Tony, he was kind and understanding.

"Do your thing, Crystal. My love for you is not only deep, but everlasting. I trust you, and I trust you will follow your heart."

"Damn! I've been wasting my time," Crystal thought as she packed her bags.

She did manage to catch Damion before he got on his plane. He was sitting by himself looking lonely. He was dialing a number on his cell phone. He seemed pleasantly surprised to see her. It was hard for Crystal at first, but the more she talked, the more emboldened she became, until she was able to tell him goodbye forever. She wished him the best and gave him a big hug and one last kiss on the lips. The flight attendant made one last call for flight 733 when she and Damion heard a loud boom.

Damion—Flight 733
September 2000

Damion was waiting for the phone to ring. He was expecting the offer of a lifetime. He and Madison attended the Chicago party the week before during the Congressional Black Caucus. She excused herself to interview some of the figureheads for *The Chocolate City Voice*. While Madison was off doing her thing, he'd run into one of his old golf buddies from Chicago. Medaris was also in the business, and was headed to L.A. at the end of the month to enter a Director's training program for improvisation and sketch comedy for a year. He wanted Damion to cover him at his radio station WCHI on the south side. Medaris had asked someone else, but the guy was leaning towards moving to Boston with his wife, who was an Orthopedic surgeon. Not too many of them in the country. He told Damion he would call him the following week, once the first guy made his decision. Damion was banking on the assumption that dude was pussy-whipped, and would tag along with his wife. Who wouldn't? Ten to one his wife would always make more cheddar than him. He just needed to man up and say, "Honey, would you like your underwear packed separately?"

As Damion chuckled at the thought, his phone rang. Although he was expecting a call, he still jumped. It was Madison. He let it go to voicemail. Now was not the time to deal with whatever she had cooked up. Hanging with her had been cool the past few weeks, but Madison had a tendency towards drama. Not the obvious kind, but subtle. And when it finally bubbled to the top, it wasn't really necessary in the first place. Madison was one of those honeys that lived life carefully, and planned most everything, so nothing much was ever wrong. But if something happened outside of the "plan," it took her a minute to adjust, to adapt. He didn't know how she would react to this sudden change in plans, if it happened. He hadn't mentioned it to her, didn't want to until he knew for sure. But Damion felt he would get it in his bones. He had been preparing all his life for this very moment, and Madison would just have to deal with it. The phone rang again. Damion looked expectantly at the Caller ID display. Now THIS was the call he'd been waiting for. The voice on the other end was cheerful and positive when he picked up.

"Good news, dawg, Chicago is yours for one year. It's time to bring your black ass home!"

"Damn! Thanks, dawg. Good looking out for a brotha!"

"No problem, D. But remember, I'm like the terminator, nigga, I WILL be back!"

"Yep. I'll keep your whip and your woman warm while you're gone!"

Both men laughed good-naturedly and ironed out the details of Damion's new gig.

"Alright, man," Medaris said after about an hour, "you should be straight, you'll just have to find a place to stay. I would let you stay at my crib, but my cousin is coming up from West Virginia. He's going to school at Northwestern, and he can save money by staying here his first year."

"Not a problem, man. I'm just thankful to have the opportunity."

"Alright, man. Don't fuck it up by sleeping with all the assistants at the station, 'cuz there are some fine ones, but they're young, and hungry. So watch out."

"Alright, man. Good luck out there in L.A., and don't come back with an Asian chick, 'cause I know you!"

"Well, ain't nothing wrong with that, man. She'll love me long time!"

Both men hung up laughing, understanding all too well that there is some truth to every joke.

Again the phone. It was Crystal. Damion picked up to tell her about his good fortune. Although they were in a weird place, their friendship was rock solid, surviving the years of drama and other women. Crystal had been pretty low-key lately, especially after the Potomac incident. But Crystal expressed her happiness for Damion's good fortune, and even suggested he call her uncle Phil who owned rental properties in Hyde Park.

"We'll have to do dinner, and celebrate," she said.

"Yeah, Houston's," Damion said nostalgically. "That is our spot!"

It was true. Whenever one of them had especially good news, they would head to Houston's and order the same thing, every time. They'd contemplate ordering a different item, but their palates were set; Damion's for the Hawaiian steak, and Crystal, for the ribs and baked beans. She might have been little, but she could throw down! Damion's line clicked again, and it was Madison. Damion told Crystal he'd give her a call so they could hook up. He clicked over before he could hear her response. Damion arranged to meet Madison for an early dinner so he could tell her in person. It was hard for Damion to quell his excitement and try to balance it with the melancholy he felt he'd have to muster when he told Madison. But, contrary to what he thought, Madison took the news quite well. She was supportive and encouraging, and felt this is just what his career needed. She even talked about coming to Chicago one weekend a month. The distance, she reasoned, would make their relationship stronger, keep it sizzling. Madison continued to surprise him with her maturity and wisdom. She was like an old young person. She mentioned a friend of hers at work may need a place to stay for a while, and could house-sit for him, as her relationship fluctuated like an out of control see-saw.

Damion spent the next two weeks preparing for his trip, getting his affairs in order, and tying up loose ends. He and Crystal did hook up and go to Houston's. They accidentally slipped into each other's arms afterwards, for old times' sake. But there was no use discussing trying to get back together again. Crystal wanted marriage. Damion didn't; well, at least with her. But, they had to admit, they had history, and still loved each other. Damion knew Crystal wouldn't be single long, but didn't want to think about her treating another man the way she treated him. She asked when he was flying out, and he told her his itinerary without thinking much about it. She told him she'd be out of town for a leadership summit, but would give him a ring to make sure he'd made it to Chicago safely.

The morning he was scheduled to fly out, Damion jumped up early, packed the last of his toiletries and waited for Madison. She'd spent the night, but went home to change. She didn't want to start a habit by leaving her clothes over there. Her philosophy was that she didn't live there, so why should her things be there? Must be her father's influence, but Damion didn't fight her on it. 15 minutes before she was to pick him up, Madison called in a panic, and said she had to go by the office, the system crashed and they needed all personnel on hand to try and resolve the issue, whatever it was. She was crying profusely, and Damion could barely understand what she was saying. An emotional, out of control Madison? Another side Damion hadn't seen. Although it had been about a year, he still felt he had a lot to learn about Madison, and this Chicago gig would definitely be a test; a BIG one. Damion consoled Madison, and told her not to worry, he'd jump in a cab, and would hope to see her if she could escape before his flight left.

"Don't worry baby," he said. "It'll be alright. I'm a grown ass man. I will make it to the airport on time, and if I don't see you, we'll start our monthly moments this weekend, I'll buy you a ticket."

Madison was just whimpering, now.

"I love you, Damion Eric Cross."

"I love you—Madison Paige Robinson."

At the airport, Damion kept looking down the hall to see if Madison was going to make it before he left. He tried to call her when the first call to board his flight crackled over the loudspeaker. When he looked up, Crystal was walking towards him with her suitcase in tow. That's strange, she was supposed to be at a leadership summit in Lake Tahoe. He greeted her warmly, she seemed different somehow, but nothing he could put his finger on. She was pretty calm, and wanted him to hear her out. Crystal began hesitantly, and seemed as if she had prepared a speech, stuttering and stumbling on her words, but once she got warmed up, she became more confident. When Damion asked her what had gotten into her, she stood up straight, and said, "Tony is what has gotten into me."

"Tony? Tony who?"

"My friend Tony."

"You talking about gay Tony?"

Damion suppressed the urge to laugh, but felt a twinge of believable disbelief nagging at his gut.

"He's definitely not gay, Damion."

"Crystal, baby. I've seen the nigga coming out of a gay club before."

"Oh, he told me about that. Tony was celebrating a childhood friend's promotion to VP of the marketing department at his company."

"Well, I'll be damned."

Crystal actually looked smug. Well, she could sleep with the gay guy if she wanted to, Damion felt glad he'd chosen Madison, she was definitely more level-headed. Damion arched his neck to look down the hall one more time. Madison wasn't rushing down the hall, heels clicking and hair blowing in a mini and some high heels, like he imagined she would look. He stood up to gather his things, and Crystal reached out her arms to give him a hug. He squeezed her tightly, and wished her the best. She snuck a kiss and he kissed her full lips for the last time. The loudspeaker made a last call and then Damion heard a suppressed scream and breaking glass.

Madison—Flight 733
September 2000

I can't believe this, people! The day my man is supposed to leave for three months, I get an emergency call at work. This is bullshit! I am hot! And Damion was depending on me to take him to the airport, too. I was going to ask my neighbor Sabreena to take him, but she would show up late to her funeral. I hated calling him to break the news; but, Damion didn't pay the bills, work did. Well, he didn't pay the bills, yet. But he was cool about it, said he'd jump in a cab. Hopefully whatever the emergency is won't take long to rectify.

I grabbed his goodie basket I'd been preparing since last week. It had 3 new CD's, 2 bottles of Voss sparkling water; we both loved the stuff, 3 bags of M&Ms, a box of golf balls, a love letter from me letting him know he had my heart, a 60-minute phone card so we could have phone sex and not worry about the minutes, a VHS of one of his favorite movies, *Cornbread, Earl and Me*, he loves the part when Larry Fishburne runs down the street hollering, "They shot Cornbread!" and a framed 5x7 picture of us when we went to Deep Creek Lake. I'd placed it all in a closed-lid picnic basket, so he wouldn't have any problems transporting it on the plane.

When I got to work, one of our servers had crashed. But Drew, my new coworker, was on it. She was pretty cool, and broke all the rules of tech people. She had a sparkling personality, and could make anyone laugh. I often told her she should be on stage. She would have been a big hit on the black comedy circuit. I would have liked to hang out with her, but I was a little cautious about getting too close too fast. I was still tripping off of Pilar, and how I allowed her to use me, when I was just trying to be a good friend. Do you blame me? Ah well, I'd take this one slow.

"Go on girlfriend. I got this," Drew whispered after we wrote the ticket. "You have way more important things to do than wait for our server to be restored, now go!"

"Don't take this the wrong way, but I love you girl!" I grinned as I hugged her.

"Don't you take this the wrong way, you're not my type!" Drew laughed at my back, 'cause I was out of there." I almost ran into Demetrius, who'd been sniffing around Drew every since she started there. Who knows, she might like the thug type. I could definitely make that an editorial, middle-class women and thug life. Speaking of life, I couldn't wait to get to the man that I'd decided I wanted to spend the rest of my life with. Thank God I didn't work far from the airport. I sped across the 14th Street bridge. It was 7:30. Damion's flight left at 8:00 am. They would be boarding soon. I took a chance and zipped in the HOV lane. Hopefully I wouldn't get stopped. People had gotten desperate with all the traffic issues, even going so far as to put dummies in their car so it would look like two people. How funny is that? At any rate, God knows I need to see my man before he leaves. It wasn't as if I wouldn't see him soon, it was just seeing him off that was so important to me. Parking was a breeze. I was on the elevator getting ready to enter the terminal when I realized I left Damion's goodie basket in my car. By the time I got to the gates, it was 7:50. He was leaving from gate 13. I should have put my sneakers on. The heels weren't doing it for me. When I approached the gate, it was nearly empty, but I saw Damion on his mobile. I wonder if he was trying to call me? Of course I'd left my cell in the car. Ah well, I was here. Then I saw Crystal. What the fuck was she doing here? She had a roller bag suitcase with her. I slowed down to a crawl, and my heart began to pound so loud I could hear it. She approached Damion, gave him a big bear hug, and kissed him squarely on the lips. I felt like things were in slow motion. Nausea overcame me. The loudspeaker replaced my muffled scream.

"Last call for flight 733. Last call for flight 733."

I tried in vain to blink back the tears that had already formed rivers down my cheeks. The scream came as the goodie basket fell from my hands. Broken glass, and M&Ms rolled over the shiny marble floor. I looked at Damion. Crystal looked at me, and Damion's face registered surprise, then the deepest regret. He reached for me, and I reached for the nearest trash can. I threw up violently, wretchedly, without regard for who was watching. I didn't care. My world had been turned upside down. Again. I sobbed, out of control. Damion hovered over me and tried to hold me. I snatched away from him.

"Madison. Madison. It's not what it looks like," he said nervously.

I couldn't speak. I looked at him through burning haze-covered eyes, and saw airport staff out of my peripheral vision trying to clean up the mess I'd made. I was having a crisis, and everything was continuing normally. That was the world for you. It didn't stop rotating on its axis because one woman had been stupid for the last time.

Damion gingerly tilted my chin towards him like he did when we first kissed.

"Madison, she was telling me good-bye, she's found someone. It's just you and me, baby. Just you and me."

"Damion, how can you say some shit like that and I just saw you lip-locked with your ex, excuse me, your girlfriend? And you have the NERVE to say it's just you and me? You have lost your cotton-picking mind, Damion. I am sick of this!"

"Final call for flight 733. This is the final call for flight 733. Damion Cross, please come to gate 13. Damion Cross, please come to gate 13."

My head was going to explode. I was sure of it. I couldn't think, couldn't breathe, could barely stand, but I'll be damned if I continue to look like boo boo the fool.

Damion pleaded with his eyes. I stood on my tiptoes, mustered up some strength from God knows where, and got as close to his face as I could get.

"Fuck you, Damion. Fuck you. Fuck us. Fuck this."

I smacked him as hard as I could and walked back the way I'd come less than five minutes ago. My parking shouldn't cost that much. All in all, I'd been here less than 15 minutes.

EPILOGUE

Madison—"Her Name Will Be Grace"
Three Years Later

I jumped on my man's back while he was brushing his teeth to stage a mock protest so he wouldn't go out of town. Usually I wouldn't mind, but today was a special day. He tossed me aside after I pulled his arm, making his toothbrush slide from his mouth, leaving white foam across his cheek.

"Madison you play too much," he teased.

I giggled and watched him like a child watches *Sesame Street*, although I can't count the hundreds of times I'd watched him, whether he was getting dressed, shaving, watching sports, playing pool, cooking; whatever he did, he was so sensuous. God, I loved this man. Truly loved him. Loved him like I'd never loved another. Well, except for Damion.

"I can't help it. I don't want you to go," I pouted.

"Baby, this is the only conference I have to go to all year, this is it, you gotta understand. You're going to be jet setting all over the place, and what am I supposed to do, then? Do you know what the odds of—" I interrupted him.

"Honey, please! Not the odds! I mean, what are the odds, though, that you would have to go on my big day?"

"Ha ha ha. Madison has jokes. You know I'm the only actuary in this house."

"Yeah, I think you're the only black actuary in Washington, DC."

"You better hurry up and get dressed, if you're going to take me to the airport, Mrs. Terry."

#Place the numeral 6 by the CD to indicate song #6.

7:33 am

I sprinted towards the drawer in our master bedroom. My husband was right. I was stalling, and wasn't quite sure why.

"Look, love. I know you don't like early morning flights, but this one couldn't be helped."

"Yeah, I know. I know. I'll bring breadcrumbs with me this time."

"No need. I don't need any man driving you around trying to find where you parked the car. We'll just tie a string to you and the car door handle," my husband said jokingly. I was reminded of the time Christopher Pannell Terry found me three years ago, wandering in the airport parking lot, tears streaming down my face and disoriented as a new born baby calf. He offered to drive me around the lot to find my car. I refused him with some not so kind words, 'cause you know, the love of my life had just sliced my heart open. He walked around with me for close to half an hour. Then he stopped. I stopped. He logically explained to me how long it would take to find my car out of the hundreds there on foot versus the time it would take using his car. Little did I know his habit of calculating the odds was his money-maker.

"I won't hurt you," he'd said. His choice of words, his thoughtfulness and calm during my personal disaster made an impression on me. Christopher had left a business card in my passenger seat. I'd emailed him the following week to thank him for his kindness. We stayed in touch via email, and 6 months later, I accepted his invitation to dinner. The rest is history. Everyone liked him. Even Stacey. So ladies, if you think you can't move on, or there won't be another one like the jerk you thought was "the one," be patient, because it will happen for you, just when God knows you need it. I just happened to be lucky enough to bump into my life saver. Literally.

I chuckled, and began to put on my clothes, though deep in thought. I'd re-played the last time I saw Damion over and over in my mind, coming up with different scenarios as to how it would end. I would often ask myself, 'what if I was wrong? what if he was telling the truth about Crystal?' Then I'd shake it off, and rationalize that if it wasn't Crystal, it would be someone else. That's how he is. How he was? Who he is. Well, it'd been three years, who knew what he was up to, now. But I knew one thing. Damion didn't deserve me. He didn't deserve what I gave him unconditionally. I had so much love pent up inside me to give to the right person. My love was too big for Damion. Period. But, moving on, I had to look at the bright side. If it wasn't for the airport scene, I wouldn't have met my husband. God sent him in the nick of time, because I think I was on my way to a nervous breakdown. For real. And no one, not

#Place the numeral 7 by the CD to indicate song #7.

my dad, mom, Stacey or Paul would have been able to drag me from the depths of blue black funk I knew I could descend towards.

"No problem, Mr. Terry. 'da car will be ready in 'jus a minute, suh…" I teased to hide my nervousness. I hadn't been near an airport in the morning since then. The thought of it put a bad taste in my mouth. I shrugged off the memory, and finished dressing.

The ride to the airport was uneventful. It was going to be a beautiful day. There is nothing like DC when the weather is just right, and the sun bounces off the wonderful building architecture and showcases the beauty and character of the city.

The airport was alive and bustling. Chris and I played the "what you're really saying game" to pass the time while we waited for his plane. The game entails looking at other people and putting conversation in their mouths. He would have been happy to read the paper with a cup of coffee, but he indulged me. That was one of the things I loved about him. He got me. Of course we were over an hour early and had plenty of time to kill.

"Honey, I'm going to the ladies room. You want a *New York Times* and a *Wall Street Journal,* right?"

"Perfect, I'll be right here."

Chris also reads like three papers a day. Here I am, a quasi-journalist, and can barely make it through the *Washington Post*. Well, I bet our kids will be smart.

I saw a couple canoodling walking into the bathroom. I played the game by myself, taking the male voice. "I can't wait until this chick leaves, I gotta get to my other woman." I chided myself for still being somewhat bitter and untrusting, so changed the imaginary dialogue, this time in the voice of the woman. "He is the best kisser ever. I am going to miss this man and miss our nookie. I can't wait for him to get back. Tomorrow." I laughed internally. When I came out of the bathroom they were still going at it. Looked like an Asian girl with a brother. They were into that here, lately. That was alright with me, as long as folk were happy. All of a sudden, I, and everyone else within a 50 foot radius, heard an unnatural sound, except the couple, who seemed to be oblivious to the world. The combination of shattering glass and a scream that sounded like a freshly wounded animal will probably haunt me the rest of my life. An absolutely stunning Ethiopian woman stood staring at the couple. She'd dropped a paper bag that apparently held bottled water. Oblivious to the broken glass, she reached in the bag and pulled out a box of golf balls, opened them and started throwing the balls at the couple, and shouting what I assumed to be obscenities in Amharic. I watched like it was a tennis match, horrified and fascinated at the same time. When one of the balls landed, the couple jumped up, and my heart stopped.

It was Damion.

When he realized what was happening, he grabbed the woman next to him, looked at the human golf ball machine like she was insane and walked off briskly. Fucking coward. The woman stood rooted to the spot. She was rendered immobile and I sympathized with her greatly.

I walked towards her and touched her gingerly on the shoulder. She looked at me with huge, tear-filled eyes. I reached in my handbag and pulled out a postcard.

"Sister, I know what you're going through. Trust me. I've stood in your shoes. But whether you believe it or not, it is not the end of the world, it may actually be the beginning. You have got to thank God for his amazing grace."

"But I love him," she managed to stammer.

"Love yourself more," I shot back bluntly, hoping she would hear the strength in my voice and understand it was for her. Understand that she was strong enough to overcome this.

"Listen, if you're not doing anything tonight, please come to this, and bring a girlfriend, it will make you feel better. I promise. Going underground and wallowing in self-pity will make matters worse. Again, I know."

She took the card from me and I watched as her eyes read the content.

"Please join author Madison Robinson Terry as she reads from her first novel *7:33 am* Recognized by the *DC Post Book World* as a must-read, *7:33 am* is about a relationship between a man and his woman, and, his woman. The book is funny, engaging, and uplifting, as the author artfully demonstrates one woman's road to healing after facing true adversity."

She looked at me. I gave her a big hug. The blue shirts were there picking up the glass and mopping up the water.

"I hope to see you," I said as I walked off, marveling how some people, no matter what, didn't change, didn't grow, just fed off society and lived for the moment. I said a quick prayer for her, for me, and for all women and men who have found themselves victims of deception and betrayal at one time or another, and walked to the newsstand.

I gave my husband a huge hug when I returned to his gate. He looked up surprised, and smiled, warming my soul.

"Hurry up and come home," I said.

"Madison, what is wrong with you? I haven't known you to be so clingy. I will be home in three days, and I'll go with you to all your book signings."

"Okay" I said slowly, and smiled like a Chesire cat. "We'll be waiting for you."

Chris looked at me with concern. He felt my forehead to check for a fever, since I was acting so strange.

I touched my abdomen and rubbed dramatically. "Her name will be Grace."

Madison's Journal: July 19, 2003

Dear Journal:

You know, you never know how your current circumstances will play into your future. I thought I would crumple up and die the last day I saw Damion in the airport, but I have to tell you. I did a Maya Angelou and "...still I rise!"

PRICELESS...for Christopher

You are so sweet and so tender
You make my heart stop and my soul tremble
A fireplace with infinite embers
Warming to your constant wit, sharp and nimble

Your spirit is so bright it lights up dark places
Daring to travel where no one really cares
Deep within the recesses of unhappy faces
Where life experiences leave tiny traces
Of hopes of dreams of disappointments untold
Your very essence challenges the truth to unfold

I don't even know if you're aware
Of how you inspire and uplift me even with things you don't say
Those kinds of qualities are special and rare
With effects everlasting and lovely, like sun rays

You are astute, compassionate, confident and blessed
With talents too many to name
Your hard work and determination has me impressed
And your positive outlook stays the same, unchanged,

Kindled by a burning desire to be healthy and happy
Your excitement and joy of life spreads like wildfire
Although every day the sun doesn't shine and the weather inside your soul may be crappy
You live by example and that makes me respect and admire…
You
Your resolute faith in me
Gives me the strength to be the best woman I can be
I thank God I'm your wife
And I'm confident that we'll be together for life

Discussion Questions:

1. What is the significance of time in the novel? How does time affect our everyday lives?
2. It's been said that you should always listen to your gut; follow your instincts. What are some of the signs Madison could have recognized in order to have a different outcome with Damion?
3. Why does Crystal stay with Damion when she knows they aren't really together?
4. Against her will, at Pilar's request, Madison took Pilar's lover to Pilar's house and posed with him as her boyfriend. What does this kind of decision-making say about Madison?
5. Why is Stacey such an important character in *7:33 am*?
6. At some point, did either Crystal or Madison love Damion more than themselves?
7. Do you think Damion will ever change? Why or why not?

Real People, Real Places
Gargantuan thanks to all of my friends who lent their tremendous support as I raised funds for this self-publishing effort. For the locals, when you visit Washington, DC, look them up, use their services, stop by their shops and say "hello," and for my musician buddies, buy their music, you won't be disappointed.

Merchants, Musicians, Entertainers and Specialists

Kwame Alexander, Author, poet, playwright, producer
www.kwamealexander.com
www.myspace.com/kwamebooks

Jackie Ashton, Owner
Jackie Ashton Gloree Bags
www.jackieashtonbags.com
(301) 899-2800

Ayinde, Stylist and make-up artist
(202) 360-5620

Yvette Baldwin, Jewelry Maker
Distinct Designs
(240) 994-6492

Syvella Brantley, Owner
BeginningTwoEnd
Premier Event Planning Services
www.BeginningTwoEnd.com
www.myspace.com/partycoordinator

Amber Brown, Seamstress
(202) 288-8561

Donald Byrd, Certified Financial Planner
(301) 257-9529

Laura Cambridge, Owner
Dynamic Organizing
www.dynamicorganizing.com

Raheem DeVaughn, Singer
www.theloveexperience.com/index_main.html
www.myspace.com/raheemdevaughnenterprises

Maisie Dunbar, Owner
M & M Nails and Wellness
www.nailandwell.com
(301) 585-4770

Foluke, Sensorium Healing
Massage Therapist
(202) 459-8575

Georgia H. Goslee, Attorney at Law
www.georgiagosleelaw.com

Winston P. Goslee, Consultant
Kitchen and Bath Design

(202) 352-3727

Ayanna Alex-Harris
Pampered Chef
(410) 493-4841

Brenda Harrison
www.vinolovers.net
"Love the Wine You're With"

Bruce Johnson, Owner
Avatar Salon & Wellness Spa
www.avatarwellness.com
(301) 608-9344

Marcus Johnson, Jazz Pianist
www.threekeys.com
www.myspace.com/marcusjohnshonphoenix

Sashia Jones, Event Management
Mosaic Partners, LLC
202-369-7156

Michael Koch & **Pablo Solanet**, Cheese Artisans
Firefly Farms
www.fireflyfarms.com

Temika Moore, Singer
www.temikamoore.com
www.myspace.com/temikamoore

Todd Rexx (T-Rexx), Comedian
www.toddrexxcomedy.com
www.myspace.com/rexxtacy

Kenny Rittenhouse, Jazz Mucisian
www.kennyrittenhouse.com

Safori, Artist
www.houseofsafori.com

Heather Smith, Director
Certified Fitness Instructor, Aspen Hill Club
Silver Spring, MD
(301) 598-1100

Rashaud Wayns, Owner
Excellent Carpet Cleaning
(240)-205-3558
www.excellentcarpetcleaning.net

7:33 am Companion CD. Songs written and arranged by Hermond Palmer and Asheley Jenkins. All songs performed by AJ Phoenyx. © 2007 Hermond "Scoot" Palmer and Asheley Jenkins.

1. **"Satisfy"** Chapter 11, Crystal—Big Surprises Come in Small Packages (Fall 1999) Love scene
2. **"Undeniable"** Chapter 21, Madison—Unexpectations (Fall 1999) Love scene
3. **"If I Give In"** Chapter 25, Damion—Mission Madison (Winter 1999) Love scene
4. **"I Believe"** Chapter 32, Madison—Pride Goeth Before a Fall (Summer 2000) Church scene after the "episode"
5. **"Keep Wanting"** Chapter 33, Crystal—Flight 7:33 (Fall 2000)
6. **"The Way I'll be Loving You"** Madison, Before Epilogue (2003)—As chapter begins
7. **"Over You"** Madison, Epilogue (2003)—Bedroom Scene

Lyrics may vary slightly with recorded version

1. Satisfy

Baby
Baby
Baby
I'm 'bout to drive you crazy

Crazy
Crazy
They say don't be hasty

I say Maybe
I'm just crazy

But I got to get with you
With you
I'm Amazing
Hell Raising
Worth tasting

Your other girls don't phase me
Erase me
Can't replace me
I am emancipated

Don't waste it
Come taste it

They can't do what I'll do
For You

Many guys have tried and many failed
To find my love
But it's not hard to tell
Do you think you can satisfy me
I know I can satisfy you
Come correct or you won't come at all
I can have more fun here on my own
I need a real man come and find me
Kiss me

Touch me
Oooh just satisfy me
Tease me
Please me
Believe me

I'll be your special treat
Oh so sweet
Take you deep
You'll find that I'm unique
At my peak
Closet freak
All this you'll see is true
It's true
I'm exotic
Erotic
Hypnotic
I'll be your best narcotic
Just one shot will have
You locked baby
Watch me as I drop it
I'm so hot it...
It can't be stopped
The best I've saved for you
Just for you

Many guys have tried and many failed
To find my love
But it's not hard to tell
Do you think you can satisfy me
I know I can satisfy you
Come correct or you won't come at all

I can have more fun here on my own
I need a real man come and find me
Kiss me
Touch me
Oooh just satisfy me

2. Undeniable

What you do to me
You see right through me
I can't resist your charms
I just can't seem to resist your charms

Come let me ease your pain
I'll make you scream my name
When we're finished hold me tight inside your arms

When I see your face
I know love's a place
That's always right there by your side

I just want you so
I'm never let-ting go
You're the passion
I just can't deny—

It's undeniable
You're incredible
Every dream is a scene of a moment
with you baby

I'm never letting go
How I want you so
Can it be you want me
Just as much as I want you

It's undeniable
You're incredible
Every dream is a scene of a moment
with you baby

I'm never letting go
How I want you so
Can it be you want me
Just as much as I want you

It's undeniable
Undeniable
Undeniable
Undeniable

What you do to me
Your touch it moves me
I just can't seem to resist your charms

I can't fight it—I tried it
But Oooo somehow you get through to me
My body comes alive in your arms

When I see your face
My heart it starts to race
It's like I'm burning up inside

I try to let go
But my heart tells me no
Then I'm right back in your arms
I'm right back in your arms…

It's undeniable
You're incredible
Every dream is a scene of a moment
with you baby

I'm never letting go
How I want you so
Can it be that you want me
Just as much as I want you

It's undeniable
You're incredible
Every dream is a scene of a moment
with you baby

I'm never letting go
How I want you so
Can it be that you want me
Just as much as I want you

It's undeniable
You're incredible
Every dream is a scene of a moment
with you baby

I'm never letting go
How I want you so
Can it be that you want me
Just as much as I want you

It's undeniable
You're incredible
Every dream is a scene of a moment
with you baby

I'm never letting go
How I want you so
Can it be that you want me
Just as much as I want you

3. If I Give In

If I give in
Will you love me then
Will you be much more than my friend
If I give in—
Or will you hurt me when
When the sun climbs high again

Don't tell me you love me
Your heart's beating for me—just for show
If you truly love me then this
Then this won't be the start of our end
Then you won't ask to be just a friend

If I give in
Will you love me then
Will you let go in the end
If I give in—
Will you hurt me when
When your eyes start wan-der-ing

Don't say that you love me—oh no
Your dreams are all of me—did you know
If you truly love me then this
Then this won't be the start of our end
Then you won't ask can we be just friends

No, don't hurt me and
Oh, swear that you'll never desert me
I don't want to wake up to an unhappy ending
Don't you make me realize that you've been pretending—

Don't tell me you love me – if you don't
Your heart's beating for me – if it won't
If you truly love me
Your actions will show me

Hold - me - close - and - don't - let - go
Hold me - close and - never let go
Hold me close and don't let—go

Don't let me wake up and not have you, there
(Repeat and Fade)

4. I Believe

They marched Him out
On a cold and callous day
They cursed and scorned Him
In a vile and evil way

They couldn't see His manner was the manner of a King
The Son of One most holy, that He was the Son for whom we sing

I be-lieve there is a Savior
One who died upon the cross
I believe I am a sinner
And without Him I'd be lost
I believe He brings salvation
Paid the price with all His blood
And if it weren't for Him
Salvation would be lost

On Calvary
When they nailed Him to the cross
They sinned a great—sin
Yet forgiveness was not lost

He prayed and asked His Father to stay His great and vengeful hand
To forgive the righteous, those who would accept Him as the lamb

I believe there is a Savior
One who died upon the cross
I believe I am a sinner
And without Him I'd be lost
I believe He brings salvation
Paid the price with all His blood
And if it weren't for Him
Salvation would be lost

Jesus died at Calvary
For you and for me
All our sins He washed away
So that one day we'd see
We would see
His righteous majesty
Through his sacrifice we would see
All His might and majesty…

I believe there is a Savior
One who died upon the cross
I believe I am a sinner
And without Him I'd be lost
I believe He brings salvation
Paid the price with all His blood
And if it weren't for Him
Salvation would be lost

And if it weren't for Him
Salvation would be lost

And if it weren't for Him
Salvation would be lost

5. Keep Wanting

Don't run your fingers through my hair
Don't try to share how much you care
Don't run your silly games boy 'cause I'm hip to you
Don't try to promise you'll be there
Don't play this game of truth or dare
It's time you see our truth now from my point of view

Don't even try to kiss my lips
I banked your love and I got jipped
I was a fool to place so much faith, trust in you
Now's not the time for me to trip
The lovin's good but I'm not whipped
I've got faith and trust that I'll find somebody new

And yet I keep wanting
keep wanting—you
Even though boy you'll never be true
wanting
keep wanting—you
I keep wanting
keep wanting
wanting
keep wanting—you
Now what am I to do—?

When you walk by the girls all stare
They like the stylish clothes you wear
Love is a gamble now, that can sometimes be cruel
You've got a certain savior fare
The other guys just don't compare
But I've got the inside scoop now and I know the truth

You're just a dream that won't come true
The one you love is Y-O-U
Now that I've had a taste I know where you come from
You're full of talk and that comes cheap
You're not Don Juan you're just some creep
And every time we speak I swear to you I am done

And still I keep wanting
keep wanting—you
Even though boy you'll never be true to me
wanting
keep wanting—you
I keep wanting
keep wanting
wanting
keep wanting—you
Now what am I to do—?

I can't take it
Can't shake it
Because you got a hold, control of me
I don't want to go
I try to make it
Can't shake it
Ba-by
You-r love
You-r love it just takes control
Let me go
Let me go
Won't let me go
Won't let me go, no, no ,no
Your love has a got a hold—on me
so please let me be
Let me be
Let me be
Let me be
Don't want to lose you
Don't want to lose me
Don't want to lose you
Don't want to lose me
Don't want to lose you
Don't want to lose me
Don't want to lose you
Don't want to lose me
Don't want to lose you
Don't want to lose me
Don't want to lose you
Don't want to lose me

6. The Way I'll be Loving You (Wedding Song)

I want you to want me
I want you to want me
I want you to want me
the way I've wanted you
to say you want me too

I need you to need me
I need you to need me
I need you to need me
the way I've needed you
to say you need me too

the moment
I call you my wife—
the happiest day
of the rest of my life
I'll have and I'll hold you
thank God I'm alive
I'll love you forever
my one perfect treasure

I never imagined
these tears in my eyes
this way I am feel-ing
the way I'll be loving you—

I need you to hold me
I need you to hold—me
I need you to hold—me
the way I'm wanting you
for me there's only you

the moment
you call me your my wife—
it will be the happiest day
of the rest of my life
I'll have, hold you
thank God I'm alive
I'll love you forever
my one perfect treasure

I never imagined
those tears in my eyes
the way I am feel-ing
the way I'll be loving you—
I—thank God that I found you
and there's no other dream
no better dream
in this world

with you I have my perfect world

A love everlasting
to ca-all my own
someone I can care for
to whom I belong

Now that I've found you
you're never alone
our love is forever
love will forever be strong

I want you

7. Over U

Woke up this morning kind of empty
Got the feeling
You're doin wrong

Time keeps passing and you're not here
I've fought the thought that we are better off a part

Tears keep rolling down my face
Swear I'm through playing your games—
I'm so tired—it's a damn disgrace
Loving you's brought nothing but pain
So...

I've pulled myself together somehow
I found the strength to claim right now
I am over you
I'm so over you

I finally fought and conquered my fears
Tomorrow's gonna start right here
I am over you
I am over you—

Can't help laughing it's so funny
To think you could ever really care
This situation now is over
I'm in control, you can go somewhere

I'm clear in my mind—, back to loving me
I'm through playing your games—
I once was blind—, but now I see
Loving you was simply insane

I've pulled myself together somehow
I found the strength to claim right now
I'm over you
I'm so over you

I finally fought and conquered my fears
Tomorrow's gonna start right here
I'm over you
I am over you

I've pulled myself together somehow
I found the strength to claim right now
I'm over you
I'm so over you

I finally fought and conquered my fears
Tomorrow's gonna start right here
I'm over you
I am over you

Now that you and I are through
Sorry baby it's true
You and I will never be
Leaving you was right for me
(Repeat and Fade)

...
...